Liberation

by

Katja Desjarlais

The Haunt Vault, Book Seven

Liberation

Cover Art by *Diana Carlile*

The Wild Rose Press, Inc.
PO Box 708
Adams Basin, NY 14410-0708
Visit us at www.thewildrosepress.com

Publishing History
First Edition, 2024
Trade Paperback ISBN 978-1-5092-5622-8
Digital ISBN 978-1-5092-5623-5

The Haunt Vault, Book Seven
Published in the United States of America

Dedication

For Trina, Noriene, and Kaylan

CHAPTER ONE

Harper uncrossed her legs and straightened in her seat as the conference room door swung open and a stunning brunette glanced around the remaining candidates before frowning at the clipboard in her hand.

"Harper Strauss?"

Rising to her feet, she extended her hand. "I'm Harper."

The woman held the door open and gave her a bright smile before schooling her expression into one of complete disinterest. "Molly Wagner. Follow me."

She followed Molly into the meeting room and approached the long table where two other women sat, one with striking feline eyes and the other with wild golden-brown curls and a stunning array of rainbow-colored ringlets softening the hardness of her gaze.

"You can set your resume there," the cat-eyed woman instructed, tapping one of the few empty spaces on the table. "Please. Sit."

She obeyed immediately, smoothing her skirt as she sat. "Thank you for taking the time to look at my online application," she stated, folding her hands onto her lap to avoid fidgeting. "I admit I was surprised to receive a call so quickly."

"We're on a rather tight timeline," the woman replied, flipping through the resume absently. "My name is Audra Verdi. This is Simone Mahler, and you've already been introduced to Molly. We'll be conducting the interview process for the caregiver position you expressed interest in." Setting the resume aside, Audra leaned back in her chair. "I'll get right to the point. Your social media screening, health records, criminal history check, and the psychiatric assessment you graciously completed through our hiring portal all came back impeccable."

Giving the women a tight smile, she shifted in her seat. "Thank you?"

The phones of the interviewers buzzed incessantly, drawing Molly's attention every time. Audra turned hers over and glared at the screen for a moment before placing it facedown and giving Simone a look of exasperation. "Would you please answer his texts before I drive back there and put a pencil through his heart?"

With a huff, Simone got to her feet and strode to the corner of the room, typing furiously on her phone.

"My apologies," Audra said with a huff before blinking slowly and giving her head a slight shake. "This position requires intensive monitoring on your behalf for a minimum of two, possibly as many as seven nights, followed by eight weeks of basic observation and supervision. All equipment will be supplied. All meals provided. As stated in the ad, it's a short-term live-in position requiring you to remain on site until the contractual obligations are fulfilled."

Nodding, she leaned forward a fraction and clasped her hands a little tighter. "The patient…is he or she terminal?"

Molly and Audra exchanged a look as Simone sat back down, and the room went quiet.

"The patients are two vampires," Audra finally

replied. "The three of us will be on the premises for the initial treatment phase to assist in anything that may not go according to plan. Once we deem the procedure a success, you will be in charge of rotating our pre-approved donors through the feeding regimen until the vampires are strong en—"

"I'm sorry," she interrupted, brows knotting. "This is a caregiver position for vampires?" Reflecting on how little she knew about vampire physiology, she cringed. "I'm not sure I'm qualified. I know nothing about their biological makeup."

Audra's harsh tone softened. "The procedure itself requires little more than observation and the changing of a few IV bags. The vampires will do the heavy lifting, so to speak. Our priority is security, and I'm sure you can understand why we've chosen to narrow our focus to individuals who won't threaten the existence or health of our colleagues."

Harper's eyes drifted to the raven-haired Molly, who was shifting in her seat, her fingers noisily flipping through the short stack of resumes on the table. "Of course," she murmured, biting her cheek when Audra's hand slammed down on the crinkling papers, stilling Molly's movements. "So the excessive money offered for this position is danger pay?"

"Silence," Simone stated, rocking her chair back and typing away on her cell. "We're compensating you for your silence." Her green eyes narrowed, and she tossed a stapled stack of papers across the table. "If you sign on, this will be a real lucrative deal for you."

Leaning forward to take the contract, she scanned the first page. "May I?"

Audra nodded and scooped up her phone. "Please

do. If you have any questions, feel free to ask."

Reading through the meticulously laid out details of the agreement, her eyes widened at the financial clauses at the end. "This twenty-thousand-dollar payment? Is that per year?"

"Yes," Audra confirmed, not bothering to look up from her cell. "Twenty grand for every year of silence, with the option to renegotiate on your fiftieth birthday."

Tucking her hair behind her ear, she exhaled slowly. "And this starts when?"

"Tomorrow."

Dozens of thoughts swirled through her head.

She had a dinner date on Saturday.

Coffee with Zoe on Wednesday.

Her housemate was two weeks late with his rent.

And her severance pay was quickly trickling from her savings account.

She swallowed and pursed her lips. "What are the dangers involved? The risks?"

All three women straightened in their seats. Audra cleared her throat. "The vampires themselves will pose little threat, providing you adhere to the safety guidelines we'll be putting in place. The donors are thoroughly vetted and will receive the same compensation for their silence and discretion, which should remove most hazards on that front."

"But?"

"But the chance of being discovered by the Species Purifiers still exists," Simone interjected, pushing away from the table and pacing the room while her cell buzzed incessantly in her hand. "This area is a hotbed of activity, which is why we're anxious to get this done. I...Audra? I'm about ten seconds from staking Nichol myself.

Could you put him on speaker or something?"

Audra scoffed. "Do you mind, Harper? Our coworker is a control freak."

Shaking her head, she inched a pen off the desk and clutched it tight while the phone rang, and a gruff voice answered.

"You're on speaker," Audra stated, sliding the phone into the middle of the table. "Watch your manners."

"This should have been over six minutes ago," the guy barked. "Is she holding out for more money? Did you inform her of the signing bonus?"

Harper's jaw dropped as Audra's cat eyes narrowed into slits. "No, Nichol. We were just reviewing the haza—"

"This is the oilfield nurse?" Nichol interrupted. "Harper Strauss?"

"Medic, sir," she replied, hoping her nerves weren't coming through in her voice. "I have a resumé here with my qualifica—"

"Can you run an IV?"

Taken aback by his abruptness, she nodded toward the phone. "Yes, sir."

"Any firearms training? Self-defense courses?" he pressed. "Martial arts classes or something comparable? Preferably advanced enough to reach weapons training?"

She glanced over at Audra, grateful when Audra held up her hand and took over.

"Simone already told you she'd work on that during our time here," Audra snarled, giving Molly a sharp look when the brunette's mouth opened. "I'll update you once we arrive on site this evening and see exactly what we're up against. Until then, we're collectively muting you."

The three women powered down their phones at the same time, and Harper bit her lip. "Is he the boss?"

"He likes to think so," Audra snorted, her posture relaxing as her phone went black. "We work as a collective. Unfortunately, some of us struggle with letting go of the reins." She looked down at the contract in Harper's hand. "Are you still interested in the position, knowing you'll be in periodic contact with that miserable old goat for the duration of your employment?"

The numbers on the last page flitted through her mind, and she clicked the pen. "I'm in."

****

Harper swung her purse onto the kitchen counter and opened the fridge, mulling over the freshness of the takeout containers stacked on the top shelf. "Austin? How old is this chicken Alfredo?"

Her roommate stuck his head out of the living room. "Six days? I dunno. When did I drive down to Camrose?"

Wrinkling her nose, she tossed the foil package into the trash. "Almost two weeks ago. Right around the time your rent was due."

"I'm good for it," he replied flippantly, slipping his belt through the loops of his jeans as he looked her up and down. "Where were you today, dressed all responsible and mature?"

Switching her attention to the freezer, she pulled out a pizza and turned on the oven. "Interview for a temp job." She dug her thumb into the plastic packaging and tore it open, sending flakes of cheese onto the floor. "Speaking of, I start tomorrow, so you'll pretty much have the place to yourself for two months or so."

Austin knelt down to help her clean up the mess.

"Another one of those respite things? You're not going to be refereeing money-hungry family members while some poor bastard lies alone in his room again, are you?"

Setting the pizza on a cookie sheet, she shook her head and eased her phone from her purse. She opened her banking app and checked the balance again to ensure she hadn't imagined it.

Yup.

Ten thousand dollars, right there in her checking account where it was deposited the moment her signature hit the contract.

"No boxing matches should break out during this gig." She laughed, sliding the pizza into the oven and shoving her phone back into her purse. "Just a recluse who needs a little post-operative care until he's back on his feet."

It wasn't a total lie. Vampires were reclusive. In a roundabout way.

Austin spun a chair around and sat, his eyes locked on the blackened window where the pizza was barely visible. "Those speeding tickets took a good chunk of my last payday, but I'll make sure to transfer rent over on the fifteenth, kay? The overtime I've been putting in should make this one sweet check." He ran his hands through his short brown hair and reached back to grip his shoulders, groaning as he dug his fingers into the muscles. "That's what I keep telling myself every time I get on that goddamn ladder."

Setting two plates on the table, she pulled up a chair behind him and sat, rocking her knuckles into his shoulder blades to loosen the knots that always formed when Austin worked overtime at his roofing job. "How much longer are you going to do this to yourself?" she grunted, leaning forward to add more pressure. "The damage you're doing to your body isn't worth it."

"Oh, right." He crossed his arms over the back of the chair and dropped his head onto his forearms. "I completely forgot that doctoring degree I have sitting in my sock drawer." Relaxing a fraction, he closed his eyes. "Once the oil prices pick up again, I'll get back on the northern rigs and leave those shingles behind. Deal?"

Patting his head, she got to her feet and checked on the pizza. "Deal. After we eat, I need to pack and get a few things organized. You staying in tonight or heading out?"

"Out," he confirmed as he stood and turned his chair around. "So, will you be reachable? How will I know you haven't been offed by some lunatic or eaten by one of those biters they say are still creeping around the fields taking out livestock?"

Keeping her back to him while she sliced the pizza, she cringed at the bigoted statement. "You know damn well those vampire stories are just rumors and you shouldn't be feeding into it," she chastised while she placed their meals on the table and sat. "And yes, I'll have my phone on me. I'll text you every day if it makes you feel better."

"Feeding is the whole problem right there," Austin argued back, pointing his slice of pizza at her. "The only good biter is a dead one. An actually dead one. Ryker sent me an article last week that showed vamps are the number two cause of death in Canada now."

Swallowing her first bite, she rolled her eyes and swatted at his hand. "Ryker's a Purifier," she snorted. "Anything he sends you is probably from that propaganda site he calls a news outlet. There's been a grand total of one vampire-on-human killing in this country since they started tracking it, what, ten years ago? And that was ruled self-defense during the civil suit investigation, so we can't even count that."

Austin shook his head and took another bite. "Whatever. Those things have been paying off the media for decades to keep their kills silent. The freaks are so moneyed up, they totally control the mainstream spin machine."

The ten thousand dollars sitting in her account flashed through her mind. "I'm not getting into this argument again," she grumbled, knowing from experience the discussion would turn loud if they kept going. "Where are you off to tonight?"

Taking a deep breath as the conversation took a calmer turn, he shrugged. "The guys and I are going to hit the bar, then maybe go for a midnight quad ride in the eastern fields."

"Make sure you know where the wire fencing is," she warned, finishing her meal and setting her plate in the sink. "Want me to wake you before I take off in the morning?"

He pulled the last half of the pizza in front of him. "Of course, dumbass," he grunted. "I want to see what you're wearing so I can issue a proper police report when you go missing."

CHAPTER TWO

Harper closed Austin's bedroom door, smirking when he continued his incoherent, drunken mutterings long after she said her goodbyes.

He'd been renting a room in her house for four years, and it took almost that long for her to become accustomed to how chatty he was when he'd overdone the drink.

She didn't want to think about how many hours she wasted attempting to engage in one-sided discussions during the first three years. Once she realized he would talk whether she was there or not, any guilt she felt over walking away mid-conversation dissipated.

Her coffee was almost done when there was a loud knock on the door. Peering through the window, she frowned at the taxi sitting at the curb and answered the phone call buzzing her cell to life.

"Hello?"

"Hey, Harper," a smooth baritone replied. "Nichol told me to give you a call to let you know a cab is picking you up to take you to the hotel where Audra, Simone, and Molly are staying."

Opening the door, she gave the driver a tight smile and covered the phone's mic. "I'm so sorry," she whispered. "I'll be ready in a minute." As the driver walked back to his car, she knelt beside her open suitcase and shoved her clothes in tight. "I'm sorry, I didn't catch

10

your name," she said to the unknown caller, glancing down the hall and wondering if waking Austin would be wise.

"Dominic," the voice replied cheerfully. "I'm Molly's fiancé. Nic will pay for the taxi once you get there, so no worries on that end, okay?"

Nodding, she zipped up her bag, tugged the handle up, and flung the closet door open to grab her boots and coat. "That's very generous, thank you. I'm almost ready to go."

"No rush," he reassured her. "I was supposed to touch base with you earlier, but I had your number written on a super tiny piece of paper and I lost it. If you could maybe not tell Nichol, I'd be really grateful."

Recalling Molly's incessant fidgeting from the day before, she grinned at the thought of a sweet, forgetful vampire proposing to her. "My lips are sealed. Okay, I'm heading out to the cab now."

A second voice spoke in the background and Dominic laughed as the sound became muffled. "I'm not saying that, you sick pervert." There was a pause before he returned to her. "Sorry about that. I'm going to text you a list of names and numbers you need to keep on hand at all times. Nichol will always be your emergency contact, but the rest are there in case you can't get a hold of him for some reason or if Nic gets to be a little too much. Which he will."

Smiling at the memory of Audra and Simone's interactions with Nichol, she handed her suitcase to the driver and mouthed a quick thank you while she got into the taxi. "Does the driver know where I'm going?"

"Sure does," Dominic replied. "Safe travels and thanks for signing on."

Her cell went black as the call disconnected but lit up moments later with a dozen phone numbers and names, some of which she recognized.

Nichol. Audra. Simone. Dominic. Molly.

Her brows rose as she read down the list and her mind connected the dots between the names on her phone and the reports filling the news cycles for the past few years.

Jagger. Bianca. Mikhail. Louis. Jonathan.

She sat forward in her seat when the last two confirmed her suspicions.

Rhys. Lis.

Her thumb was shaking while she texted back a thank you to the Kaius haunt vampire who sounded so young and not the least bit intimidating.

The Kaius haunt dominated global news since Rhys Kaius and Lis Bruckner took center stage as the first vampire-human couple to be sentenced to the Deepfryer in North America, a public execution carried out through UV rays in a glass enclosure for the world to see. Rhys, with his dark flirtatious eyes and self-assured swagger, captivated audiences around the world. At his side was Lis, the vampire killer who looked like a delicate fairy from the hills of Scotland.

Their faces monopolized the news circuits for months, from the moment Lis participated in an exposé revealing the dark side of the vampire training and trading of women to the explosive rescue mission which played out during the live broadcast of their Deepfrying.

From then on, the Kaius haunt was front and center of every news cycle.

They established the only vampire sanctuary city in the world, working with officials in Denver to defy the

American government and create a safe haven for vampires amid the rising exterminations. Two months ago, they launched a massive evacuation of vampires stranded outside the fortified city limits, an event seeing dozens of losses from both species. The globally televised memorial for those losses resulted in the only existing video footage of the elusive Nichol Kaius, the rumored leader.

Overnight, the name Jonathan Minks was synonymous with the pro-vampire movement alongside Jagger Kaius and Bianca Schumann, noted vamp freedom fighters. Jonathan's entire haunt was wiped out during the evacuation when the members sacrificed themselves atop a bomb. The emotional reading of their names during the memorial service became the rallying point for many politicians in both the USA and Canada.

Glancing over to her driver, Harper tilted her phone to ensure he couldn't read the text she was scanning over and over.

Most of her initial knowledge of the Kaius haunt came from Austin's snide ramblings about the vampires and the women who worked alongside them. He and his friends shared links and opinions amongst themselves, spreading the misinformation far and wide on social media and cawing in victory with every agreement posted in the comments.

According to Austin, the Kaius vampires were the scourge of the earth, and their elimination would end the vampire stronghold he believed responsible for destroying the global economy, keeping him from the lucrative oilfield worksites where the two of them met before the market crash.

Harper wasn't on the same page as the anti-vampire

groups.

But although she often softly defended the right of continued vampire existence in human society, she was careful to keep her strongest feelings on the subject to herself in light of the recent violence breaking out between the pro and the anti-vampire movements.

The Species Purifiers wasn't a group she wanted to agitate online or in person.

So she spoke in maybes and perhaps, quietly pushing against the rising misinformation drowning the internet. Stronger posts she put forth on social media when the anti-vamp rhetoric first began were deleted, her admission of finding Rhys Kaius sexy eliminated within days of posting it when friends and family went on the offensive.

Staring out the window at the industrial buildings signaling the entrance into the city of Edmonton, she gripped her phone and wondered if the rumors of government investigations into search histories for signs of vampire support were true.

She really needed to remember to erase her laptop cache once she was settled in her temporary home. Although nothing more than an unconfirmed rumor, the thought of an intelligence agency seeing just how much Rhys Kaius fan fiction she read last year wasn't anything she wanted to experience or explain.

Her cheeks flamed, and she kept her head turned from the driver.

She always skipped most of the Jagger Kaius stories, preferring to delve into the pieces about the reckless, sensual Rhys, which were often accompanied by photos and still shots taken from the hundreds of news articles and videos about him.

His partner, Lis, was always cropped out.

Dating at thirty-four wasn't easy. Dating at thirty-four in the hotbed of anti-vampirism when you were pro-vamp was harder.

And dating regular guys when you were inundated with the antics of dangerous, seductive vampires was almost impossible.

"We should be at the hotel in five minutes," the driver informed her, snapping her out of her daze.

Arranging her purse on her lap and checking to ensure nothing had spilled out, she smiled. "Thank you. I hadn't expected this much traffic around here today."

"The protest caravan is gearing up over on 167th Avenue," the man replied, nodding toward a line of trucks blocking traffic in the far right lane. "They posted their route online, so try to avoid coming back this way if you're traveling later. They're aiming to circle those two churches, giving vamps sanctuary north of here."

Her throat tightened when she considered where her final destination might be. "I heard nothing about it," she said slowly, reading the hateful banners hung across the back windows and tailgates of the protesting trucks. "Are there actually vampires there?"

"Actually vampires everywhere," the driver grunted. "And they're going after babies now. My sister is a nurse in the neonatal unit, and she said they amped up security because they keep getting calls from biters threatening to take the newborns to eat."

Holding her tongue against the absurdity of the accusation, she returned her attention to the caravan. "How many vampires are hiding in the churches?"

The cab slowed as they turned into the hotel parking lot. "Last I heard, thirty. But don't you worry," he cooed, apparently mistaking her expression of disbelief for one of concern. "The Purifier Army is well-armed. None of us will get hurt in the battle."

Fighting the urge to roll her eyes, she smiled. "Well, thank you for the ride. Do you need me to wait until you get the payment?"

He tapped his phone and shook his head. "No need. The trip was paid for upfront, so I'm just waiting for the tip once you inform your boss you made it."

Hauling her suitcase out of the back seat, she smirked. "I'll be sure to message him right away and let him know."

As the cab drove off, she pulled her cell from her purse and fired off a message to the number assigned to Nichol.

— At the hotel now. Driver very informative. Claims there are 30 vampires in hiding in 2 churches outside the city. Lynch mob 300+ heading that way. —

Nichol's reply was immediate.

— Evacuated the last vampires from that region two months ago. Depositing reduced payment for driver now. Will monitor regional news.—

Pleased the notoriously miserable Nichol Kaius didn't swear at her, she walked into the hotel lobby and looked around for a moment before her phone buzzed again, Audra's name lighting up her cell.

— Room 143 —

She hesitated.

The signing bonus sat in her account untouched and could be returned with a few keystrokes.

Walking away was still an option.

Peering out the glass doors of the entrance, she watched the rows of trucks inch past on their way to the meeting point. The drivers were hooting and hollering nasty callouts from their windows, oblivious to the disgust on the faces of several onlookers. Hers included.

— On my way up —

CHAPTER THREE

"I apologize for the mess," Audra huffed as she opened the door for Harper, revealing an impressive level of disarray in the small hotel room. "We've misplaced the cord connecting the echocardiogram to this," she said, holding up something that looked like a small white taser.

Joining in the hunt, she knelt beside Molly and helped tilt the heavy dresser forward to allow Simone a better look. "Is that for the sick vampire?" she asked, easing the furniture back into place and following Molly to the suitcases that were torn apart, their contents scattered throughout the room.

"It was supposed to be," Simone called out, balancing on a chair to see the top shelf of the small closet. "It has to be in the SUV. I knew we should have just left it all in there."

Molly snorted inelegantly. "Was that really the fight you wanted to have with Nic last night? Because I sure as fuck wasn't going to disobey."

Simone's eyes narrowed as she hopped off the chair and pointed a long, thin stick at Molly. "There's a difference between obeying and compromising. Don't make me shoot you with this."

When Molly merely turned and wiggled her hips, Simone motioned for Harper to help repack the suitcases, tossing the stick on top. "Nichol likes to have control over everything, and he isn't handling this mission with as much composure as he should," she explained, folding a pair of cargo pants that looked suspiciously militaristic.

"And with his girlfriend and his best friend thirteen hundred miles away from his sphere, he's way worse than usual," Molly added, tossing a pair of neon orange underwear at them.

Simone snatched them out of the air and flattened them into the suitcase. "Says the chick whose fiancé has called fifty times since sunrise."

Harper smiled at Molly. "Congratulations. Dominic, right? I spoke to him when the taxi arrived to pick me up."

The brunette's dark eyes lit up, and she waggled her ring finger in the air. "He's a sweetheart." She stuck her tongue out at Simone. "And he calls to connect with me, not to be bossy and demanding."

Audra stepped between the women, a small white cord in her hand. "Who was supposed to be checking the outlets in the bathroom?" When Molly's eyes widened and she turned away to busy herself with packing her bag, Audra blinked slowly, wrapped the cord around an industrial-looking laptop, and arranged her own suitcase. "We'll be leaving for the property once this place is organized."

Tossing a blanket aside to ensure nothing was missed on the bed, Harper jumped back. "Oh, wow. A gun."

"Throw that over here," Molly called over. "I meant to store that between my shirts and jeans."

"Why—" she blinked and backed away when Audra lifted the weapon and handed it to Molly. "Will that be needed?"

Simone opened the doors of the large television cabinet and removed an intricate bow, scooping up more of the long sticks scattered throughout the unit. "Let's say yes, and be pleasantly surprised if the answer is no." She lifted the bow and peered through the scope, aiming it at the far wall. "Do you have any firearm experience?"

Slowing her movements to avoid startling any of the armed women, she shook her head. "Not really. I went to a shooting range once. I'm not…good…at violence."

Molly grinned and pushed down on her suitcase, yanking the zipper closed. "Once you get a taste for it, it's pretty addicting."

"In the correct circumstances with the proper motivation and goals," Audra interjected, setting the last of their bags beside the door. "Senseless violence is never our intent. But we have the capability to defend ourselves and our family from anyone seeking to do harm."

"Or to keep our lovers in their place," Simone hushed under her breath, earning a loud guffaw from Molly as the women collected their things and passed Harper her own suitcase. "Ready?"

****

Harper clenched her teeth when Molly spun the back end of the SUV out to make the tight turn and the tires slid out before they found their hold on the ice-covered road.

"Oops." Molly laughed when Simone barked out a curse. "Should I park behind the house, by the shed, or just pull up here?"

Audra's fingers unhooked from the armrest, and she exhaled slowly. "Out of sight from the main road is best. The aerial footage Nichol sent shows a small garage at the back of the property that may be accessible once we can check it out."

The women climbed out of the vehicle, Harper holding back while the others fanned out and scanned the area.

"Mickey would've been able to scent out if this was the place," Audra muttered, her nose wrinkling as she removed the pins from her bun and allowed her long black and blue hair to tumble down her back. She pulled out her phone and glanced over her shoulder at Harper. "I'm going to confirm location with Nichol before we head inside."

"Do you mean Mikhail Kaius?" Harper ventured, keeping one eye on Molly's fingers as they spun her handgun.

Audra's piercing gaze softened a fraction. "It is," she confirmed. "Do you know much about the Kaius vamps?"

Burrowing deeper into her coat to hide the pinking of her cheeks when Rhys's fan fiction flashed through her mind, she shrugged. "Just what I saw on the news. I pieced it together this morning when Dominic texted me all the contact names."

Simone joined them, crossing her arms while she appraised the tree line surrounding the property. "Then you'll know we aren't senselessly violent." She smiled with a cheer Harper hadn't seen before now. "Only appropriately so." Reading Nichol's response over Audra's shoulder, she led the group to the front door. "Boy's expecting us. Let's go."

Staying tight to Audra, she followed Molly and Simone up the snow-covered path to the front door, surprised when it opened without a key. "I live twenty minutes south of here," she murmured, tapping the snow from her boots before entering the house. "Leaving the door unlocked is kind of risky in this area."

Audra chuckled and toed her shoes off. "I'll remind Boy this isn't the haunt, and he needs to be aware there's no perimeter security here." She wandered the small house and returned to the others. "I found the entrance to the basement. We'll bring in our stuff now and get—"

A low howl rumbled through the house, and Harper startled, grasping Simone's arm. "What was that?"

The women exchanged concerned looks before Simone finally spoke up. "That would be Kaius Khthonios, leader of the Kaius haunt. He's one of your patients. Boy is the other one."

Her stomach knotted when the howl morphed into an animalistic snarl. "That sounds like one of those zombie-things crawling around the towns and cities," she whispered, unsure if it was their presence agitating the vampire below them. "I've seen a few videos of them."

"Deviants," Molly stated, tucking her gun into her back pocket. "Those zombie-things are Deviants. They're vampire turnings gone wrong. Kaius and Boy's creator unleashed the hoards during the Denver evacuation."

Swallowing when the basement went silent, she took an involuntary step back toward the door. "Why is one down there?"

"The Deviant downstairs is Kaius," Simone replied. "We'll get to the hows and why later, but we assure you, he's contained, and Boy has a handle on him."

Nodding slowly, she held her position. "And Boy is who?"

Audra gave her a sympathetic smile, motioning for the others to head outside. "Ladies, could you bring the supplies in? I'll fill Harper in on the basics." When Molly and Simone squeezed through the door and strode toward the SUV, she sat on the dusty sofa in the living room and patted the seat beside her, ignoring the sharp yelp from the basement. "Boy is an ancient, a sweet soul who sired Kaius a long, long time ago. But he made an error in the turning and Kai went Deviant. It was Boy's creator, Khthonios, who completed Kaius's transition into a vampire."

Harper tiptoed across the floor and sat. "But Kaius is a Deviant again now?"

"Nichol shot him down with a wooden bolt during a battle. It was a hit that should have killed him instantly, but all it did was kill off the part of Kai that had been properly turned. His Deviant side is still very much alive," Audra explained. "Our goal is twofold: figuring out how Kaius existed as both and how to correct it. Nichol has been researching the issue for months and has his theories. We're acting on those this week."

Attempting to take in the information, she frowned. "Why did Nichol try to kill him?"

Audra's eyes darkened and she sat back, thumping her heel on the hardwood floor when the howling resumed. "Their creator, Khthonios, is a vindictive bitch. She essentially pitted her haunt against Kaius's in a twisted competition for her entertainment, and since Kaius was deemed hers, Nichol did what he needed to do to ensure the survival of the rest of us." Molly and Simone reentered the house, their arms loaded with bags and suitcases which they dropped unceremoniously on the floor, earning a stern look from Audra. "Smashing our medical equipment is probably not helpful right now," she called out while the women returned to the car for another load.

"So you're attempting to re-vampirize Kaius?" Harper clarified, her fingers tightening on the sofa cushion when the beast downstairs growled. "Why am I needed?"

Audra leaned forward and rested her elbows on her knees. "We can't stay long. The Denver sanctuary needs all of us working to ensure no one becomes overloaded and nothing is overlooked. We need you to be our organizer, our communicator, and our first line of defense." When Harper visibly recoiled, she smirked. "By defense, I mean reporter. Boy is more than capable of fending off anything coming his way. And Nichol has been coordinating a drone-based defense of the area should the need arise. We need you to be a lookout and an advocate while we try to bring Kaius back to us." When Molly and Simone stumbled back inside and slid the last of the suitcases across the floor, she rolled her eyes and smiled. "Ready to meet Boy?"

Nodding, she got to her feet. "Let's do this," she stated, her voice shaking. "I've had a decent life."

Molly snorted and followed Audra through the house, grabbing Harper's hand. "You'll be fine. Boy looks scary as hell, but—"

"But he's an absolute sweetheart," Audra finished for her, opening a small hatch in the corner of the dining room. Securing it against the wall, she descended the ladder into the dim basement below. "We're coming in, Boy."

Harper climbed down slowly, moving out of the way to allow Simone and Molly to enter and squinting when

Audra flicked on the light switch to illuminate the barren room. Her eyes adjusted to the brightness as a door opened on the other side of the space and a tall blond with shoulder-length hair ducked through the frame and eased the door shut.

"Oh, honey!" Audra said with a smile, jogging across the floor and wrapping her arms around the guy's waist. "It is so good to see you. Come, I have someone I want you to meet."

The howling resumed, echoing against the cement walls while Audra dragged the blond over to her and gently pushed his hair back from his bowed head.

"Boy, this is Harper. Harper, Boy," she stated, nudging Boy's arm forward and smiling when he extended his hand hesitantly, his hair falling forward and covering his face.

Harper shook his hand and swallowed, plastering a smile on her face when he tugged his cool hand from her hold. "Nice to meet you, Boy."

The vampire's shoulders remained hunched, his arms hanging awkwardly at his sides while Audra smoothed his wrinkled, blood-splattered shirt. "You're going to have a nice, hot shower tonight while we guard Kai," she ordered, glaring at his filthy jeans. "And we brought along some fresh clothes for both of you."

Boy was so obviously uncomfortable with the attention, Harper felt bad for him. Molly and Simone crossed the floor and stood in front of the door, where a quiet rumbling continued to reverberate through the room, their weapons at the ready.

"We're less than an hour from sundown," Simone called over. "Why don't we get those blood coolers down here so Boy can eat before we figure everything out."

Harper stood back while Audra climbed back up the ladder. She watched Boy retreat as far from the women as he could, his head cocked toward the door hiding Kaius from sight. Molly and Simone talked quietly to each other, neither paying any heed to the vampire standing motionless in the corner.

"We'll be doing a good cleaning of this place while we're here," Audra announced as she descended, a white cooler hefted onto her shoulder. "Come eat, Boy."

The vampire skulked like a lion to the cooler and opened it, selecting a bag of red liquid and returning to his place against the wall in the darkest corner of the room. When he lifted the bag to his lips and bit in, Harper got a good look at his face, and her eyes widened.

"Pretty, isn't he?" Audra whispered, smirking when Boy froze for a moment before turning toward the shadows again.

Harper nodded and tried to disguise the pity in her eyes when Boy's shoulders hunched farther. He quickly polished off the bag, rolled it neatly, and slipped the empty container into his pocket.

"Could I take that for you?" she ventured, holding her hand out instead of advancing on the wary vampire.

His bright blue eyes caught hers for a moment, the emptiness of them sending ice through her veins as he shook his head and walked over to the door holding Kaius at bay. Opening it, he disappeared from view while another howl of rage blasted through the basement.

"Okay, ladies," Audra finally huffed, her back straightening. "Let's get organized for nightfall. Harper, you're about to get a crash course in Deviant restraint."

CHAPTER FOUR

Harper watched in amusement as Boy sat at Audra's feet in the living room, his head bowed while a brush was pulled through his wet, tangled hair.

"Nichol theorizes Kaius has a heart defect resulting in his ability to be essentially turned twice," Audra said, leaning closer to examine the ends of Boy's hair. "Once I'm done here, we'll be subduing him, hooking him up to the monitor, and linking to Nichol for a diagnosis so we know how to proceed."

Spraying down the small dining room table, she wiped the years of dust away and folded the paper towel in half. "So the whole stake in the heart thing is wrong?" she asked, cringing when she caught sight of Boy's shoulders tensing.

"Not at all," Audra replied, dragging the brush through Boy's long hair a final time and patting him on the back. "It usually decimates vampires on impact, but in Kaius's case, the wooden bolt embedded and somehow killed off the Khthonios blood without touching Boy's contribution. Once we know how, we can hopefully copy Khthonios's successful Deviant-to-vamp turning and these two can come home. Right, Boy?"

Boy pushed himself off the floor and slunk away, glaring at the brush in Audra's hand without a word while his fingers tugged at the hem of the fresh shirt he'd put on after his shower.

Tossing the filthy paper towel into a black garbage bag, Harper rinsed her hands in the sink and dried them on her jeans. "Should I change? Or is this, okay?" she asked, looking over Audra's militaristic uniform.

"You're good." Audra got to her feet and walked over to the hatch, climbing down the ladder. "This shouldn't get too messy. Boy?"

Boy held off until Harper joined the women in the basement, his eyes locking onto the door where Molly and Simone continued to stand guard. The women stepped aside to allow him into the room, and he paused at the doorway before looking over at Audra.

"We just need to keep him immobile," Audra said softly. "We won't hurt him."

With her heart pounding in her chest, Harper followed the women into the room, inhaling sharply when a huge beast flung itself against the bars of a makeshift cage, its snarling amplified against the clanging metal. Boy pulled up a small stool and remained within reach of the Deviant, the cooler of blood bags tucked at his feet.

"We'll need to get in there," Simone stated quietly, moving a safe distance around the cage. "If Boy can hold his body still, Molly can tie the gag around his mouth to avoid any accidental bites. I'll tether his legs and Audra, you'll get in there and get those readings as fast as you can."

Harper remained on the periphery while the others organized their supplies and got into place at the entrance to the cage, Boy leading the way.

"Harper?" Audra called over, the echocardiogram in hand, "Molly is going to run the wand across his chest while I watch the screen and input the images. Are you okay being at Kai's head? His mouth will be bound tight, so there's no risk. And Boy will be watching closely." She swiped her phone to life and tapped it. The ring pierced the room and drew the attention of the Deviant in the cage. "I'm putting Nichol on speaker so we can communicate. Ready?"

Her throat tightened, and she nodded, keeping her eyes off the beast throwing its weight against the bars and sending a deafening clang through the small room. As Nichol's voice rang through the speaker, Simone cocked her bow and Boy opened the cage, catching Kaius mid-air when he launched toward the escape.

The movements were too fast to track, a blur of activity which stopped within seconds. Boy lay on his back on the cement, his grip restraining Kaius's arms and torso while his legs wrapped tight around Kai's.

The women moved in, Simone wrapping heavy chains around Kaius's ankles and securing them to the bars with a practiced finesse while Molly wrestled a scarf into Kai's mouth, tying it with impressive force.

Audra flipped the monitor open and passed Molly the wand, glancing up at Harper when she remained rooted to the spot. "It's okay. I promise."

Exhaling, she inched along the perimeter of the cage and crouched at Kaius's head, her terror lessening slightly when she noticed the Deviant's strength was nothing compared to Boy's iron grasp.

"I need access," Molly called out, grinning when Simone reached up and tore Kai's shirt up the middle with her bare hands. "Practice much?"

Simone merely lifted a brow while Molly pressed the wand against the exposed chest. "His heart's on the left, dummy."

The muscles along Boy's forearms strained and Harper zeroed her attention on Kaius's thrashing head, determined to keep the deformed fangs still visible over the scarf away from her veins.

"Go back an inch," Nichol barked through the phone speaker. "Hold it there."

Boy adjusted his grip while Kai arched against him, and Harper instinctively placed her hand on Kaius's forehead. "Almost done," she whispered, more for herself than for the mindless animal snarling and bucking his restraints. "Shhhhhhhh."

For a moment, the vampire stilled under her hand until Nichol let out a curse. "Got it. Get the hell out of there."

Kaius's brief serenity evaporated, and he slammed his head back into Boy's shoulder, the unmistakable sound of bone breaking turning her stomach. Audra evacuated the medical equipment while Simone unlocked the chains securing Kai's feet. Molly hefted Harper up and shoved her toward the exit before loosening the scarf, darting out of the cage, and slamming the door shut.

While the Kaius haunt women reconvened on the other side of the bars, she watched in terrified fascination as Boy released his grip on the thrashing Deviant and sat up, holding his arm out. Kaius latched on. The crunch of his fangs through skin and muscle pierced her mind while Boy methodically removed the chains entangled around Kaius's ankles. Boy's right shoulder hung at an odd angle, a peculiar protrusion jutting out along his collarbone.

"Audra?" she whispered, enthralled by the serenity

Boy projected while feeding the snarling animal attached to his forearm. "Is he okay?"

Audra glanced over and nodded. "Broken clavicle. Simone can align it once he's done in there." She returned her attention to her phone and the screen of the echocardiogram. "Are you meaning that mass at the bottom, Nichol?"

Nichol's voice took over the room, the mayhem of earlier leaving the room oddly subdued. "I suspect the fifth chamber was never filled during the initial turning attempt. Khthonios may have given Kai enough blood to breach the membrane separating the extra chamber from the rest of the heart. Boy?"

Boy's head cocked toward the phone, his attention still on Kaius.

"He's listening, honey," Simone confirmed, a soft smile crossing her lips when Nichol cleared his throat and there was a jostle of noise in the background.

"Boy," Nichol barked out, his voice clipped as a loud *thunk* came through the speaker and the background noises ended immediately. "Was Kai sickly when you chose him? Rasping breathing? Perhaps a peculiar rhythm to his heartbeat?"

Easing himself off the floor, Boy extricated his forearm from Kai and gripped him by the back of the neck, holding him at arm's length until he was out the door, and the cage was locked tight. Audra passed her phone over. He hunched over it to the sound of Kaius's howls, tapped at the keyboard clumsily, and gave it back to Audra.

"Yes, to all," Audra confirmed aloud over the growling. "He was also supplementing Kaius in the night with his blood since childhood, as Kai was often weakened and unwell."

Harper backed into the corner of the room and the snarling ceased as Kai's attention focused on her.

"The position of the extra chamber aligns with the angle of the bolt I hit him with," Nichol stated, his voice brasher. "Since a standard human heart has four chambers, this fifth one means our turning attempt will require constant monitoring of that extra chamber to ensure Kaius's entire heart is filled. I'll put together the specific process in an email and forward it to everyone once I do a little more research."

Kaius stumbled toward the bars separating him from Harper, and she flattened herself against the wall while a deformed hand slipped through the cage in her direction. Her voice caught in her throat as one finger hooked into her shirt.

"Audra?" she whispered, stilling when the Deviant pinched the fabric between his thumb and finger, his head bowed low against the bars while he studied it.

"Oh, fuck!" Molly gasped. "Boy—"

Boy's hand closed on Kaius's wrist before Harper saw him move, but the Deviant refused to release her shirt. A sickening snapping sound echoed off the walls as Boy forcibly unhooked the fingers from her clothing. Kaius snarled, yanking against Boy's grip until he was free to retreat to the back of the cage, cradling his broken hand.

She heard Simone and Molly calling to her, but her feet refused to obey, remaining anchored in place until Audra tugged her arm and dragged her from the room.

"I'm so sorry," Audra apologized as the door closed and Simone took her place in front of it, bow in hand. "Are you okay? I should have warned you he has a long reach. Let's get you topside and settled. We can review the necessary information after you get some rest."

Exhaling, she shook her head and ran her hands through her hair. "I'm good. All good," she said, smoothing the spot on her shirt where Kaius grabbed her. "Shouldn't we get Boy's clavicle set?"

Simone jolted and reached behind herself to open the door. "Damn. Right." She stuck her head into the room. "Come on, Boy. We need to get you fixed up." Closing the door again, she gave them a tight smile. "He's feeding Kai again. How the hell can he spare this much blood without a fresh influx coming in?"

Boy wiggled the knob and Simone stepped aside to let him through, sliding the locking bolt in place before reaching up to his injured collarbone. Muttering half-hearted platitudes, she snapped the bones into place and took up her position again, kicking her heel against the door when Kaius let out a low growl. "Molly and I will stand guard while you three work out tomorrow's procedure."

Harper followed Boy up the ladder, accepting his hand when he held it out to help her. Audra set the echocardiogram on the table and crossed her arms, giving Boy a hard glare. "Simone had a good point," she stated, crossing the floor toward him until she backed him into a corner. "You need fresh blood with the amount you've been giving Kai. And I know for a fact the evacuation into Denver interrupted Nichol's supply line. So where are you getting it? There isn't a single verifiable report of vampire attacks in a four-hundred-mile radius."

His jaw set, Boy turned to the front door and walked outside barefooted. He waited at the end of the path for

Audra and Harper to pull their boots on before he led them around the house to the thick tree line dividing his property from the next.

Audra's eyes closed for a moment, and she took a deep breath as she looked into the adjacent field. "Tell me you aren't subsisting on cow blood." When Boy merely shrugged, she lolled her head back. "I won't tell Bianca, but you know damn well this is beneath you."

At the mention of Bianca, Boy appeared to shrink into himself despite his immense size.

"Okay, go." Audra sighed, leading Harper back to the house. "And next time you come out here, I expect those shoes we brought you to be securely on your feet. Understood?" Boy nodded, ducked between the trees, and disappeared out of sight as Audra turned to her. "Poor guy. He's had a tough go of the past few millennia. If Kaius's re-turning goes as planned, they're going to need you around to stay on top of these little things while they gain their strength back enough to travel home."

Kicking the snow off her boots, she glanced into the darkness. "I'm sorry," she murmured when her brain caught up. "Did you say he's had a tough few *millennia*?"

CHAPTER FIVE

Harper looked at the clothes laid out on her bed while she ran a brush through her wet hair.

"Molly?" she called into the hall, unsurprised when Molly flung the door open instead of knocking first. "What would be best to wear tonight?"

The fidgety brunette scanned the choices, looking down at her own torn jeans and oversized concert shirt. "General rule to follow when dealing with vamp missions is to wear something that you won't miss when it's wrecked, something you can easily move in, and comfortable shoes because you'll probably have to run at some point."

Selecting black leggings and a plaid button-down she'd inherited from Austin, she held her towel tight around her bosom while Molly made herself comfortable on the bed. "What happens if this doesn't work?"

Molly draped her arm over her eyes and leaned back on the pillows. "There's no option," she stated. "We need Kaius and Boy back. Even if Boy freaks me out."

"Doesn't say much, does he?" she mused, pulling on her underwear and leggings under the towel.

"He's mute," Molly replied. "Did Audra tell you anything about him?"

Hooking her bra around her waist, Harper twisted it around and eased her arms through the straps, turning her back to her unintended guest. "Nothing much. Aside from the fact he's been alive since forever."

Snorting, Molly shifted on the bed. "Get this," she opened, her husky voice lowering in volume. "Kaius was the leader, right? I mean, Nichol is right now, but Kai is technically the lead vamp and has been for over two thousand years. But he always kept Boy around. Poor guy never had a name and was treated like total trash by everyone because they all assumed he was some rogue Kaius felt bad for and took on."

While Harper draped her towel on a hook to dry, Molly got up on her knees, her dark eyes glinting. "This is where things get weird. Kaius's creator, Khthonios, is this lunatic female vamp. She shows up one night deciding the Kaius vampires should fight her vampires because Kai said something a billion years ago about how he could create the ultimate haunt, and she wants her battle to prove him wrong. So Kai fights on her side along with an ancient named Chen, and an ass named Dovidas. Nichol, Rhys, and Boy take them on, but they're totally outnumbered in age and strength. The older vamps get, the stronger and faster they get. Not a good combo when Rhys was still recovering from his public baking."

Joining Molly on the bed, she leaned in. "Is this when Nichol shot Kaius?"

Nodding, Molly's eyes widened. "Simone was on site and took out Dovidas. Nichol took out Kai by accident. But instead of killing him, Kaius went Deviant. So Boy jumped in and tried to save Kai, and Khthonios tells him *Mommy isn't fixing it this time*. Like, fuck, right? None of us knew Khthonios created Boy, so we were all totally blown away. And since Boy was Kaius's original creator and Kaius went Deviant initially, and the

whole Kaius haunt is actually part vamp, part Deviant."
She scooted closer. "It's a sensitive issue for them, the
Deviant thing. So never mention it. Especially as a joke.
Trust me on that."

"So Khthonios—"

A shudder went through Molly, and she shook her
head frantically. "Still around. No one knows where.
She's terrifying. She's the one who ratted out the
evacuation to the FBI Vamp Division, and she's
responsible for the Deviants that rose up in St. Louis and
the huge second wave that rose during the sanctuary
evacuation. Personally, I put all those deaths of the
humans and vamps that night a hundred percent on her
head. Fucking bitch is what she is."

The fact Molly's voice dropped to almost
imperceptible levels while she talked about Khthonios
spoke volumes.

"Ready?" Audra called from the hall. "We have
everything set up downstairs for sunset in ten minutes. I
just need help getting this old mattress squeezed down
that hatch."

Jumping off the bed, Harper took one end and
helped guide it down the hall, struggling to bend it in half
while Audra shoved it through the small opening.
Simone barked out a curse of surprise and she bit her
cheek to suppress her laughter.

"What the hell?" Simone yelled up at them. "You
almost killed me."

Harper could hear Nichol's voice hollering through
Simone's phone and Audra winced. "Tell him it was an
accident, and you're fine before he drives up here and I
have to stake him."

Simone thought long and hard, making a production

of it while Nichol's voice continued to holler in her hand. "What do I get for my cooperation?" She grinned as the women descended into the basement.

"My undying devotion," Audra replied, kissing the air. "Now give that poor vamp some peace of mind."

While Simone calmed Nichol down, Molly and Audra dragged the mattress toward the door where Boy was hiding out with Kaius until sunset, the deadbolt in place under Nichol's orders.

"Harper?" Audra called over. "Molly and Simone will head topside to meet the donors as they arrive. Could you set up the IV and prep those blood bags in case we need them?"

Setting to work on her assignment, she kept one eye on the door and listened for signs of movement on the other side as nightfall hit and all levity was erased from the room.

"Okay," Audra stated with finality. "Let's open this door and get this party started. Simone, you're on exterior patrol. Keep your phone on vibrate and stay in contact. Molly, you're interior patrol and hostess as the mea…donors pull in. We only want to yank one pint from each to ensure we can keep them on rotation, so don't go overboard."

"No dead men," Molly confirmed, saluting Audra. "Gotcha."

Unamused, Audra turned to Harper. "You and I will monitor monitoring that fifth chamber and ensure Boy isn't accidentally drained in the process. Kaius will be weakened by the time we need to get a good look at his heart, so I don't anticipate any issues. I'm more concerned about Boy ingesting that much Deviant blood."

The possibilities blasted through her head, and she paused. "You think he'll become one?"

"I think he'll get a stomachache," Audra clarified. "Or become too full and get sluggish before he needs to reverse the blood transfer. And the last thing we need is Boy's strength significantly compromised."

"What happens if he's too weak to complete the process?"

Clicking the deadbolt open, Audra shrugged. "We deal with it."

Deal with it.

She took a deep breath and followed Audra into the cage room, keeping well out of Kaius's reach. He remained silently crouched in the corner of his enclosure, his blackened eyes locked on her movements while she busied herself with the IV stand. Tracking the Deviant's position, she checked the lines and dragged the cooler of blood bags over before inching past Audra and exiting the room, startling when Kaius broke his silence with a low snarl.

"No," Audra barked at Kai. "Behave." Turning to Harper, she pursed her lips. "He knows better. Whatever piece of Kaius is still in there knows better than to be a jerk. Let's set up in the main room so we have the space we need to move."

The growling hitched for a moment, resuming at a lower volume while Harper shuffled the IV stand into place beside the mattress and Audra went over to the ladder and called up for Molly to drop a blanket down. When a large, ratty comforter fell to the floor, Harper picked it up. "If we do this in here and Kaius gets loose, won't he go up there? Could we lose him?"

Audra arranged the echocardiogram beside the

makeshift bed and shook her head, lifting a flashlight. "UV light," she stated. "It'll slow him down enough for Molly to shoot him off the rungs."

Her eyes widened, and she glanced toward the doorway where Kai was visible, his large form hunched against the bars and his gaze locked on her. "What happens to vampires when you shoot them?"

"Metal bullets hurt, but aren't fatal." Opening the computer monitor and swiping her phone to life, Audra sat back on her haunches and tightened her ponytail. "Pulling them out can be gross, though. Boy can handle that if it comes down to it." She got to her feet. "That reminds me. Boy? Nichol wants to go over a few things with you, so come listen."

Harper stepped back to give Boy room to pass her without crowding him. As he crouched down and Nichol's voice filled the room, Kaius went silent again. She turned to watch him while he zeroed in on the phone, his lips moving wordlessly and exposing the gnarled angles of his fangs.

They looked nothing like Boy's long, smooth enamel with a faint silver hue shimmering in the light.

The blackened Deviant eyes lifted from the cell and narrowed at her. For a second, she thought she saw a hint of blue irises before the onyx took over again.

"Audra?" she murmured, squinting as she tried to get another glimpse of the blue eyes hidden behind the beast now watching her with the patience of a predator. "What was Kaius like? Before this?"

Rubbing Boy's shoulder as she got to her feet, Audra walked over to her and leaned against the door frame, studying Kaius. "Much like Boy. Sedate. Contemplative. Controlled. He's well over two thousand years old, pragmatic as they come." The Deviant gripped a malformed hand around the bars, and she smiled sadly. "He walked away from the haunt on bad terms. None of us knew anything about his creator at the time, or how much he was trying to shield us from her sick games." When Kaius pushed off the cage with a howl and booted at the lock, she blinked slowly and turned away. "His hauntmates will watch through the video app on my phone when we begin the procedure." With a deep breath, she straightened her shoulders. "Please ignore their reactions if they become emotional. This has been a difficult pill to swallow. For all of us."

Nodding her understanding and glancing over at Kaius one more time, she joined Boy at the mattress and sat quietly while Audra placed the call on video feed and propped the phone up.

Nichol Kaius's hazel eyes filled the screen, the faint movement of his jaw giving away his grinding teeth. "Ready?" the old vampire asked, sitting back and allowing the screen to fill with the rest of the hauntmates, their arms crossed, and faces locked in matching unreadable expressions.

Audra motioned toward the cage, and Boy walked to the bars. "We're ready. Are you?"

CHAPTER SIX

Harper used the back of her hand to wipe the sweat from her brow while Nichol's voice bellowed through the phone speaker.

"This is the cusp. Get Boy off the fucking floor and bleed him out down Kaius's throat."

With the last of the death tremors shuddering through Kai's body, they hit the critical turnaround point. After almost an hour of restraining the bucking, snarling beast, he now lay grey and lifeless on the blood-covered mattress, motionless except for the infrequent tremors rippling through him.

Jumping to her feet, she joined Audra at Boy's side and helped pull the enormous vampire upright into a position they could work with.

"Pass me the knife," Audra panted, angling Boy's arm over Kaius's throat while the ancient vampire lurched forward and heaved the polluted Deviant blood from his system for the countless time. "I'll steady him. You make the cut."

Her hand shook as she lined the blade up with Boy's wrist, Nichol's voice dropping to an abnormal serenity.

"That's it," Nichol reassured her. "Deep enough to hit the artery. I personally guarantee you he'll heal."

She shoved the knife against Boy's skin with as much force as she could muster and averted her eyes when the first stream of blood missed Kaius's mouth and coated his neck. Steadying Boy's arm, she reached across Audra and grasped at the echocardiogram wand, her eyes flicking to the depleting IV bag supplementing the amount of blood Boy was quickly losing.

"Molly?" she called toward the exit, abandoning the wand. "We're getting low again."

Molly dropped down the ladder at an impressive speed, two guns shoved in her back pockets and three fresh bags of blood in her hand. Taking over Harper's position, she tucked the knife at her knees and focused on Audra and Nichol's instructions while Harper sprang up and changed out the bags. Ignoring the disturbing amount of foul-smelling Deviant blood covering the floor, she instinctively knelt at Boy's side and placed her fingers along his throat to feel for a pulse.

"If you feel a heartbeat, we're more fucked than we thought," a smooth voice called out over the din and she looked toward the phone, snatching her hand away from Boy when Rhys smirked, his eyes holding none of the levity in his voice.

"Sorry," she muttered, grabbing the wand and ultrasound gel, and stretching it across Boy's back while she positioned herself at Kaius's head. "Okay, I'm going to get this lined up with his heart. Let me know when you have the visual you need."

Keeping her arms arced over Boy's bleeding wrist, she moved the wand across the still chest, her view of the monitor blocked by Audra.

"There," Nichol yelled out. "No, back down half an inch. There."

Wisps of hair escaped her ponytail and clung to the sweat on her neck and forehead. The muscles in her legs and arms protested the awkward position while Molly sliced Boy's wrist open again on Nichol's order.

"Two chambers filled," another voice updated them from the phone. "Boy, time's getting tight, man. We need a more prolific artery."

Boy pushed himself upright, his movements unsteady and lethargic as he held his bleeding arm over Kaius's mouth and reached across to grab the knife from Molly. The depth the blade sunk into his throat had Harper yanking a corner of the blood-soaked blanket free and she moved to press it against the wound while he lowered his neck toward Kaius.

"Harper," Nichol called out over Molly's disgusted groan. "Give the wand to Audra. I need you to angle Kaius's head back and hold it steady. And keep an eye on those IV bags. Boy won't bleed out as long as we do this fast."

Assuming her new position, her gaze moved between the depleting blood bags, the arch of Kaius's throat, and the paling of Boy's skin.

"Four chambers," an unfamiliar voice reported from the phone, and she looked over to see a vampire with long blond hair not unlike Boy's on the screen.

Mikhail Kaius.

The vampires went quiet, and Audra stilled, her hand holding the wand tight to Kaius's chest while Boy's arms shook violently.

Turning to Molly, she nodded at her hands. "Could you hold him steady? I need to switch those bags out now."

Molly took over at Kaius's head and Harper scooted back, her socks wet and cold from the Deviant blood soaking into them. Ignoring the stomach-churning slurping of her feet as she crossed the floor, she called up to Simone. "Are there two more?"

The seconds ticked by before Simone appeared at the opening, bags in hand. "We have another on the go, and I arranged for three of the later donors to arrive on site within the hour." She glanced at the mayhem in the basement. "Goddamn it. We may need to offer a vein ourselves if this goes much longer."

"Almost there," Mikhail hollered, his voice bouncing off the cement walls. "The fifth chamber's been breached. Just a few more minutes, Boy."

Boy's left arm gave out and his balance wavered as Harper ran over and attempted to hoist him back up into position by wedging herself under his shoulder. Tugging his IV line gently, she inched the stand over and grasped the pole, tilting it over and cinching his line long enough to switch out the blood bags. His weight on her back held her nearly immobile and she let out a quiet curse as she struggled unsuccessfully to right the stand.

There was a flurry of activity over the phone while Boy's skin continued to pale. She doubled her efforts to right the IV stand as Nichol's voice cut through the din crystal clear. "You did it, Boy. We have circulation."

Easing herself out from under him, Harper knelt on the floor, tipped the stand, and ran her fingers along the line to ensure there were no kinks.

Boy rolled off the mattress and onto his back while the wound on his neck continued to bleed profusely.

"Audra?" she called out. "Is this supposed to happen?"

Audra snatched her phone and angled the camera toward Boy while Nichol and Rhys barked instructions. "Harper, Molly needs to get topside to help Simone with those donors. We need all the bags we can get right now.

I need you to monitor Kaius until we get this little problem fixed, okay?"

Backing away from the bleeding vampire, she crawled over to Kaius and crouched at his side, ignoring her phone while it buzzed incessantly in her back pocket.

"Harper," Nichol snarled. "Answer your goddamn cell. Mickey is going to help you monitor him while Rhys, Audra, and I get Boy patched up."

Nodding, she grabbed her phone from her damp pocket, cringing at the streaks of blood crisscrossing the screen. "Hello?"

"Hey, Harper," Mikhail greeted her. "Tap that little video icon so I can get a good look at my dad."

Her hand shook as she tapped the video feed to life and Mikhail's face filled the screen, his image jostling as he moved. "Here," she said, clearing her throat when her voice cracked. "Can you see him?"

Kaius lay motionless on the crimson mattress, his short blond hair matted and streaked with blood. Mikhail went silent for a moment before replying. "Yeah, I see him. First thing we're going to check is his hands. Hold one up and examine his fingers for signs of straightening. The bones may be realigning already."

Lifting one heavy arm, she placed it on her lap and angled her phone while she ran her fingers along each gnarled digit. "I can't tell if they've improved."

"Neither can I," came the hard response. "Okay. Jagger says we need to do a fang check, but with Boy out of commission, I don't know if it's wise."

Glancing around the room, she slid out from under Kaius's arm and skirted around Boy and Audra. Eying the blood bags, she scanned around the base of the echocardiogram for the UV flashlight. Once she spotted it, she grabbed it and held it in front of the camera. "Will this work if he wakes up?"

"I'm texting Simone now to tell her to be on guard," Mikhail replied. "If he snaps—hell, if he moves even the slightest—blast him with that and hold it on any exposed skin. You'll burn a hole through him, but it's nothing he won't recover from."

"It won't kill him?" she confirmed, glancing back at Boy and exhaling at the faint improvement in his color.

Mikhail chuckled and Audra's head turned toward her, a small smile on her face. "No, it won't kill him in the dose you'll need to incapacitate him. Put one knee on his chest and be ready to move."

Gingerly lowering herself onto the motionless vampire, she turned the camera to Kaius's lips. "I can see them."

"We need to see the shape," Mikhail stated. "Use your thumb to push his lip up and try to snap a few pictures if you can. We can maybe track the morphing that way if there isn't enough change yet."

Steadying her phone, she gently pushed Kaius's lip up with her thumb, snapping a dozen pictures of the mangled fangs. Being so close to them, she could see the faint yellowing of the enamel, contrasting with the slight silvering of Boy's long viper teeth. The delicate curve all vampire fangs held was gone, the Deviant metamorphosis apparent in the serrated, brittle teeth that were chipped and jagged.

Keeping her weight on his chest, she fired off the images to Mikhail. "Are those good enough?"

"Yeah," Mikhail replied, his voice flat. "A good starting point, I guess, right? I mean, we'll be able to see the difference once the transformation completes." He said something quietly to someone else and returned to the phone, his expression less hopeful than it was moments earlier. "Now that Boy's stable, you and Audra will need to secure Kai and begin twenty-four-hour monitoring on both vamps until they recover. Harper, thanks for doing this. Audra?" he called out. "I'll call you later, baby."

The call disconnected, and she studied Kaius's still face. She was leaning closer to get a better look at the tips of his fangs when his eyes snapped open and she screamed, jumping away, and fumbling for the flashlight.

"What?" Audra and Nichol hollered simultaneously as Kaius's black pupils elongated, a glimpse of blue appearing before they shut tight.

"Nothing," she stammered, her thumb on the light's power switch. "I'm sorry. He just opened his eyes."

Audra sank back to her knees and lifted her phone, oblivious to the amount of blood coating her hands. "That's a good sign." She grinned, inching over to Harper so they could both see the screen. "Right, Nichol?"

Nichol nodded and reported the update to the vampires behind him, the tension in their faces noticeably draining as they slouched back in their chairs.

"You ladies were incredible," Rhys called out.

"You ladies," Nichol interjected, "completed phase one. Now get Kaius back into the cage, set Boy up on something a little cleaner than that mattress, get a few IV drips going for him, and shower."

CHAPTER SEVEN

Harper's head snapped up, and she blinked, rubbing her eyes hard enough to see black spots while she felt around for her phone and tapped the reset on her alarm.

"Okay, Boy," she murmured, pushing herself off the floor and staggering over to the blanket where he lay silent. "Let's rotate those bags out and check the IV site."

He remained still while she stopped the IV drip, traded the empty blood bags for full ones, and sat at his side to inspect the place where the line ran into his vein. "I'm going to need you to move your hand," she instructed, frowning when he did, and the catheter fell to the floor. "How long were you holding that in place?"

Shrugging, he kept his vacant eyes averted from her.

Examining the place where the IV had been inserted, she shook her head and got to her feet. "I suppose that fast healing rumor is true," she muttered as she walked over to the bin of medical supplies and searched through it quietly to avoid disturbing Audra's rest. Gathering her supplies, she sat at Boy's side and ran the pad of her thumb over his inner arm. Satisfied with the vein she found, she tied a tourniquet and waited until the vein became clearly visible. "Just like last time, this will sting."

Boy didn't flinch when she inserted the needle and threaded the IV line back into his body.

Of course, he hadn't flinched when Molly sliced his

wrist open.

Or when he took the blade to his own throat.

A little poke was likely the least of his traumatic events over the past twelve hours.

Adding a few extra layers of tape to hold the line, she opened the drip back up and stood, noting the direction of his gaze. "I'll go check Kaius," she reassured him, following his attention to the cage room where the door remained propped open with Audra's shoe. "You need to rest up."

Stepping around the plastic covering the bloody mattress and floor, she tiptoed to the bars of the cage and watched the lifeless vampire for a few minutes. Under Nichol's repeated warning, she avoided unlocking the cage and going in for a closer examination.

But the temptation was there.

The Kaius haunt vampires had shown such relief when they received the report Kaius had opened his eyes. The decreased tension in a room a thousand miles away could be felt in the little Alberta acreage. Audra, Molly, and Simone were more relaxed as they spent the rest of the evening stocking up on blood donations and cleaning what they could from the basement before exhaustion got the better of them.

One peek at Kaius's fangs, a quick photo, might give another burst of hope.

"It always throws me how young they look when they're sleeping," Simone said softly behind her. "All the stress and pressure completely gone for a few hours. They look almost harmless."

Harper glanced over her shoulder and smiled, taking a step away from the bars. "Almost," she replied. "It must be easy to forget how lethal they are."

Hiking her crossbow onto her shoulder, Simone smirked. "Everyone's lethal under the right circumstances."

With a final look at Kaius, she walked out of the cage room and checked Boy's IV again. "If you need to sleep, I'll be good for a few more hours."

Simone's curls bounced as she crossed her arms and shook her head. "No deal, medic. I'm well-versed in staying awake for thirty-six-hour stretches. You, on the other hand, we need alert and functioning by nightfall. Head to bed. If I need anything medical, Nichol's on call and he can walk me through it."

Taking a deep breath, she nodded and trudged to the ladder. "Good night, Simone."

"Night, Harper. Rest now because when you wake up, you're training under me. And I'm going to be overtired and cranky."

Her nose wrinkling at what that training would entail, she crawled up the ladder slowly, her legs heavy from exhaustion. By the time she reached her bed, her feet were barely lifting off the floor.

The quick shower she'd taken hours earlier had left her long chestnut hair damp, and it sent a chill through her as she settled into bed, tightened the blanket around her, and closed her eyes.

What. A. Rush.

The adrenaline was still pulsing through her veins. Hours of the constant pressure and stress to balance two vampires between life and death had wound her muscles and kept her mind thrumming in anticipation of the next emergency, the next decision.

Focusing on her feet first, she tensed and relaxed rhythmically in an attempt to make her body as tired as her mind.

Her years as a medic and caregiver had many moments of fear and strain, when seconds counted, and every choice made had lasting impacts.

But this was different.

It wasn't an unexpected accident bringing the patients to her. There was no doctor on the way to take control, no ambulance stocked with supplies zipping her way with a team of support. The onlookers weren't family members well-versed in hospice care protocol, knowing their loved one was at the end of their life and grateful for whatever relief her skills could provide.

Instead, she'd done everything she could to avoid meeting the eyes of the vampires who watched in anticipation while she, Molly, and Audra brought two vamps to the edge of death with purposeful decisions. There was no acceptance of final death from them, no acknowledgment the procedure could fail. No human error could be detected through expensive equipment. No textbooks had step-by-step instructions for what they did.

All she had were Nichol's barked instructions, Molly's quick movements, and Audra's cool head.

Shifting her attention to her legs, she stretched them out and held her breath for ten seconds, exhaling loudly and forcing her muscles to relax.

Once the turning was deemed a hesitant success, she worked quietly to clean what she could, assisting Audra and Molly in lifting Kaius and transporting him back into the cage where he would be contained until they could assess his condition. She caught snippets of phone conversations as the excitement lessened and the Kaius haunt women touched base with their partners.

Molly was the loudest, her side of her talk with Dominic filtering into the basement from her position topside. Between reassurances she was safe and promises she was eating were comments on the distance between them, guarantees she would be home soon.

Simone was briefer. Her clipped report to Nichol was softened at the end by concerned instructions for him to rest, to walk away from the computer, and to trust they had everything under control for a few hours.

Although she wouldn't place money on it, Harper was certain Simone's voice wavered when she signed off with a hushed reminder that she missed him.

Laying back on a blanket by the cage room, Audra spoke softly with Mikhail, talking through plans for the next evening before her voice dropped to a whisper, the term *bloodslave quarters* hushed while her cat-eyes scanned the basement room. Whatever Mikhail said in response drew a small smile and she sat up to lean against the wall, her arms crossing over her knees as she listened to him. A few minutes passed before her forehead dropped to her arms and her phone fell from her hand, its brightness letting Harper know Mikhail's end of the call was still going.

Tossing her arm over her eyes to block the sunlight breaching the tattered curtains, her mind brought Boy's blank expression to the forefront.

He was truly a gorgeous specimen.

But it was whatever the pretty package hid that had her pushing past the urge to recoil every time he inadvertently looked her way.

Molly seemed to react in much the same way. Simone, to a lesser extent.

Audra obviously had some sort of rapport with the

vampire, but Harper got the feeling few things scared the domineering woman.

And Boy was scary. Maybe even scarier than the Deviant Kaius with his jerking movements and black eyes tracking her with sniper precision.

The leader of the infamous Kaius haunt, who was locked up like a rabid animal.

Exhaling slowly, she relaxed into the lumpy mattress and hoped for sleep.

CHAPTER EIGHT

Harper handed her laptop and phone to Audra and backed away, grateful she remembered to clear her browsing histories when she woke.

"There's no password on either," she volunteered while Audra called Nichol and put him on speaker.

"He could break through whatever security is in place anyways." Audra grinned. "Any folders you want him to stay out of? Private pictures for a boyfriend?"

Her cheeks flushing, she shook her head. "No, no nudes or anything."

Nichol's voice broke through the discomfort, making it almost less awkward with his abruptness. "I'm not looking for nudity. I'm looking for questionable site cookies and will link your computer and phone to our secured server to ensure all communication over the next few weeks will stay secure. This will also ensure any photos you do send to a partner will be safe from hacking efforts."

"Great," she muttered, picking up her phone. "I'm going downstairs to remove Boy's IV line and check on Kaius. I'll bring this back up as soon as I'm done."

While Audra and Nichol invaded her electronics, she descended into the basement where Molly and Simone were taping plastic around the mattress. Boy stood in the corner of the room, the IV stand beside him.

Her brows lifted as she took in the neatly rolled

catheter line, the empty blood bags removed and folded at his feet. "You unhooked it yourself?"

"He ran all the lines in the bloodslave quarters," Molly volunteered from across the room. "Dominic says he can find a vein blindfolded with one hand tied behind his back."

Recalling her first failed attempt to insert a catheter in him, she winced. "Sorry for the extra poke last night. It's been a few months since I did it." Boy responded with nothing more than a quick bowing of his head and she walked over to Molly and Simone, peeking in on Kaius. "How has he been?"

"Subdued and silent," Simone replied, widening her stance when the lump in the cell stirred. "Still no obvious sign it worked, though. Aside from the fact he's not trying to eat us."

Easing her phone from her back pocket, she slipped past the women and crouched out of reach of Kaius. "I need to take a few photos to send to Mikhail for assessment. I can get his hands from here, I think, but I'll have to get in there to examine his fangs, and Nichol wants me to run an IV line to ensure he's getting enough into his system."

Boy appeared behind her with unnatural speed, and she startled. Clutching her heart, she stood and backed away from the cage door while he opened the lock and stepped inside.

"Okay then," she said as she followed him in. "How do you want to do this?"

Rolling Kaius onto his back, Boy hooked his feet around the sprawled legs and gripped Kaius's wrists, holding him prone on the cement.

Moving quickly, she snapped a few pictures of the

gnarled fingers, narrowing her eyes at the pinkies that looked somewhat straighter than they had the previous night. "Molly? Can you grab the IV lines and that box of medical supplies while I check his teeth?"

Molly saluted her and skipped across the basement, a clamoring of metal and hushed curses echoing through the room soon after.

"Boy? Am I okay to touch him?"

Boy nodded and adjusted his knee to keep one of Kaius's arms immobile while he held the slack jaw steady for her to lift his top lip and capture the images of his fangs.

The jagged edges made to hook and dismember prey were smoothing out. The yellow hue was completely chipped away to leave a crisp white enamel.

"This looks better," she mused aloud while Molly rolled the IV stand into the cage and slid the medical box in behind it. Opening a fresh needle and catheter line, she held it out to Boy. "Do you want to do the honors?" He shook his head and she shrugged, finding a good vein with ease given the tight hold Boy had on Kaius's arm. "I'd feel a lot better if we had antiseptic or something."

"Vampires don't get sick," Simone offered, her bow trained on Kaius's stomach. "Infection is impossible."

Suddenly aware of the weapon aimed at them, she ran the line and began the drip, getting out of Simone's line of sight as fast as she could. "I think we're done here for now. I'll check on him in two hours."

Simone smiled at her while she and Boy left the cage, and Boy locked it up. "Molly," she called over her shoulder, "you're on guard duty. Harper, Boy, and I are going to do a little attack preparation."

****

Harper's shoulder dropped with relief when Simone's phone timer chimed. "I'll head inside and crawl down to the basement and check on Kaius. I shouldn't need more than..." Five? Ten? "Twenty minutes," she stated, buying herself enough time to gulp some water and rest her aching muscles.

"I'll give you fifteen," Simone retorted, reloading her bow, and looking pointedly at Boy. "You have a meal arriving in one hour. No arguments." When his eyes darkened and he slunk off to the back of the property, she glared. "He's slower and weaker than expected. Which makes him useless as a defender when we leave."

Harper pulled off her boots and brushed the clumps of snow from her clothes.

Simone used Boy as Harper's live target for the past two hours to demonstrate a variety of offensive techniques she insisted Harper needed to master prior to their departure.

The poor vampire was kicked, hit, pummeled, tackled, and tossed into the snow more times than she could count. Any potential break during the practice was filled with Simone's demands, sending him running through the trees, watching him drag fallen logs, and scrutinizing his form while he shimmied onto the roof of the old house.

"Too damn slow," she would bark out after every attempt before growling out another order Boy obeyed immediately.

Climbing down the ladder, she jumped from the second-last rung onto the floor and jogged over to the cage, slowing when she caught sight of Kaius sitting up in the cell with his long arms draped over his tattered jeans and his head bowed.

"Hey." She greeted hesitantly, looking over her shoulder for Molly and wondering where the woman had disappeared to. "I'm not sure you remember me. I'm Harper. I'm here to help you and Boy for the next few weeks." When he remained still, she inched forward and squinted at his IV line. "Can you turn your arm a little? Like this?" she asked, demonstrating in case he didn't understand her.

Kaius tilted his head a fraction and extended his hand slowly, turning his arm with the same slow motion she had used.

"Good, good," she cooed, glancing at the empty blood bags on the IV stand as her voice took on the cheerfulness she easily adapted with patients. "Want me to free you up until your next feed? I can disconnect you from the stand if you like. It may make you more comfortable."

She trailed off with her final statement, looking around the barren cell with the steel bars and cement floor before her eyes fell on Kaius's bloodied clothes and hair.

There was a loud thump in the basement room as Molly called out. "Harper? You aren't supposed to be in there without a weapon." She skidded to a stop in the doorway. "Sorry. I was shoulder-deep into the fridge."

Harper smiled, keeping one eye on Kaius when he recoiled farther against the back of the cage. "We were just getting acquainted."

Yanking her gun from her back pocket, Molly flipped the chamber open and counted the bullets, her lips moving as she did. "Audra and Nichol said no getting within reaching distance of Kai unless you're armed and accompanied. We don't know what he'll do, and we don't have time to bring in a new nanny."

Turning her attention back to Kaius, she frowned. "Could you maybe put the gun away? I think you're making him nervous."

Laughing, Molly shrugged and pocketed her weapon. "There isn't a gun on the planet that could spook Kaius Khthonios. He's a fucking beast. Probably faster than the bullets."

"Perhaps," she murmured as the vampire hunched tighter over his knees and she caught sight of his blue eyes for the first time. "I'll be back later to check those hands and teeth out, okay? I'll bring some clothes and blankets by, too."

****

Kaius watched the Harper woman turn her back and walk away, the scent of her O-negative blood still drifting through the stale air as she disappeared from view.

The other woman, the brunette with the loud voice who paced the floor with heavy steps, gave him a long, hard look and returned to her post, closing the door behind her, and leaving him alone.

The vague familiarity of the loud brunette's face was somewhere deep in his mind, somewhere he knew existed but couldn't access. It was in the same place the female with the colorful curled hair resided, the woman with the weapon trained on his body every time she opened the door and checked in on him.

Pushing himself off the floor, he crept to the bars of the cage to wait for the blond vampire to return.

CHAPTER NINE

Harper crossed her legs and sat on the ratty sofa while Audra placed her phone and laptop beside her. "Do I need to press anything to link up with the Kaius server?"

"It will automatically channel through until the end of your time here," Audra assured her, keeping her eyes averted and biting her lip. "Your phone is untraceable to anyone outside the haunt, but all communication will be monitored until the contract expires and Nichol disconnects you." Giving her a pointed look, Audra repeated herself. "All. Communication. And websites."

Nodding her understanding, she tapped on Austin's texts and fired off a quick check-in to let him know she was fine. "You all probably know my housemate isn't the most vampire-supportive guy," she posited. "He's a decent man. Just easily led."

Audra shrugged and stretched out on the other side of the small sofa. "We're no strangers to vamp hate." She lowered her voice. "Simone was a vamp-killing assassin. I was a bloodslave. Molly was kidnapped by one and sold to another." When Harper's eyes widened, her nose wrinkled. "Long story. The Kaius haunt blew up his house and Simone eventually killed the vamp. The point is, Nichol tracked your online presence going back a decade and if he's happy, we all are. You can't control the thoughts and words of others."

Simone stomped out of the bedroom she was sharing with Molly, her hair wild and mood sour. "I thought you were going to wake me at sunrise so we could get a good start on the drive."

"Too many loose ends to wrap up," Audra stated. "Harper and I had to review the blood donor schedule, Mickey uploaded the donor photos to her computer for identification, and I needed to make a few lists of reminders. Besides," she smiled, "you're so much more pleasant to travel with when you're rested."

Grunting, Simone tossed her bag by the front door and returned to her room, growling at Molly to get up.

Harper watched silently while the women collected their things. Simone lay an arsenal of knives and UV flashlights on the kitchen table while Molly threw a gun onto the pile and deposited three boxes of bullets unceremoniously onto one of the chairs.

"If you need refills, Nichol will take care of it," Molly called out while she loaded her backpack with food from the fridge. "You might want a grocery delivery made soon. Like, tomorrow soon."

Audra held a set of keys out to her, kneeling to tie her boots up. "These belong to the SUV in the shed at the back of the property. You aren't stuck here, but it might be a good idea to do any errands you need in a town where you aren't known. Or drive into the city. And always text Nichol your plan, your destination, and keep him updated on any detours."

She bit her lip and stood, pocketing the keys. "So you're all going now? Are you sure Kaius is going to be, okay? Or Boy?"

The women exchanged a look, and Audra blinked slowly. "Kaius will survive. Boy is weak, but still strong enough to do a decent amount of damage should the need arise. And as long as he feeds on human blood instead of that damn cow blood, he'll get stronger every night." She straightened and gave her a tight smile. "We need to get back to our posts in Denver."

"What she means," Molly interjected, "is we need to get back to the guys. They don't do well when we're separated, so right now they're working distracted and getting sloppy and cranky."

"Sloppy, cranky vampires cause deaths," Simone added, slinging her crossbow over her shoulder. "You got this, Harper. Just follow Nichol's lead, never let down your guard around the donors or Kaius, and remember you have backup zipping all around this place even if you can't see it."

Glancing at the window, she swallowed. "Okay then. I, um, I got this."

Within minutes, the women were backing out of the property, leaving her alone with two ancient vampires hidden in the basement.

"I don't got this," she muttered, closing the door tight and flipping the meager lock.

****

Harper knocked softly on the door to the cage room before cracking it a fraction. "Boy? Kaius? Is it okay if I come in?"

Met with expected silence, she inched the door open farther and stepped inside, holding her phone out toward the far corner where Boy sat hunched on a small stool. "Rhys asked for updated photos of Kaius's hands and fangs before the donors arrive, so—" She trailed off, knowing the pictures were necessary but not eager to watch Boy restrain the currently subdued Kaius.

Boy walked past her and opened the lock, his dead blue eyes cast downward until he came within reach of Kaius and Kai growled low in his throat.

Before she could blink, both vampires were on the ground. Boy's fingers wrapped around the back of Kaius's neck as he pressed him flat to the floor with his knee. The growling amplified briefly, cutting short when Boy's grip visibly tightened.

"Oh, wow," she exhaled, glancing at the open cage door. "Are you sure I should I come in there?"

With the quick shake of his head, Boy lifted Kaius off the floor and walked him to the bars, restraining both arms behind his back as they came within reaching distance of her. Lifting one of Kaius's arms, he forced the fingers to splay, releasing his hold only long enough to reposition his grip when Kai's arm stretched too close to the bars.

Snapping a few pictures as fast as she could, she cringed when Boy locked the first arm against Kaius's body and held up the other, repeating the same rough treatment until Kai bared his fangs. Boy pushed him to his knees and shoved the side of his hand into Kaius's mouth.

"Oh. Oh, wow," she breathed, crouching down and trying to ignore the barbaric handling. "I need a few shots of his teeth, but maybe a little more gently?"

Boy's blue eyes darkened with what almost looked like exasperation. He yanked his hand from Kaius's mouth and knelt, wrapped his arm around Kai's chest, grabbed his jaw, and forced it open.

The long white fangs were pristine, the silvery sheen mimicking Boy's and arced with a viper elegance. She paused a moment, snapped back to attention when

Kaius's lip snarled up and his eyes locked on her throat, his pupils ovaling. She managed to take a single photo before Boy hauled the vampire to his feet again and walked him to the corner of the cell. He forced Kai into a wide stance in the corner, hands wrapped on the bars while Boy backed out of the cage. Every flicker of movement from Kai brought Boy flush up against him again, the repositioning roughly methodical until Kaius held the pose long enough for the lock to click.

Keeping close to the exit, she watched the manhandling play out, her phone tight in her hand and her attention on Kaius's motionless form. "I'll send these off and, um, the first donor should be here within the hour."

She climbed out of the basement, shaking off the violent treatment of the vampire in the cell as she brought up Rhys's number and sent off the pictures.

He called her moments later.

"Hey, sweetheart," a low voice purred. "Those pics look good. You getting all settled?"

Wincing at the flippant endearment, she sat on the sofa. "Yes, sir. I'm just waiting for the sun to set and the first guy to arrive."

"Sir," Rhys scoffed. "We're way past formalities, angel. Call me Rhys, call me god, but never call me sir. Nichol wanted me to remind you he'll be monitoring the arrivals and departures of the donors with drones, and you need to be armed at all times when you're expecting company."

Frowning at the collection of weapons on the kitchen table, she slumped back. "So, Rhys?" she posited, her cheeks flaming as one of the steamier stories she'd read about him zipped through her head. "I had a question about Kaius."

Her statement hung in the air for a moment before he responded. "Shoot."

Taking a deep breath, she dropped her voice to a whisper to avoid being overheard by the vampires below her. "Boy was really rough with him earlier and I wasn't sure if maybe he might be a little too rough?"

"Define rough," Rhys ordered. "Are we talking hand removal? Flayings?"

"Oh my god, no!" She gasped, sitting up straighter. "Nothing like that. He was restraining him, though. Holding Kaius on his knees. Even pushing the palm of his hand into his mouth. It was—"

"Discipline," Rhys finished for her, all tension gone from his voice as he chuckled. "You ever babysit?"

Blinking at the sudden shift in topic, she nodded. "Yes. Lots. Why?"

"Ever babysit toddlers? Overtired toddlers?"

Humming in agreement, she glanced outside again to watch for movement in the darkness.

"Vamps are nothing more than toddlers for the first weeks or months of their existence," Rhys continued. "Except they can bench twelve hundred pounds out of the gate, have the speed of a hummingbird, and could drain a human in eight minutes flat. You're in the unique position of witnessing those crucial first nights. Boy is establishing dominance. If he doesn't do it now, it'll be a fuck of a lot harder when Kai's strength returns, and he becomes more calculating."

Thinking back to Boy's methodical corrections, she walked over to the kitchen table and picked up one of the flashlights, holding the phone tight to her ear. "What if Boy hurts him?"

"He'll heal."

Shoving the light into her back pocket, she gingerly lifted one of the sheathed knives. "What if he hurts him bad?"

"Sweetheart," Rhys interjected. "I know you've seen the Deepfryer footage from LA. What you didn't see was every inch of me baked almost to the bone. And I healed up just fine, wouldn't you say? I know you have a thing for the boots."

The phone vibrated, and she looked at the screen, wincing when she got an eyeful of Rhys Kaius standing in front of a mirror in nothing but boxers and black boots. "I, um…yes, you healed nicely," she stammered, deleting the image immediately out of guilt. "Your point is made."

A woman's voice came across the speaker, cutting in and out until it came through crystal clear. "Hello, Harper? Lis here. I am so, so sorry. Rhys lacks a filter. And decency. And pretty much everything that keeps normal people from being creeps."

Covering her mouth, she closed her eyes tight as Rhys defended himself in the background, claiming vampirism set a new standard of normal. "It's okay," she finally got out. "I was just a little taken aback."

"He has that effect." Lis laughed. "I'm passing the phone back to him if he promises to behave. Talk soon, Harper."

She could hear them whisper to each other, a soft murmuring followed by Lis giggling when Rhys took over the call again.

"Okay, princess," he said. "We'll be watching over you from the drones tonight. After every feeding, text me or Nichol about your observations of the donor. We want everything: demeanor, reaction, anything odd or too normal. Nichol worries recording them could result in altered data, so we'll go strictly by your instinct and Boy's, if he makes any concerns known. Deal?"

"Of course," she replied, her mind back on her responsibilities. "I'll be in touch."

"I'm sure I would have found your touch rather enjoyable," Rhys purred. "It's a pity I'm taken because your reading habits have me a little intrigued. Though I should warn you that as much as it kills me to say it, some of those fanfics have slightly exaggerated my endowment. Have a good night, angel."

The phone went black, and she covered her face with her hands, the heat of her cheeks warming her palms until headlights lit up the small house and her first night of solo vampire babysitting began.

CHAPTER TEN

Harper stood in the doorway and wrapped her arms around herself as the truck drove off, the red taillights spreading their glow across the ice. "He seemed nice," she called over her shoulder to Boy, waiting until the vehicle was out of sight before shutting the door and flipping the lock. "I thought he was going to cry when you bit him, but he took it like a champ, don't you think?"

Boy gave a quick nod, his blond hair falling into his eyes as he stood in the corner slouched and silent, his fangs extending past his bottom lip.

"I'll let Nichol know," she continued cheerfully, tapping the UV light subconsciously while she walked toward the basement hatch. "I suppose you must be feeling better now after a warm meal. A little more invigorated, perhaps?"

The one-sided conversation came naturally, a result of her years caring for many who were too weak to speak but enjoyed the company and the relative normalcy of casual discussions.

Descending the ladder, she hopped off the second last rung with a flourish and stepped aside. Boy followed, jumping from the sixth rung, and giving her what almost appeared to be a challenging smirk.

"Yeah?" she snorted, following him to the cage room. "Well, if I was fifty feet tall like you, I would've jumped from the top. So there."

He paused and glanced over his shoulder at her, his blue eyes flat and unamused as he opened the door and walked up to Kaius's cell, where Kai sat cross-legged in the far corner. Boy gestured for him to rise, staring the vampire down until Kaius reluctantly got to his feet and took a step forward, halting when Boy shook his head and unlocked the cage door, leaving it wide open.

She stayed in the doorway and watched Boy skulk over to Kaius to adjust his stance: straightening his back, squaring his shoulders, and forcibly clasping Kai's hands behind his back when he met with resistance. Once Boy was satisfied, he scored his wrist with his fangs and held it up to Kaius.

Kai locked his attention on her for a moment before his fangs buried into Boy's wrist and his gaze dropped to the floor. She looked away, scanning the area for something she could busy herself with to combat the urge to watch the feeding. Seeing the IV lines scattered on a small wooden table, she crept over and wrapped them, meticulously aligning the loops, feeling Kaius's eyes on her every movement.

Fumbling the last one, she knelt down to pick it up off the floor, propelling herself against the wall when a scuffle broke out in the cell. The blur of motion came to an abrupt halt with Kaius on his knees and one of Boy's arms locked tight around his throat, the other restraining Kai's wrists.

She swallowed and pushed herself to her feet, brushing the dust from her pants. "Boy?" she called out warily, increasingly conscious of Kaius's blue eyes tracking her while she inched toward the cell door. "Should I lock that up again?"

Boy's muscles flexed as Kai attempted to arch away from him, relaxing only when Kaius relented and held position. Shaking his head, Boy yanked Kai back onto his feet and roughly readjusted him, blocking her from Kaius's view until Kai remained in place with his focus on the wall. Boy backed out of the cell, locked it up, and stood on the other side of the bars with her, his arms crossed as though daring Kaius to move. When he was satisfied Kai wasn't going to disobey, he motioned for Harper to leave, turned the light off, and left Kaius in the dark.

She held her tongue until they were back upstairs, checking the clock against the donor schedule before she sat on the sofa and Boy paced the floor like a caged lion.

"Rhys said you're disciplining him," she opened. "Would it be better if I wasn't down there with you when he needs to feed? He seemed uncomfortable eating in my presence."

Boy stopped in front of her and crouched down, holding his hand out for her phone. He opened her note app, typing and deleting with intense concentration. Glancing at the extra space on the sofa, he sat on the floor and passed the cell back.

Until Kaius can maintain complete control in the presence of one human, he cannot be exposed to others. He requires your presence to acclimate.

Nodding, she bit her lip and frowned. "Makes sense. I just feel like some kind of Peeping Tom watching you feed him."

He took the phone back gently and methodically typed another message.

Kaius would benefit from you bringing a meal downstairs. If you are not too bothered by the feeding to eat. It would also allow him the opportunity to practice blocking and targeting scents.

Brows lifting, she smiled at the suggestion. "I'd like that. Why don't I get something prepared after our next donor comes by?"

****

Kaius squinted when his keeper flicked the light on without warning. The room flooded with an artificial glow, tinting everything yellow and humming with the buzz of the electrical feed. He could smell the woman's proximity before she entered, an intriguing combination of the artificial fruit scent clinging to her skin, the fabricated floral in her long, dark hair, the underlying pulse of O-negative enhancing everything she touched, and...salted meat?

Forgetting his place, he rose to his feet to get a better look at what the Harper woman was carrying in her hands, wrinkling his nose when he was accosted with the overpowering stench of aged cheese and pickled cucumbers. He was vaguely aware of the lock to his cell opening, of the creak of the cage door while he stepped toward her for a closer look. But it wasn't until the vampire Harper called Boy had him skidding across the cement on his knees, he realized he'd walked halfway across the cage, his attention on the woman and her plate of food.

Against his instincts, he relented immediately, even going so far as to stand at attention once Boy hefted him to his feet. When the huge male stepped between him and Harper, he dropped his gaze to the floor and clasped his hands behind his back until Boy was appeased.

"I hope you don't mind," Harper called into the cage, her voice softer and sweeter than any other stored in his jumbled mess of a memory. "I'm going to have dinner with you tonight. It's quite lonely above ground."

Boy moved aside and Kaius held position to avoid another confrontation. Even with his head bowed, he could track her movements along the exterior of the cage. He heard the gentle placing of her plate on the table and peeked at the prim crossing of her ankles as she sat in the rickety wooden chair. He could see the faint bounce of her knee, hear her knife scrape across the ceramic. The smell of Boy's blood hit him, and he felt his fangs lengthen involuntarily when the vein was presented to him.

He hesitated.

"There's something so communal and comforting about sharing a meal," Harper stated, her legs angling toward the cell. "Eating alone can feel so isolating. Being observed while eating alone is infinitely worse, though." She laughed and took a bite of cheese, pointing her fork toward him. "It's very disconcerting. So, please. Eat."

With her permission, he sank his teeth into Boy's wrist.

"I think this is my favorite kind of meal," she mused, as though she wasn't dining with the caged, blood-thirsty animal he knew he was. "A little of this, a little of that. No rush to finish something before it gets cold. I could probably have this every day." He lifted his eyes to her, and she gave him a cheerful smile. "In fact, I very well may do just that while I'm here."

She continued to chat amicably between bites, a steady stream of commentary about the weather outside, the dreariness of the cage room she deemed needed a little less grey and a little more blue, and the saltiness of the ham.

73

It wasn't until Boy nudged at his jaw that he realized he'd been feeding slower and slower while she spoke. His drive to satiate his hunger was tempered by the lilting one-sided conversation that was simultaneously boring and fascinating. He unhooked his fangs without pause, lowering his gaze when he noticed Boy watching him closer than usual.

"Oh, darn." Harper sighed as she stood and collected her plate. "Boy, we need to get up there before the last donor gets here." She took a small step toward the cage and put her hand on the bar. "We'll be back down soon, okay? Thank you for keeping me company during dinner."

As Boy locked the cell and followed her from the room, Kaius remained in place and sifted through the lingering scents, locking on the ones that were distinctly Harper's and committing them to memory.

CHAPTER ELEVEN

Harper glared at the ceiling and debated hanging up the call. "Those rallies are disgusting displays," she hissed, rolling onto her side. "I can't believe you're going. You're better than that, Austin."

Austin let out a long, pained groan. "See? This is why I didn't say anything."

"Then maybe posting about it on a public forum wasn't a good idea." She seethed. "What purpose does attending this thing have? You've never even met a vampire, let alone talked to one long enough to form an opinion."

"I read," Austin countered defensively, his voice clipped. "We're protesting them for people like you, you know. Those things do some horrible shit to women. Kids, too. We're in a war here."

Sitting up, she slammed her hand on the mattress. "Stop using the word 'war'. You aren't soldiers, no matter how much camouflage you wear or how many of those stupid UV lights you strap to your trucks."

"Fucking symp," Austin retorted, catching himself only after he'd spoken. "Jeez, sorry, Harper. You know I don't like arguing this stuff with you. I just don't get why you don't see how dangerous those things are to us. Between the global market manipulation, the attacks, the fact they've already taken over a whole city and put their laws into place? As a woman, you have a lot to lose when they take over and start enslaving people."

Closing her eyes to center her temper, she took a deep breath. "Don't go, Austin. Those rallies are poisonous. They're filled with a bunch of angry, scared men, creating an enemy out of nothing. And don't 'as a woman' me. All that does is make me want to throat-punch you." She could hear him grin over the phone and she laid back on her pillow. "Call me tomorrow evening, okay? And keep your ass home tonight. You're not that guy, Austin."

His noncommittal hum was all the answer she needed as he hung up.

Pursing her lips, she tossed her comforter off and got out of bed, trudging to the shower, and letting her simmering anger spiral down the drain with the soapsuds. With two hours until sunset, she took her time brushing out her hair and dressing, the decision between her grey yoga pants and her black ones taking far longer than necessary.

After a quick glance outside at the snowfall, she poured a cup of coffee and descended the ladder into the basement to check on her wards. Boy lay sprawled out on the floor in the middle of the room, one eye opening when her feet touched the ground.

"Just peeking in," she whispered while she tiptoed past him, waving her phone as she opened the cage room door. "Nichol wants updated photos. I'll be quick."

When the azure eye closed, she crept up to the cell, using the light of her phone to scan it in the darkness.

"The blue light that contraption emits is off-putting," a low voice rumbled from the corner of the room. "I would prefer the temporary blinding of the florescent if given the choice."

Fumbling her phone, she shoved it into her pocket and felt along the wall for the light switch. "I am so sorry," she whispered. "I didn't realize you were awake. Close your eyes."

The brightness hit her, and she blinked rapidly to gain back her vision, finding Kaius leaning against the bars at the back of his cell, arms crossed, and shoulders slouched.

He gave her a tightlipped smile. "The warden may not appreciate your unguarded presence in here."

"The warden," she smiled, keeping out of reach, "is finally getting some much-needed rest. I'm here to take a few photos and I'll leave you alone."

He cocked his head and narrowed his eyes. "What's the purpose of all these pictures you take of my hands and fangs?"

Glancing out the door at Boy and finding him deathly motionless, she inched along the wall and sat on the small stool Boy often used. "Well, the vampires you lead—or used to lead—are tracking your recovery. The state of your fingers and teeth is one way to ensure you're healing up."

He visibly swallowed, his back straightening a fraction. "The vampires I lead," he echoed. "Who are they, exactly?"

"I'm not sure how much I'm supposed to say," she replied, folding her hands in her lap. "I don't know much myself."

Kaius chuckled humorlessly. "From whom shall I seek the information? The mute warden?"

Cringing, she lowered her gaze to the floor while she debated the problem, flinching back when she caught Kai stepping toward her in her periphery.

"My apologies," he murmured, returning to the back bars. "Perhaps we can start with something simple. Who is Boy?"

Sitting up, she exhaled loudly and smiled. "That's an easy one. He's your creator."

Kai shoved his hands into the pockets of his shredded, filthy jeans. "How old is he?"

"Older than you," she stated. "And you're well over two thousand." She could see a flicker of wariness flash through his eyes before he locked down his expression and his jaw. "I'm sorry. That's probably hard to take in right now. But Nichol said you should start regaining some of your memories in the next few days." Her voice trailed off while Kaius continued to stare past her. "Would you like to talk to him? Nichol, I mean?"

Kai shook his head slowly. "Who is Nichol? Is he one of the vampires you claim I lead?"

Wishing Boy would intervene, she shrugged helplessly. "He's running the Kaius haunt," she opened before launching into as much detail about the group of vampires as she knew from their public personas, the media coverage, and her own limited time with Audra, Molly, and Simone.

Kaius stood still against the bars, his only reaction the tensing of his muscles when she described what she knew about Jagger's time in a human jail, Rhys's time in the Deepfryer, and the vampire evacuation into Denver, skirting carefully around the information Molly shared about Nichol's role in his current situation. His eyes remained locked on the wall behind her, the blue shifting from light to dark as his irises ovaled.

"So here we are," she ended, gesturing around the cell. "I'm sure Nichol would answer any questions you may have."

Kaius's attention shifted to the door and Boy slunk in, his expression unreadable as he opened the cell's lock and joined Kai, motioning for him to hold out his hands and bare his fangs.

"Right," she said with a sigh, getting to her feet and taking out her phone. "Talk time is over. Smile."

****

Kaius lay face down in the cell's corner, Boy's booted foot holding him firmly against the cold cement.

"I'm sure it wasn't intentional," Harper called out behind him, her words doing little to ease the guilt and shame creeping through the fog in his mind.

Boy's heel dug deeper against his spine, and he forced his muscles to relax, willed his body to stop fighting the stronger, faster male who had yanked him from the cell bars and tossed him across the room like a rag doll. The sound of Harper's shocked scream echoed against the shattering of plates and looped in his head, giving him something to focus on while the onslaught of raging hunger subsided.

As though sensing the shift in his mind, Boy hauled him to his feet and forced his hands to grip the bars along the back of the cell, his fingers cracking under the harsh hold of his sire. He braced himself for whatever came next, unwilling to risk a glance over to ensure Harper was okay.

He'd scared her.

Bad.

The thrum of her heartbeat pounded against the walls, a pulsing reminder of his unexpected lunge at her when she'd moved to leave the room.

Whatever propelled him toward her had caught him

off-guard as much as it had her.

"Kaius? I'm fine. And it was an ugly plate anyway. No harm, okay?" she said softly from behind him, the calm of her voice at odds with the rapid beating of her heart. "Boy? It was an accident."

It was no accident.

It was a humiliating loss of control, a moment of weakness he was unprepared to combat.

Boy released his hands with a final squeeze of warning, and he held position, his head bowed as the lock clicked open and the metal door slammed shut. He tracked Harper's footsteps out of the room, catching the slight falter in her gait when Boy's joined hers and the light was turned off.

Pathetic animal.

The words wormed through his mind as he remained still, a woman's vaguely familiar voice sending ice through his veins.

****

Harper scooted her chair to the side so Boy could fit in the camera view on the laptop, frowning when he ducked his head forward enough for his blond hair to cover his face while Nichol rattled off a checklist of skills the two of them needed to practice for Kaius's assessments.

"Contain nightly sparring to the cell for now," the miserable vampire stated. "But eventually, you'll need to move the ring outside, where you can examine his stamina and tracking capabilities."

Boy nodded in agreement, and she put her hand up, waiting for Nichol's acknowledgment.

"What."

"Kaius was asking questions about you tonight," she

said, side-eying Boy. "I'm not sure how to answer what he wants and probably needs to know."

There was a flash of strain across Nichol's face before it hardened again. "We'll give him a little more time to stabilize and then we can arrange to reintroduce him to the haunt."

"But he nee——"

"Needs time for his brain to complete the rewiring necessary to recover memories he will require moving forward," Nichol interrupted, leaving no room for further discussion. "I'll be emailing a document of his physical and mental growth that you can complete during the nightly assessments. Boy, we'll trust your judgment on how far you can push him, but we don't have the standard year to get both of you back."

Nichol's computer jostled and moved back, Rhys's smirking face joining the conversation. "Hey, gorgeous. How are the guys treating you up there in Buttfuck, Alberta?"

Trying unsuccessfully to control her blushing cheeks, she mimicked Boy's trick and bobbed her head forward enough for her hair to drape down. "We're doing well, thank you."

When he ran his tongue along one fang, she knew he'd caught the reddening of her cheeks. "I'll be taking care of all your needs from here on out," he purred. "Text me a list of anything you want, and I'll make sure you're satisfied, sweetheart."

"What was our discussion about inappropriate suggestiveness in work settings?" Audra's voice called out from somewhere behind him. "Word choice is important for clear communication."

Leaning forward on the table to give Harper an

unobstructed view of the infamous tattoos lacing around his biceps, Rhys licked his lips. "All right, Audra. Let's try it your way. Harper, angel? If my soul wasn't tethered to a master-killer, I'd definitely take care of every fucking need you have, and all the ones you never knew you had." He turned away from the camera. "Did I do it right?"

"Out," Nichol snarled, angling the laptop back to him. "Maybe text me anything you require for yourself, or the household and we can have it there in twenty-four hours."

Boy sat up straight in his chair and cocked his head, holding his hand up for silence and listening as a faint growl came steadily from the basement.

Harper tapped his arm gently, snapping him back to attention. "Is he okay down there? Maybe you should go and check." While he got up and descended the ladder, she looked back at the screen to see Nichol leaning back in his chair, his arms crossed and eyes narrowing with suspicion. "Boy's just going to make sure Kaius is okay. He's sounding like he might be a little agitated."

"He's sounding like he might be making this a fuck of a lot more complicated than it needs to be," Nichol stated. "Take tomorrow night off, head into town, and maybe stay away until sunrise. Boy can handle things for one evening."

CHAPTER TWELVE

Harper leaned against the worn pool table and watched Austin sink the last ball before he tossed his cue onto the table in victory, grinning at her. "What's the score now? Seventy-nine games to three?"

She bit the inside of her cheek in a fruitless attempt to maintain a straight face. "Seventy-nine to four. I took that one out at the camp last year."

Sauntering up to the bar to cover the tab, he pulled out his truck keys and aimed them toward the large, tinted windows, pushing on the command start until the fob beeped in his hand. "I'll give that one to you, even though you totally double-tapped. Because I'm a nice guy."

She handed over a sizable tip to their server and followed him outside, cinching her coat together as the wind kicked up a flurry of snow. "You heading out or coming home?"

The flicker of guilt in his eyes almost went unnoticed.

Almost.

"You aren't," she stated, opening the door to the SUV she'd borrowed from Boy and turning on the ignition. "Come on. You were just saying the last rally was a total shit show."

He crossed his arms and glared at her. "Well, yeah. It was, like, too organized. The cops were all in our faces about having routes and maps, and it was just a lot of driving around for nothing." Glancing at a couple exiting the bar, he stepped closer to her and lowered his voice. "They were probably tipping the biters off about where we were headed. I read that vamps pay off local cops to keep their locations hidden. Big bucks, too."

With a deep breath, she cranked up the heat in her car and closed the door, rolling the window down halfway to keep as much warmth as she could inside the vehicle. "How about I come with you, then?"

"Why?" he scoffed. "So you can pick a fight?"

"No, so I can see what it is you're seeing in this group," she countered. "Because obviously, you get something out of it that I'm just not grasping."

He eyed her with suspicion and tugged his phone from his pocket, firing off a quick text and watching for the response. "Fine. We'll ditch your car here and you can ride with me. I don't think your employer would be too happy with you taking that beast onto the side roads."

Ensuring the SUV was locked tight, she crawled into Austin's truck, her stomach knotting as they hit the highway.

****

"What the hell?" Harper whispered, stepping closer to Austin as three of the louder men in the group shoved past them, beers in hand and voices hollering calls for unity.

Austin shoved his hands in his pockets and shrugged, refusing to look at her. "They're just gearing up. You know, psyching themselves up for the hunt." He accepted a beer from one of the few women wandering through the small crowd in the old farm garage. "We're hitting the backroads in a minute to check on some places those guys over there said were hiding vamps."

Those guys over there stood at the entrance of the building, chests puffed as they zipped up their camouflage jackets and straightened their red Species Purifier hats. They barked out instructions to the others, their statements punctuated with words pulled from the headlines of the articles Austin often used to back his flawed arguments.

"So the whole purpose of this is to drive up to strangers' homes and what, break in to look for vampires?" she asked under her breath.

Austin rolled his eyes and downed the last of his beer. "No one's breaking into anything. We're staking out the places. Taking pictures and shit we can send to the authorities."

"But you just told me the cops are paid off," she countered snidely.

Ignoring her, he jogged over to the ringleaders, joining in the chanting. The doors opened and everyone filed out to their trucks, the night lighting up as the vehicles revved to life.

She held her tongue and hopped into Austin's truck. The group sped off, skidding out on the ice in a blast of snow. The glare of UV lights bounced along the ditches, reaching into the tree lines dividing the farms and acreages along the way.

"Is this one of them?" she asked when the trucks slowed to a crawl, windows rolling down en masse. "That little house there with the living room lights on?"

Austin leaned out and called over to another driver, giving the thumbs-up confirming the location. "Yup, this is it. The guys on the snowmobiles are going to circle the yard and get as close as they can for the pictures."

Squinting through the flurries of snow that swirled in the wind, her lips drew into a thin line. "What are they doing? Austin…Austin, I don't like this," she hushed as the snowmobiles came to a stop tight to the house and small flames lit up in their hands.

"Shit," he groaned, tossing the truck into gear, and backing up. "We gotta be ready to move."

Arching back to see fireballs smash through the windows of the house, she covered her mouth with her hand and shook her head. "Why are they doing that?" she shrieked as the truck lurched. "We can't leave! Stop!"

The snowmobilers bounced out of the ditch and fish-tailed in front of them, spraying ice and snow across the windshield of the truck. Austin slammed on the brakes to avoid clipping the last of the riders and spun to the left, flinging Harper against the passenger door.

"Austin, for god's sake, we need to go back and help those people!" she yelled, ignoring the ache in her shoulder as she turned in her seat to see flames flitting inside the house's picture window.

"Would you just stop?" he snarled, righting the truck, and tearing ahead to catch up to the others. "We're not going back. We need to get the fuck out of here and…fuck." He took his hat off and shook his hair out before tucking the longer stands behind his ears and tossing the hat on the dashboard. "They're sympathizers, okay? I mean, there's probably no vamps there now, but we know they were hiding them a couple years back. And they…they're sympathizers." He looked over at her as they hit the main road, desperation on his face. "Harper, you can't say anything about this. You know you can't. If you do, you'll be an accomplice and you could get in a lot of trouble."

Her jaw dropped open as she yanked her cell from her purse. "Are you kidding? We need to call someone. People could die, Austin."

He shook his head frantically, reaching over to knock her phone from her hand. "What part of jail time do you not get?" he hollered. "Look, I didn't know they were gonna do that, but we can't play innocent now, can we? We just gotta keep our heads down." He nodded and took a deep breath. "Yeah. Heads down. Okay? There were, what, six Molotov's tossed into the house? Those won't be hard to put out. And everyone has smoke alarms." He swallowed and scanned the rest of the group as they veered toward an exit. "I'll call it in once I drop you off at the lounge. Give everyone enough time to clear out of the area."

Grasping her purse, she nodded, one eye on her phone. "This isn't right, Austin. These guys aren't playing around."

Slowing when they approached the town's turnoff, he exhaled. "I need you to swear you'll stay quiet. I can't lose my job for this."

She held her tongue until the truck pulled up to Boy's SUV. Swinging the door open, she snatched her phone from the floor. "Not a word. This time. Now call it in."

He nodded and continued to stare straight ahead, a slight tremor in his fingers as he gripped the steering wheel. "Night, Harper."

And with that, he peeled out of the lot.

"Damnit," she whispered, getting into the car, and starting the engine. Her cold hands fumbled her cell when she tapped on Nichol's number. "Come on. Answer."

"What."

Closing her eyes, she sank back in her seat. "I need help."

****

Harper gave Boy a grim smile as he opened the front door for her and stepped aside, his blue eyes scanning her over with an unnerving seriousness.

"I'm good, Boy. Thanks." She toed her boots off and tossed her coat onto the sofa while she brought her phone back to her ear. "Okay, Nichol. I'm inside."

There was a momentary pause before Nichol responded, exasperation tinging his words. "Perhaps you should remain on site for the duration of your contract," he finally stated. "I have enough shit to deal with around here without having to hack into emergency responder reporting systems up there."

Wrapping her free arm around herself, she slumped against the wall. "I will and I'm sorry," she replied, her throat tight from the tension of the night. "Thank you for sending help to those poor people."

"We'll discuss this further tomorrow."

The call ended, and she looked at her black screen before glancing over at Boy, a rush of guilt flooding her veins. "Did everything go well tonight? When did the last donor leave? Did Kaius get his final feed of the night?"

Holding up one finger, he grabbed a plate of meats and cheeses off the kitchen table and nodded toward the basement ladder. He stood back to allow her to descend first before following her to the cage room where Kai sat at the back of the cell, his long arms draped over his knees and his gaze locked on the floor.

Boy passed over her meal and she pulled the small

stool tight to the bars, attempting to erase all the evening's strain from her expression. "Good evening, Kai." She smiled. "How has your night been so far?"

Jumping to his feet with the fluidity of a gazelle, he placed his hands behind his back and stood motionless while Boy approached him. "Uneventful."

"Uneventful nights are truly the best," she replied, taking a bite of a pepperoni stick when Kaius's fangs sunk into Boy's wrist. "No moral dilemmas, no danger, no Molotov cocktails." She picked up a slice of cheese and studied it. "I definitely prefer uneventful nights."

Kaius continued his assessment of the cement floor while she ate and the night's events replayed in her mind, every moment she should have walked away highlighted in slow motion.

At the lounge.

In the parking lot.

At the barn.

When the first calls to fight rang in her ears.

"Your heart rate is rising," Kaius stated quietly, snapping her attention to the cell where he remained in place, gaze on the floor. Boy stood at his side, arms crossed and assessing Kai with detached interest. "My apologies for pointing it out. It's just very noticeable."

Taking a few deep breaths, she set her plate down and folded her hands in her lap. "Do you hear it or is there a pulsing in the room?"

Kaius's eyes flicked to Boy before he responded, his continued refusal to look her way unnerving. "The sound of your heart valves opening and closing is quite loud for me, but it's easy to tune out when it remains steady."

"And it's not too steady tonight, is it?" She smiled, tilting her head. "How far can you hear it? Is it just in this room because of all the cement, or can you track it farther?"

He licked his lips and side-eyed Boy. "I can track you eighteen steps outside the house," he said slowly before he caught something in Boy's expression and sped up his explanation. "But I do my best to avoid monitoring you at all."

"Of course," she murmured, narrowing her eyes at Boy. "Well, I suppose I should head upstairs, get cleaned up, and ready for bed. Have a good night, Kai. You too, Boy."

****

Kaius held position until the rush of shower water gurgled through the old pipes, his control snapping while the stench of human male continued to pummel his senses in the small space.

He was vaguely aware of Boy standing calmly in the corner of the cell as he slammed his fists repeatedly into the concrete wall at the back of his cage, the bones of his knuckles breaking and healing throughout the assault. The scent of his own blood overpowered the stench of human man, the red haze of his mind evaporating as he gained his footing again.

Again.

And again.

Weak, pitiful animal.

The female voice rang in his ear as he slouched against the bars and ran his bloodied hands through his hair. His thoughts whipped through his head, churning with images he knew he should recognize and split seconds of moments he couldn't recall. Flashes of faces and scenes he didn't remember brought about waves of rage, pride, or joy.

The pipes above him groaned, the water reduced to a slowing trickle. Tracking the simple thumping of the heartbeat above him, he squeezed his eyes shut and focused on it until everything else drained away.

CHAPTER THIRTEEN

Harper balanced her coffee mug while she descended the ladder, resisting the urge to flinch when the hot liquid sloshed onto her hand. Nichol's updated evening schedule lit up the phone tucked into her bra strap, his only mention of the previous evening's events a clipped reminder for her to remain on site for the night.

It was a rather anticlimactic message compared to the possibilities keeping her awake long into the morning hours. She was certain she would wake to a lecture, a salary cut, or Nichol outright firing her.

Stay on site. I'm too busy to arrange for the disposal of your body was not the expected response.

But she'd take it.

"I have good news," she called out into the basement, knocking gently on Kaius's room before opening the door. "Nichol sent a revised schedule for the night."

She trailed off when she caught sight of Boy and Kai in the dim light. Both vampires were shirtless and grappling on the floor, their low growls punctuated by the slap of skin against cement. Staying tight to the wall, she swiped her phone to life and pulled up Nichol's number, pausing when the fight stopped and Boy hopped to his feet, gesturing to his stance while Kaius nodded.

Tiptoeing across the room, she sat on the small stool and continued to observe the training session, ignored by the vampires while they took their respective corners and began another match.

Despite his silence, Boy was obviously an excellent teacher. For a solid hour, she watched him demonstrate moves, staying Kaius's movements in a flash to correct position and trajectory, and showing no sign of frustration or boredom.

And to her untrained eye, Kai was an excellent student.

Complete focus and determination replaced the lost expression that often flashed across his face as his blue eyes tracked everyone of boy's movements. From the fastest hit to the most subtle weight shift. Wounds marring his body healed swiftly with periodic feeds from Boy, the numerous injuries drawing her attention to the definition of the muscles stretching and flexing with every motion.

The paramedic in her was itching to assess the damage.

Her inner minx was far more focused on the V-cut of his hips. A more-than-fleeting thought pinked her cheeks and drew a quick glance from Kaius, resulting in a rather violent tackle by Boy.

As the older vampire righted himself and gave Kai a flat stare, Kaius glanced over at her with a sheepish smirk before he schooled his face and backed into his corner while Boy shook his head.

Taking advantage of the break in action, she passed Boy her phone through the bars. "Nichol adjusted the schedule for tonight and called off all donors," she reported as he ducked his head, his hair falling forward while he read over the message. "You two are a step ahead on the sparring practice, but Nichol has an outdoor session slated for midnight. That's in one hour."

Boy straightened up and turned to Kaius, the slight lift of one brow mirrored by his protege. Apparently appeased by Kai's response, he stalked over to the cell door and opened it, stepping between Harper and the exit while Kaius hesitantly walked out.

****

Car exhaust tinged with synthetic oil wafting on the wind.

Two coyotes gnawing on the remnants of a rabbit carcass a mile east.

Vehicles rumbling along a road seven miles to the north, three of them diesel engines.

Twigs snapping under the weight of snow.

Pine needles tapping branches as they dropped to the ground.

Kaius zeroed in on each sound and scent one by one, assessing their threat levels before filtering them out of his consciousness. Pushing the rapid breaths of squirrels to his left aside, the slow approach of Harper's footsteps behind him grounded his thoughts when she stopped at his side, pulling bright red mittens onto her hands.

"Are you okay?" she asked, her thick coat brushing against his bare arm and sending a small shiver through him. "Nichol had a shipment of clothing delivered last night with one of the donors. There may be a jacket in there."

Catching Boy's look of warning, he took a small step away from her and shook his head. "We don't feel the cold. I'm merely adapting to the surroundings."

A third coyote had found the carcass, and the snarls of the scavengers were a distraction.

Not as much of a distraction as the soft-spoken

woman beside him, but definitely on the top ten list of things pulling his attention from his mute sire.

His mute sire who was drawing Harper's gaze while he scuffed out a sparring ring in the snow-covered field.

A low growl rumbled through the still night and Boy was on him in an instant, kneeing his stance into place and forcing his arms behind his back in the submissive pose he now knew meant he breached Boy's unspoken rules. And expressing possessiveness over a woman he had no claim over was one rule Boy rightly enforced without lenience for the past three nights.

His head bowed as Boy's large fingers splayed across his skull in a death grip. He locked his eyes on the snow at his feet and willed his body to cooperate, to relax against the burning impulse to fight, to break away from the threat at his back. The growling ceased and Boy's hold loosened once he proved he regained full control of his mind and body.

It was, in a word, humbling.

With a gentle nudge, Boy drew his attention back to the sparring practice and outlined the parameters of the match.

A single tap of the fist and fang indicated the approved weapons. Palm to the forehead meant full strength.

Nodding in acknowledgment, he joined Boy in the makeshift ring, his back to the woman who was sitting hood of a large black SUV and watching them intently.

When Boy made the first move, he blocked the hit with ease, Boy's tell giving away his intent.

The slight flexing of his sire's calf muscle under his jeans.

A tell Boy hadn't revealed to him.

A tell he just knew, and had known, from the moment their first sparring match began.

A tell which drew a counteraction that was as instinctive for him as feeding.

His body knew what to do. His mind just needed to get in sync.

Even now, with Boy's significant strength advantage, he knew the vampire's weaknesses. Knew Boy's left knee would lock up for a split-second if it was hit from the correct angle. Knew Boy had a stronger, faster left hook, but his recovery time between hits was a fraction slower with his left than his right.

And when thousands of years of technique and power came at you, those milliseconds were crucial.

When the opportunity finally presented itself, he took full advantage of Boy's knee and gained the upper hand for the first time, pinning his sire to the snow-covered ground long enough to earn a nod of respect from his creator.

And a round of applause from their spectator.

"Five more minutes," Harper called over, scrunching her nose as she gave him an excited smile. "Take that big ol' guy down once more and we'll head in so you can shower."

Her encouragement was all the incentive he needed to barrel back into the match.

And it took under four minutes for his distraction to get the better of him. Harper's enthusiastic cheers sang in his ears while Boy flipped him up and over his back and slammed him onto the cold ground.

****

Harper stole another side glance at Kaius, lowering her eyes immediately when he looked up from her laptop screen and caught her.

"So all we have to do is press that key and you'll be connected with your haunt," she continued, acutely aware Boy was observing her and Kai from the corner of the kitchen.

Kaius leaned closer to tiny camera, shooting back in his chair with a glare. "That's an unflattering image, isn't it?"

Unable to hide her smile, she adjusted the computer a few inches farther from him, doing her best not to ogle the freshly scrubbed, clean-clothed vampire who twenty minutes earlier was caked in mud, snow, and week-old blood. "When you grow up with this tech, finding your best angles becomes second nature. But I promise you, your hauntmates don't care if you get a little close to the camera." Pushing her chair back, she stood and reached over to the screen. "You're all set. Once you're done, click on that little red x and you'll be good."

His eyes snapped to hers. "Where are you going?"

Looking over her shoulder at Boy, she straightened and patted his shoulder. "Just going to give you a little privacy. I'll be in my room if you need anything, okay?"

He stared at the blank screen. "I would prefer your presence during this initial communication."

She looked to Boy for guidance, sitting when the silent vampire merely nodded and crossed his arms. "I would love to stay."

Kaius sat up straighter and tapped the call button.

Within seconds, the screen filled with the familiar faces of the Kaius haunt. Nichol was front and center, flanked by Rhys, Jagger, Mikhail, and Dominic. She watched Kaius's face for any sign of recognition, any hint the vampires on the screen were triggering a connection between them and the memories he had locked in his mind.

He dropped his hand between them and linked his pinky finger around hers under the table. Nichol's jaw tensed and he spoke. "It's good to see you again, Kaius."

She could see the gears working overtime in his head while he scanned the group over and over before clearing his throat. "It's good to be seen. I'm afraid I'll need an introduction to everyone tonight. My memory appears to be slower to recover than my body has been."

The hauntmates were visibly affected by his words, the anticipation in their eyes replaced by resignation.

When none of them replied, she eased Kaius's hand onto her lap and scooted her chair closer to him. "This is Nichol." She opened, pointing to the screen. "He's your eldest. Extremely bright and quite cranky on a constant basis." When Nichol nodded, the grinding of his molars coming to a halt, she continued. "Rhys is your second eldest, and probably the most famous among humans."

Rhys's dark eyes regained the roguish glint they always seemed to carry, and he leaned closer to the camera. "I've done a lot of shit you should've killed me for, so maybe this memory thing isn't all bad, boss."

Kaius's brow lifted and he relaxed back in his seat. "Medico della Peste. The scourge."

She watched Rhys freeze before he grinned, his fangs on full display. "Yeah. Yeah, Kaius. That's me."

Kai's grip on her finger tightened, and she took a deep breath, pointing to the black-haired vampire with the ice-blue eyes. "Jagger Kaius. He helps coordinate efforts against the anti-vamp movements alongside his partner," she reported, pulling up the limited information she retained from internet articles. "And that's Mikhail.

All I really know about him is he's very sweet."

Mickey rolled his eyes and Kaius leaned in. "The empath."

Mikhail clasped his hands on the table and flexed his fingers. "Nailed it, man."

"And that's Dominic," she finished, pointing to the vampire with the bright turquoise eyes sitting beside Rhys, his knee bouncing as he adjusted his ball cap. "Everything I've read indicates he's the typical youngest child."

When Dominic smirked and the others chimed in with calls of 'brat' and 'little prince', Kai unhooked his finger and wrapped his whole hand over hers, keeping it out of sight of the others. "I'm sure the more we speak, the more will come back to me. I have many questions about fragmented memories in my mind." With a shake of his head, he narrowed his eyes at the camera. "Nichol. We were lone comrades, you, and I."

Nichol's expression hardened, and he reached offscreen for a pen and paper. "For close to eight centuries. Although Boy was always close by. Once Harper vacates the area, we can address some of the issues and concerns you have."

Flipping her hand over to give Kaius's fingers a quick squeeze, she stood and leaned in close to him, dropping her voice to a whisper she knew all the vampires likely heard. "You can trust these guys, okay? Come get me when you're done."

He stilled, staying motionless while she walked out of the kitchen with a wave to Boy.

****

Harper skidded to a halt across the kitchen floor, grasping the wall to steady herself when she caught sight of Boy descending the ladder with Kaius thrashing and snarling against his one-armed hold.

"What happened?" she called down the opening, her question answered by Nichol's voice behind her.

"Kaius's mind isn't ready to make the connections between his past and present existence."

Spinning a chair around, she straddled it and angled the laptop toward herself, cringing when a feral howl rose from the basement. "What did you say to him? He was fine ten minutes ago."

Nichol sat alone, his hazel eyes hard. "I warned you all he would need time to filter through thousands of years of memories, that the potential for overload was high at this stage of his rejuvenation." His jaw flexed, his teeth grinding rhythmically. "But to answer your question, I made the error of detailing Mikhail's turning when he inquired why Catherine the Great stood out in his head as an important figure in his existence."

Kaius's snarling grew louder before a silencing thud sent tremors through the old hardwood under her feet. "Was it traumatic for him? Why would he react so strongly?"

The old vampire pinched the bridge of his nose and hollered a brisk *not now* over his shoulder. "Picture being in the middle of a theme park. Lights, sounds, smells, and movement everywhere. Now add in five people you're trying to converse with, but each is discussing a different important topic you have to attend to mentally and emotionally. Take that feeling, multiply it by ninety, and you'll have what Kaius experienced in that kitchen."

"Drowning." She sighed, listening for a break in the quiet downstairs. "So maybe next time—"

"Next time," Nichol interrupted, leaning back, and

crossing his arms, "will occur solely at my discretion, at a time when I deem him fit. Mikhail has reported he is sensing Kaius in spurts now. Once the remnants of his old bloodline meld with his current one, we should regain the full link. It will allow him to sense us and Mickey to monitor him to avoid situations such as this."

Glaring through the camera at him, she mimicked his pose. "And what do you propose Boy and I do in the meantime?" she demanded. "Leave him in the dark? He deserves the chance to connect the pieces swirling in his head and you have the responsibility to help him."

The sharp ovaling of his irises told her she pushed too far, his voice lowering to an almost serene tone. "My responsibility to Kaius ended with the success of his re-vamping. He's Boy's responsibility now until he is ready to be brought back into this haunt to serve in his position." He clenched his teeth and leaned forward. "My obligations lie with my brothers, our partners, and the vampires under our watch. Kaius is a detriment to us in his current state, an albatross. Exposing the others to his deficiencies weakens all of us, and we've fought too fucking hard to fall now. Were he in his right mind, Kaius would agree."

CHAPTER FOURTEEN

As Harper entered the room, Kaius willed every muscle in his body to remain static. Boy's casual slouch against the bars of the cage belied his ability to take him down in a millisecond should he deem it warranted.

"Good evening, gentlemen," she called out, her full lips turning up with the same cheery smile she greeted them with every night. "We have two donors arriving in an hour, and I want to make sure you're both presentable."

He glanced over at Boy, who gave him a brief nod. "A direct feed?" he clarified, his fangs lengthening involuntarily at the thought of sinking them into a warm human vein. "After last night's episode?"

Her smile faltered, and a hardness settled in her warm eyes as she waved her phone at him. "The boss approved it, so we sure aren't going to waste this opportunity, are we?" Turning to Boy, she tapped the lock of the cell. "Both of you need to get scrubbed up and changed. You look like you've been wrestling in dirt for the past twelve hours."

"We have been," Kaius stated, pushing himself to his feet with deliberate movements.

She crossed her arms and huffed. "I know. All the banging around down here kept me up most of the day."

Guilt hunched his shoulders a fraction, Boy's following suit as he unlocked the cage to follow Harper through the basement room and up the ladder.

It was a nice view for the few seconds he had before Boy's hand gripped the top of his head and forced his chin down, reminding him of both his place and Harper's purpose in their lives.

Leading them to the washroom, she passed him a stack of towels. "Vampires may not get that sweaty guy smell, but they still get dirty. Scrub up quick, so Boy has some hot water."

Under the spray of the shower, he zeroed in on her voice while she walked back and forth through the house, narrating her actions to her silent companion.

"After the donors leave, we're going to put together a grocery list for Nichol. A few newer towels and another change of clothes for both of you would be nice to add, don't you think?" She paused long enough for an answer that never came. "I think so, too. And maybe a few comforters. There's no reason you two should be down there in this weather with nothing. And no, I don't care if you don't feel the temperature. I do, and it makes me cold looking at you."

Wrapping a towel around his hips, he held up the clothes Harper left for him, frowning at the delicacy of the fabric as he tugged the shirt and sweatpants on. He ran a brush through his short hair and carefully hung his towels before joining Boy and Harper in the kitchen, his nose wrinkling at the sour odor of the pickles on her plate. "I'm not a fan of these clothes," he stated, tugging at the ties on the front of the pants and pulling at the elastic waistband. "They're far too easily removed in an attack."

A faint blush rose on Harper's cheeks, and he caught her staring at his bare arms. She looked away and angled her chair away from him slightly. "I'll let Rhys know you don't share his fondness for workout gear."

An image solidified in his head, the dark-haired vampire with the smirk from the night before who rocked backward on a chair in an all-black uniform identical to the one he was now wearing.

"The com room," he muttered, narrowing his eyes as the visual came into focus. "That's the room Nichol has established as his headquarters. And Rhys enjoys creating chaos amid Nichol's organization." Harper and Boy exchanged a look, and he straddled a chair, placing himself between them. "Jagger is the metallurgist. The craftsman and swordsman. I selected him for his skill with a blade and his reflective temperament."

Boy nodded as the scene continued to play out in his mind.

"Dominic," he murmured. "The woman who was here last week. Molly. She's brought him a happiness immortality never could."

Another nod, and Harper scooted closer to him. "Okay, honey. Why don't you watch out the window for our guest while I get the kitchen cleaned up?"

Recognizing the distraction for what it was, he pushed off the chair and walked over to the window, scanning the darkness for signs of life. "If I sired that haunt, should I not be able to sense them? I can sense Boy's general mood when he allows it, so why not them?"

The clanging of the dishes stopped for a moment, and he looked back to see Harper tapping away on her phone before she replied. "Nichol says the procedure altered the bloodline, so your only pure link is with Boy now. And with his creator. I'm sure the others will come back eventually, though."

There was a noticeable shift in Boy's stance. His muscles tightened and his eyes ovaled as a sharp electric impulse blasted through Kaius's head, a warning he was becoming well-versed in.

Boy's creator was not approved for discussion.

Even Harper caught on to the slight change in Boy's demeanor. She walked over to him. "Your turn in the shower. You look intimidating enough without the layer of dirt and we don't want to scare off a good meal. Go."

Knowing the shower water did little to quiet their voices for Boy, he sat back on the sofa and watched her put the dishes away. "I apologize for my reaction last night."

"No need," she replied, pouring a cup of coffee and joining him. Her proximity sent a small pulse of adrenaline through his veins. "Everyone has their limits. Even big, bad vampires, right?"

He wrinkled his nose and stared out the window. "The loss of control felt foreign to me, even in the moment. I suspect I was not one for such unnecessarily aggressive displays prior to my—" Thinking back, he closed his eyes as muffled words and commands bounced through his mind. "I can't seem to bring any sense to the event that led me here. Nichol's voice. Rhys's. I catch glimpses of two other vampires and Boy. The woman was there, the female vampire. But as much as I've tried, I can't bring the scenes together."

"Maybe it's best you can't yet," she mused, standing when headlights glared into the living room. "When you're ready to know, your brain will tell you. Now tighten the drawstring of those pants before we have an indecent exposure complaint."

****

Harper bit her lip when Boy's eyes darted to the snow-covered tree line surrounding the property, his desire to prowl around outside noticeably battling with his responsibilities.

"We'll be fine," she reassured him, nudging him out onto the steps. "Kaius passed the feeding test, right? All we're going to do is watch a movie and review the purchase requests. If he gets squirrelly, I'll call for you."

With a final glance over at Kai, he jumped off the stairs and jogged to the trees, disappearing in a blink.

Closing the door, she joined Kaius on the sofa and pulled the computer onto her lap. "I texted Nichol about your clothing preferences, and he said he knows exactly what you like. He's already added it to the order. See?"

Humming in acknowledgment, he scanned the images on the growing list. "Those pants look much more functional and sturdier. And I definitely like shirts with sleeves."

"Shame." Her eyes widened when she realized she spoke aloud. "Um, socks. The socks. Any preference?"

His thin lips turned up a fraction, and he pointed to a pair. "These. The low ones slide into my boots."

Texting Nichol his decision, she smiled. "Slide into boots you don't own yet. I'll add that to the list, too."

He sat back and stretched his arms across the back of the couch. "With every passing minute, I know more about my existence than I did seconds prior. I know I prefer a specific brand of product for my hair, and I know Nichol orders it in from Europe, but I don't know where I was three years ago."

Confirming the order, she closed out the tab and opened a rom com from the 1990s. "It's not bad to have your functional memory coming online first. At least you can exist in the here and now without confusion." Setting the laptop on the coffee table, she angled it to ensure he could see the screen. "This is probably one of my favorite zone-out films. Nothing too heavy, nothing too intense. Just a badass woman with a gun and the guy who falls for her."

They watched in silence for almost an hour before Kaius leaned forward, resting his forearms on his elbows. "You aren't intimidating or foul-mouthed," he observed, lips pursing. "Or frightening."

"Unfortunately." She scoffed, drawing her knees to her chest. "I have more of that mother-hen thing going on. So people listen to me, but only because I use mom guilt well."

With the lift of a single brow, he grinned at her, his fangs resting on his bottom lip. "You do have a rather impressive way of communicating disappointment through a simple head tilt. What is it about this character that appeals to you?"

Shrugging, she burrowed a little deeper into the sofa, adjusting her position when a rogue spring poked into her ribs. "I love the whole 'look at her go' thing. I mean, she's completely tough and crude, but she's trying to do the right thing. I guess I just like stories where people make huge mistakes and do bad things even when they have good intentions."

"Rhys struggles with that," he stated. "He's not purposefully destructive or harmful, but his actions and personality lend themselves to misinterpretation of his motives." Frowning, he pursed his lips and stared at the coffee table for a moment. "Although sometimes, yes, he is a complete asshole with full intention to be one."

She laughed and sat up a little straighter. "Even to those of us not in the vampire loop, he comes across that way. Jagger seems very chill, though. Very thoughtful."

"Thoughtful and deliberate," he agreed. "Jagg observes from the sidelines until he feels he can make the most informed move to turn the events in his favor. Even before losing his hearing, he was very adept at hiding in the shadows and gathering intel, ghosting around the room during meetings. Unlike Mikhail, who prefers to be directly in the mix and manipulating situations through casual influence."

"What about you?" she asked, moving a little closer to him as her curiosity rose. "Are you a stealthy guy, or a talker?"

He looked down at her knee as it brushed his hip and swallowed. "I'm leaning more toward stealth, but I have this feeling I had little choice in my actions prior to now." Glancing into the trees where Boy had disappeared, he reclined back again and stretched his arm out behind her, his hand grazing her shoulder. "When you aren't working, where do you live? Is it close?"

"About fifteen minutes south of here," she replied, conscious of the increase in her heart rate when his thumb skimmed along her arm. "I own a house in town that my annoying roommate is probably filling with dirty dishes and overflowing trash cans as I speak."

"What makes her annoying?"

Biting her lip as she thought about Austin and his inability to notice even the fullest of garbage bins, she grinned. "It's a guy. He's nicer than nice, but he went from living with his parents to living in work camps up north, so he has difficulty remembering to do the most basic housekeeping. I'm constantly on him to stop trying to push the garbage farther into the bin and just change the damn bag." When his hand moved away from her and gripped the back of the sofa, she side-eyed him, her pulse ratcheting up when she saw his irises elongating. "You okay?"

Pushing himself to his feet, he nodded and walked over to the door, opening it in time for Boy to come barreling inside. "Temporary irrationality," he stated, assuming the position she'd often seen him do when Boy was around, his shoulders and feet squared, and hands clasped behind him. "Though I suspect our movie time is over."

When Boy motioned toward the basement ladder, she slumped back into the sofa. "I'll pause it and we can finish tomorrow."

CHAPTER FIFTEEN

Harper pulled Boy's SUV into the post office lot, waving at Austin as he sauntered up to her. "I need to pick up a few packages for my client and then we'll head over for supper."

Austin followed her into the small store that doubled as a pharmacy. "Are you still planning on working the full month there? You've gotta be going crazy being so cooped up."

Thinking back to the previous night when she and Kaius managed to finish one movie and watch three more under Boy's constant silent presence, she shook her head. "In this cold, it's definitely not a bad thing to be holed up with a blanket, popcorn, and a whole lot of rom-coms."

"Can't believe they pay you for hanging out and eating," he snorted as he hefted the first of the large boxes up. "I need a sweet gig like that. I nearly lost my fingers on a shingle job yesterday. This cold is killing my will to live."

Piling two more boxes into his arms, she grabbed the last and balanced it against her hip while she nudged the door open. "Have you been applying up north again? The cold might be just as bad, but the pay's better."

He shoved the packages into the back of the SUV, adding hers to the back seat. "I probably pumped out fifty resumés this month alone. No one's hiring until the vamp issues are settled."

Slamming the trunk, she glared at him. "You aren't still buying into that, are you? You've seen for yourself what kind of nut jobs that movement is attracting. No one's hiring because oil prices tanked, not because vampires are manipulating the economy. Now watch your step. The snow's covering the ice right there."

"Yeah, well, I know what I read," he muttered, holding his hand out to help her maneuver the icy patches on the sidewalk.

Escaping into the warmth of the restaurant, she stepped aside quickly. "Watch your hand on that door. It slams fast."

"You aren't this preachy with your client, are you? Because it's kind of annoying," he grunted, leading her to a table in the back corner.

Smirking when she remembered Kaius and Boy's strength training outside just before dawn, she opened her menu. "Maybe a little. He's working on a new physiotherapy regime right now and my advice is probably driving him up the wall."

Advice was a loose term. Her reactions to the vampires while they boosted fallen trees onto their backs and jogged the house's perimeter probably fell more into the *unhelpful panicked noises* category.

Boy ignored her outright.

Kaius, on the other hand, always flashed her a reassuring smile, which settled her nerves while they hauled the enormous trunks around the house.

Austin closed his menu with a clap and sat back. "It sucks not having you home. Everything's messier and there's no one around to laugh at my hilarious commentaries anymore." He pulled his phone from his back pocket and swiped it to life. "So I kept a list of them. Get comfortable. I'm about to unleash some pure comedic genius."

****

Kaius could smell the stench of human male on Harper's skin the moment she opened the door. And while his logical mind recognized he had no stake in her outside life, his reptilian brain lengthened his fangs in frustration.

"I have something for you," she called over to him, standing at the entrance to his cell with a fresh set of clothing draped over her arm. Her welcoming smile did little to combat the waves of jealousy coursing through him. "Boy is already in the shower."

Getting to his feet, he stalked over to the bars, forcing all irrationality to drain before he spoke. "And what's on the docket for this evening? More landscaping?"

She shook her head and smiled. "No, thank god. That was stressful."

Reaching through the bars to take the clothes from her, he sized them up before tossing them over his shoulder. "I suppose it doesn't help for me to say again that it wasn't exceptionally strenuous?"

"Not a lick."

Chuckling, he leaned against the cell. A simple agility exercise for him and Boy had caused a lot of concern for Harper, her soft voice calling out warnings of ice and snow in their paths, worried commentary about the falling temperatures in the region, and sharp intakes of breath every time one of them adjusted their grip on the logs.

Seeing her standing on the porch and grasping the

rails was more than enough incentive for him to put in a little extra effort and speed, knowing her eyes would soften every time he rounded the corner and came into view.

He couldn't be certain, but he suspected Boy didn't receive quite the same response.

Tuning in to the rush of water in the pipes as it slowed to a trickle, he shoved the masculine scent on her skin aside and focused on her relaxed posture, the reduced tension in her shoulders and back. "Did you have a good time this evening?"

"I did," she replied with a grin. "After I picked up the packages, I went for dinner with Austin. He was definitely on tonight, and when he's on, he's hilarious. My sides are still aching."

He didn't need to dig deep into his fragmented memories to know he wasn't funny, and the realization irked him more than he cared to admit. "Humor has always been an appealing quality in both humans and vampires. It's not a quality I possess, but I thoroughly enjoy those who do."

Pulling the small stool up, she sat on the other side of the bars. "I have zero comedic timing, so you and I can be unfunny together. And Boy. I don't think I've ever seen much more than an almost-smile come from him."

"Boy—" He paused as a wave of connections were made in his head. "Boy has always been around, as long as I can recall. And no, he doesn't smile. Or laugh." A fleeting image passed through his mind, and he squinted, as though it would make the visual clearer.

He sat with his back to the door and watched Nichol and Rhys while they rested. Their bodies were motionless as the sun hit its peak. His own bones ached with the knowledge he was alert past sunrise, but his sire's insistent shocks to his mind guaranteed no reprieve from the pulsing waves until he was back within her sights.

"Boy?" he murmured to his companion, his voice low to avoid disturbing his hauntmates. "I leave at nightfall." He was hesitant to vocalize the request yet again, knowing it would not be the last time he would request such an imposition on the silent male. "You'll watch over them?"

Without pause, Boy nodded, as he always did when Kaius's sire beckoned him back to her side.

"A female," he stated, momentarily forgetting Harper was in the room. "My creator was a female."

Boy's footfalls across the floor above him sped up and Harper tilted her head. "I didn't know there were any lady vampires until Molly mentioned it," she mused. "Hey, Boy."

Boy stood in the doorway, his blond hair dripping down his bare shoulders while he eyed them and sent a low pulse of warning into his mind while he pulled his shirt over his head and unlocked the cell.

Harper walked beside him until they reached the ladder, oblivious to the tension between the two vampires. "Tonight we have one pair of donors coming, then the rest of the evening is free." She looked down at them as she reached the top rung of the ladder. "Nichol suggested we acclimate you to human scents again, so he emailed a list of preparations and routes for a little field trip tonight."

"We'll be up in a moment." He smiled up at her before turning to Boy and lowering his voice. "I won't ask tonight," he opened, tracking Harper's movements overhead. "But I need to know the power Khthonios held over me. And the power she still holds over you."

Boy's blue eyes darkened, and he reached up to tap Kai's forehead and ear gently.

"Mere whispers and ghosts in my mind," he replied to the unspoken question. "Though I suspect she screams into yours."

CHAPTER SIXTEEN

Harper tightened her hold on the seat of the SUV when Boy took another sharp turn that left her stomach several feet behind the vehicle. Not even Kaius's gentle squeeze of her forearm could reassure her the old vampire knew what he was doing on the icy Alberta roads.

"Perhaps I should drive back," she offered as they sped up, gravel kicking up behind them. "I mean, if we get pulled over, you probably don't have a driver's license on you, and that could be a problem."

Boy reached across to the glove box and popped it open, revealing a stack of identification cards covering everything from driving to health care to credit cards.

She ignored the wads of cash stacked in tight piles.

"From what I remember of Nichol," Kaius interjected from the backseat, "he is meticulous with falsifying identification to ensure it passes even the most rigorous of examination."

Gingerly lifting the cards out, she flipped through them until she found Kaius's stack. "So if you presented this to the police, you'd be fine." Holding the card up, she turned to face him, her nose wrinkling when Kai grinned at her, his clipped fangs and brown contacts matching those on the identification. "I'm not used to you looking like this."

"And I dislike having to do it," he stated, leaning

116

forward to scan the cards in her lap. "However, I understand the rationale should we encounter any law enforcement."

Depositing the identification back into the glove box, she shoved it closed and glanced at Boy, his eyes blinking unevenly against the irritation of the lenses. "Does it hurt when you cut your fangs?"

Kai ran his tongue over his blunt teeth and shook his head. "It's somewhat disconcerting mentally, but the actual clipping doesn't appear to have any physical discomfort outside of a slight tingling due to regrowth."

"Open," she commanded, checking over his teeth while keeping one eye on the lights of the city. "I don't see any change."

Snapping his mouth shut, Kai pursed his lips and wrinkled his nose. "An eighth of an inch growth in the past two hours. I'm struggling to adapt my speech to the change."

Refusing to comment on the barely detectable lisp he developed with the clipping, she sat back and watched the speedometer until Boy slowed and entered the city limits. Industrial clouds of smoke curled in the air as they drove toward a small truck stop diner in Edmonton's northeast.

Nichol's plan was detailed and held little room for negotiation. Kaius required exposure to humans and a variety of scents, but location was non-negotiable. With an unnecessarily wordy explanation of foot traffic, peak hours, and expected clientele, he deemed the diner the ideal place for a first foray into the human world.

Harper's instructions were clear. Eat a meal, casually rotate coffee cups as required to provide the illusion the vampires were drinking, and be prepared to vacate should Boy give the signal.

According to Nichol, hesitation was not an option.

Boy pulled into the busy parking lot, skirting the lights surrounding the restaurant and selecting a spot at the edge of the lot.

"Are those UV bulbs?" she asked when they exited the SUV and both males scanned the perimeter.

Kaius remained close to her side, Boy following at a distance behind them. "Only those three," he said, pointing to the lights lining the pumps. "The others are merely bright LEDs. Aggravating to the eyes, but not dangerous."

They entered the crowded restaurant, and her steps faltered. The place was packed with late night diners. Several large groups were sitting at tables pulled together in the middle of the dining room to accommodate their numbers, the booths on the sides almost full. Dozens of eyes settled on them, and it took a moment for her to realize it wasn't vampires people were seeing.

It was her two gorgeous companions.

Kaius ducked down to her ear, his voice low. "Have we interrupted something?"

Smirking, she led him and Boy to the back of the room and slid into a booth, biting her lip when more heads turned their way, the eyes of both men and women scanning over the broad backs of the guys. "Only everyone's meals as they try to get a better look at the two of you."

Boy slid in across from her, his back to the wall and head bowed to allow his long blond hair to shield him from the stares. Kaius looked between them for a second before joining her on her side, his legs jostling the table while he tried to get comfortable. "I was expecting fewer patrons."

The server approached them, giving Harper a quick smile before placing menus in front of the guys. "Did you just come from the concert?"

Harper watched with amusement as the woman's gaze fell on Boy. "No, just decided on a late dinner tonight."

"Well, there's a bit of a backlog in the kitchen," the server stated. "If you're okay with hanging out a little longer than usual, I can bring your drink orders by right away. What'll it be, sweetheart?"

Boy continued his focused examination of the table as Harper rescued him. "Three coffees, please. And we'll only need one menu. They already ate."

Giving her hair a quick toss, the waitress gave Kaius a bright smile. "Aren't you two sweet to indulge her like this. I'll be right back."

Kaius waited until she was out of earshot before he glanced around the room and angled his shoulders to block the most insistent stares. "Are meals now considered an indulgence? I was under the impression ensuring your pack was fed has always been a necessary priority, regardless of what century it is."

Amazed by the number of people who continued to watch them, Harper opened her menu and read it over. "I think she was trying to decide which one of you is available for the taking and which one is obligated to eat out with me," she explained with a laugh. "I guarantee you she has customers asking her about who is single, and which one is here with *her*." When his brown eyes narrowed, she patted his arm. "I used to try to get information on hot guys from servers when I was younger, too. So don't be too weirded out by it."

Before he could respond, Boy slid his phone across the table with a message. Kai read it over, his jaw flexing in concentration. "Seventy-eight humans on site, with one walking in the door. Forty-one different colognes and perfumes, with thirteen requiring showers in the immediate future."

Apparently appeased by his assessment, Boy erased the text and typed out another, his large hands struggling to tap the correct letters. When he was done, he turned it toward them again, shaking his head when Kai moved to look around.

Leaning back as the coffee cups were set down, Kai waited until the server took Harper's order and walked away before he replied. "The most imminent threat is the group of young men at the fourth booth from the entrance. Two of them have blades in their front pockets and there's a UV flashlight tucked along the dip between the table and the wall."

Harper turned her head to check out the group, her eyes drawn to the dangers Kaius mentioned.

"The woman working the register hovers her hand over the emergency call button more frequently than necessary, and she's quite focused on the group crossing over to the convenience store down the hall," he continued, without looking in their direction. "The large group in the center is drunk and while they may not pose a traditional threat, they will be obstacles in the event of an escape. And the couple three booths behind me are both wearing Species Purifier paraphernalia and their entire discussion is revolving around a rally planned for tomorrow evening."

Taking a sip of her coffee, she set the cup close to Boy's. "How can you see all that?" she huffed, fighting the urge to turn around and glare at the anti-vamp couple.

"Windows." Kaius grinned, pointing at the huge pane of glass behind Boy while showing off his straight teeth. "Making optimal use of reflective surfaces is a beginner skill."

Trading her cup for Boy's, she downed half the mug and placed it beside Kai's, hooking her pinky into his handle and easing it into her space. "Whatever," she grumbled, refusing to smile when he dropped his hand between them and wrapped his fingers over hers. "You could've just said you had superpowers or something equally cool."

He squeezed her hand and Boy glared at them both, his hair swaying as he shook his head.

Kai instantly brought both of his hands onto the table.

Despite the flash of disappointment running through her at the loss of the contact, she was grateful for Boy's silent interference.

Kaius was her patient, and there were boundaries, whether she liked it or not.

****

Kai rolled the back windows down while Boy sped them through the backroads to their house, the plethora of odors from the restaurant still clinging to his hair and clothes. "What else can you tell me about Jagger and Bianca's efforts with the pro-vampire movement?" he called through the rush of wind, his hands clenching his knees to force adherence to Boy's unspoken no-touching-Harper rule.

"They work primarily with the moderate supporters," Harper replied, shifting in her seat to look back at him. "The extremists are a little too unpredictable, according to some of the news articles and blogs I've read."

She looked to Boy, who merely nodded once in agreement.

"Are there pro-vampire chapters around here?" he pressed, the comments and discussions he overheard in the diner still knocking around in his head.

Her lips tightened into a thin line, her dark eyes hardening. "None that are advertised. This whole place is pretty anti-anything-different, and it's been getting worse since the USA election took over the news. Those of us who don't agree with the Species Purifiers are watching what we say now in certain company since it can be kind of dangerous."

Staring at the snow-covered fields as they whizzed by, he frowned. "Your friend, the funny one. He's anti-vamp."

She went silent and angled her face away from him, busying herself with her purse.

"Harper. Is your friend pro-vamp or anti-vamp?" he repeated, unsettled by her refusal to answer.

"He…" She trailed off and took a deep breath. "He's not a bad guy. He just spends a lot of time around anti-vampire people. I mean, he's working and hanging out with them day in and day out, so they're bound to affect his views, right? It's everywhere around here."

His suspicion confirmed, he sat back in his seat and rolled up the window. "And yet you don't buy into the speciesism. Why does he? And why does he get a pass for it in your mind?"

The silence following his questions extended into the pre-dawn hour when he was forced below ground for the day, ruining what had been, for him, a damn pleasant outing.

CHAPTER SEVENTEEN

Kaius crossed his arms and cocked a brow, his temper bubbling close to the surface while Boy unlocked the cell. "I've repeatedly requested you not address me as 'sir'," he ground out, waiting for Boy's approval before exiting the cage. "For five nights in a row, if memory serves."

Harper continued to focus on the phone in her hand, feigning the re-reading of Nichol's nightly routine as she hummed in acknowledgment. "Sorry. Speaking of memory, we have a sit-down with Nichol in an hour. You've been asked to create a list of questions we can submit prior to the call."

"Boy," he snarled, changing his tone when a shock blasted through his head. "Am I or am I not the true leader of the Kaius haunt?"

His sire stepped into his line of sight and bowed his head for a moment.

"Harper, why don't you let Nichol know I won't be submitting any questions now or in the future. Any answers I need will be provided when I demand them." The slight lift of Harper's brows let him know precisely how impressed she was with his tantrum, and he relented. "I'll make the list immediately."

Passing Boy his towels, she pulled the stool close to the door and sat, instructing Boy to shower quick so they were ready for the meeting. She clasped her hands over her knees while Boy walked away, a detached smile on her face as she launched into the evening spiel she'd adhered to for the last five nights.

"How was your day, Kaius?"

Rolling his head back in frustration, he shoved his hands through his hair. "It was uneventful as always," he lied. The constant whisperings of the female voice in his head were nothing he wanted to discuss. "Did you sleep well?"

"I did, thank you. We have a busy time ahead of us tonight, don't we?"

He knew the exchange by heart already, and it was driving him up the wall. Nonetheless, he played his part. "Do we now?"

She adjusted her hold on her knees, her knuckles whitening. "Boy wants to do some tracking through the fields, so you'll have to make sure you dress for the weather after our session with Nichol. I believe the haunt has some tests Nichol developed they would like us to complete—"

"I'm sorry, Harper."

Licking her lips, she exhaled and attempted to continue. "Complete before dawn. Boss's orders."

"It can't be easy having to censor yourself every time you step outside your home," he pushed, the business mode of the previous nights weighing on his mood and his temper. "I didn't intend to pass judgment on your friend. Or your relationship with him."

She went quiet for a moment before unclasping her hands and pulling the chair closer to the cell. "It's nothing I haven't been wrestling with myself," she said with a sigh, her eyes on the floor. "It's just hard, trying to balance who Austin can be with who he's becoming.

And although I don't want to excuse his behavior, it's not easy to accept a part of him can be so hateful."

He risked a step in her direction. Another when she didn't react. "I think many of us aren't aware of the divide our presence has made in the lives of our supporters," he mused, memories of the global awakening to vampire existence coming together in his head to give him a clear picture of the first tumultuous years. "And while I won't apologize for existing—or for wanting a continued existence—I do understand I can't fault you for walking a delicate balance between us and them."

"Them." She scoffed, sitting straighter and wiping her eyes with the back of her hand. "There's always a *them*, isn't there? Me and my world-peace-co-existence blathering doesn't hold much weight as long as *they* and *them* are the dividers."

Crouching down to reach through the bars, he linked his fingers with hers. "Humans are a competitive species by nature. There will always be a *them*, as competition has spurred on the existence of most species for thousands of years." Releasing her hand, he stood and backed away, brushing his hands down his chest. "And I don't mean to brag, but vampires have taken the competitive nature of humans and amped it a hundred-fold. We're clearly superior at it."

She leveled him with an unimpressed stare. "You aren't funny."

"Yet still funnier than you."

****

When Nichol's hard hazel eyes filled the laptop screen, the tentative peace forged between Harper and Kaius solidified. He laced his fingers with hers under the

126

table, his stoic expression belying the tension she could feel in his hold.

"Probably not a time for me to practice being funnier," he whispered to her, earning a stern glare from Boy and a perplexed stare from Nichol.

Inching his hand onto her lap where she could cradle it without being seen, she kept her lips still. "Definitely not the time."

Nichol pushed his chair away from the camera and rocked back, crossing his arms over his chest. "I received your questions ten minutes ago. I'll start at the top and work my way down. Any required clarification will be addressed after each bullet point and Boy will monitor your reactions to ensure we don't have a repeat of our last conference."

There was a slight shift in Kai's demeanor, and he noticeably relaxed. "We've often communicated this way. Through a screen."

"We have," Nichol confirmed. "Your absences from the haunt required it."

Kaius looked over at her, his eyes glazing over for a moment before he straightened. "I would like to add the issue of my original sire to the list," he stated. "My absences were tied to her, were they not?"

Taking a step closer, Boy pulled out his phone. He fired off a text and shook his head as Nichol glanced over at his own cell. "Boy doesn't feel you're ready."

"She would be an integral piece to the reforming of my memories, would she not?" Kaius pressed, his hold on her hand tightening. "Leave the list and start from the beginning. Tell me everything you know and let my mind assemble the rest."

Boy and Nichol hunched over their phones, and she

inched her chair closer to Kai. Her mind was heavy with concern for his ability to handle the information the others were so anxious to hold back, her heart aching for the confusion he was living night and day.

With a nod, Nichol sat back, and Boy stepped behind them, reaching down to untangle Kai's fingers from hers. "Your original sire was Boy. However, you were a failed turning and Boy's own maker stepped in, taking over your bloodline. Your second sire—the one whose bloodline we carry—is a female vampire by the name of Khthonios and she is not pleased with your continued existence. Or ours."

In her peripheral, she caught the tightening of Boy's muscles, his stance shifting into readiness as Kaius stared at the camera. "Then why does she allow me to live?"

****

Kaius tuned out the preservative odor emanating from the frozen pizza Harper was eating beside him, his mind far too occupied with the information it was connecting to care much for the assault on his senses.

Her proximity, on the other hand, was non-negotiable.

When she remained at his side, his focus was whole, completely absorbed with the intel Nichol was sharing and he could add his own recollections to the events. When she left him, even for a minute or two, he would feel the beginnings of an overload, the misfiring in his head settling only with her return.

"She tasked me to watch over him," he growled, his fangs lengthening in disgust. "Kaspars Dovidas is Khthonios's prized child, the one she's grooming for a takeover of the Americas."

"Kaspars Dovidas was ended the night you went Deviant," Nichol replied, his voice holding an odd tone.

Leaning back in his chair, he ran his hands through his hair as a wave of memories washed over him. "Memphis," he stated, the memories carrying a heaviness with them. "Khthonios sent me there to ensure Kaspars and his horde stayed the course during the Deepfryer negotiations. But Molly..." Images of his broken youngest child and the headstrong woman danced in the forefront of his mind. "I worked off the haunt's timeline for the mission, but you went in early. The bombs were already detonating when I arrived on site." Visions of Mikhail barreling through the fire to pull an injured Louis from the flames froze in his head. "I intended to deactivate Molly's perimeter collar before mission launch, to provide her with a fighting chance of escape."

Nichol's jaw flexed. "You were the intruder. The one Mikhail saw decapitating Dovidas's Deviants."

He nodded, a phantom ache growing in his legs. "I was ordered to follow you, to track you on your path northward."

"The horse trailer," Nichol snarled. "You tried to take us out at the goddamn gas station."

The entire scene unfolded, every scent and sound from the moment bearing down on him with disturbing realism. "Khthonios didn't want you ended. She wanted to observe your fighting skills, to see for herself what kind of haunt I curated." Harper's hand found his, and he backed out of the vision, observing from afar where Khthonios's voice was little more than a whisper in his ear. "Your success pleased her. Worthy opponents for her game."

Nichol's eyes blackened with rage. "You were aligned with Khthonios all along."

"Aligned, no," he said slowly, pieces shifting into place. "Bound to her, yes."

With a slow nod, Nichol leaned back in his chair and crossed his arms, a move Kaius recognized as a defense mechanism the vampire utilized when hiding an increased stress level. "We will continue to consider Khthonios a factor in all decisions moving forward until she proves herself irrelevant." There was a faint grinding of teeth through the speaker. "We'll speak more on that soon. Harper, I'll text tomorrow evening's schedule before dawn. Boy, once tracking practice is finished, ensure Kaius completes the examinations I'm emailing Harper now. Audra and I tweaked a few human psychological tests to assess Kai's current mental, emotional, and behavioral patterns so we can establish a benchmark of improvement now the basic physical ones have been achieved. And Kai? We need you back here. The sooner the better."

The laptop screen went black, and Harper's phone buzzed with an incoming message. She exhaled, blinking a few times before she spoke. "Are you okay? That was really, really intense."

Staring at the blank screen, he attempted to shove aside the tide of remorse accompanying the realization he'd been a threat to his own haunt. "I suspect my inability to sense Nichol may be a good thing right now." Pushing himself away from the table, he got to his feet and turned to Boy. "You know everything, don't you?"

His sire nodded, his eyes empty.

"Do I need to know everything?"

Boy shook his head without hesitation and walked

to the front door, flinging it open to the crisp wind and waiting patiently for Kaius to join him.

CHAPTER EiGHTEEN

Harper sat on the bottom rung of the ladder and sipped her coffee while she waited for the sound of the cell lock opening.

"You two done wrestling?" she asked when Boy and Kaius sauntered out of the room, her brows lifting when both had the sense to look abashed. "I know training is important, but could you maybe keep the full-blown body slams to a minimum before my alarm goes off? This place is rickety enough without hundreds of pounds of vampire slamming against the foundation."

Both of them changed trajectory, walking over to the steel posts running the length of the room and assessing their sturdiness. Boy retreated into the cage room, arms crossed as he studied the cement walls.

Kaius crouched in front of her. "Any word from Nichol?"

Shaking her head, she took another sip, tucking her hair behind her ear when his eyes drifted down to her throat. "Nothing other than the nightly donor rotation." When his jaw tensed, she squeezed his forearm. "Three nights isn't that long for a guy who's running an entire sanctuary city, Kai. He's probably just busy. The news is hopping over the issues they're having with the housing crisis. Anti-vamps are pissed off over Nichol's sliding scale for the sales of those condos he snatched up a few months ago."

He tilted his head and swallowed, the movement of his Adam's apple drawing her attention. "Sliding scale?"

Leaning forward when Boy hopped onto the ladder a few rungs up, she pulled out her phone and searched up the news reports, passing it over to him to read. "He basically reduces prices based on verifiable vampire support. But there seems to be a tipping point where the numbers start going up."

"The FANG group," he murmured. "They glue artificial nails to their teeth to mimic fangs. Louis and Rhys were quite opposed to being aligned with them."

She nudged him with her knee and smirked. "You don't like being considered a god? The Friends and Allies of the New Gods are your most adamant supporters. Now come on, you need to eat, and I need to get three cakes iced."

Without a word, he stood and stepped back, taking her coffee cup from her, and following her up the ladder into the kitchen where the first donor was already standing with Boy, his wrist pierced with viper fangs while he flipped through memes on his phone.

"Hey, Colin." She greeted him, holding her hand flat against the top of each cake to ensure it was firm enough to be frosted. "Is Carter waiting in the car?"

Colin looked at her and rolled his eyes. "He'll be here in a minute. Had to set up his evening plans with his gamer group."

On cue, Carter flung the door open, his loud arrival startling her and Colin while the two vampires merely nodded in acknowledgment of his presence.

Kaius looked over her shoulder at the chocolate cakes while Carter rolled his sleeve up. "Those smell quite good."

"They better be good," she stated without room for argument as she popped the lid of the first icing container. "It's a box mix." Using a spoon to scoop a large dollop onto the top of the dessert, she smoothed it out and nodded toward Carter. "Eat up. I need to head out pretty soon."

He pursed his lips but obeyed, his fangs sinking into Carter's arm with such finesse the guy didn't flinch from his game.

It was a normal part of their evenings, Boy and Kai taking their evening meals while she busied herself in the kitchen. Most of the donors were quiet, making little more than polite conversation before they rolled up their sleeves and continued texting or gaming or flipping through photos and articles. One guy, Barry, read. His lips moved every time he came across a word he didn't know, sometimes repeatedly until Kaius would unhook his fangs and read it out for him.

She liked Barry and his political thriller obsession.

"Okay, we're out," Colin called over to her while he and Carter tugged their boots on. "See you in a few nights."

"Night, guys." She waved the icing-covered spoon as they left, Boy hot on their heels to watch their exit and prepare the yard for whatever battle he and Kai would be engaging in that evening. "I really hope this tastes better than it looks."

Kaius spun a chair around and straddled it. "Try it."

With a laugh, she rinsed the spoon off and rifled through the drawers for plastic wrap. "It's bad form to eat the cake before the birthday boy has a chance to blow out the candles." When Kai went quiet, she glanced over her shoulder. "You okay?"

"Of course," he replied, straightening his back. "Is Nichol aware you're leaving the premise tonight?"

Ensuring the wrap was tight across the top of each of the pans, she stacked them on the table and grabbed her purse, opening her compact to check her makeup. "He approved it last week. Austin's birthday is tonight, so we're having a thing at my house." Touching up her lipstick, she smiled up at him. "I hate crowds, so I won't be long." She snapped her purse closed, grabbed her coat, and hiked it over her shoulders, feeling the pocket for the SUV keys. "Don't let Boy overdo it tonight. You look a little tired."

He picked up the cakes and walked them over to her, waiting patiently while she zipped her boots up. "You look lovely. Enjoy the party."

A twinge of something she couldn't quite place rippled through her, and she hesitated, the words she wanted to speak dying on her tongue while the expected ones poured out. "See you later, Kai."

****

Kaius's eyes narrowed when Boy picked up speed and dodged through the tree lines dividing the lands of the county farmers, the deep snow doing little to slow either of them as they approached the town. Doubling down to keep up with his sire, he pushed himself through the last field, slowing once they hit the highway where their speed would draw far more attention and questions than two men jogging along the road.

Boy came to a halt at the first subdivision, bringing up the address on his phone and angling it so Kai could see.

Three minutes away at max speed.

But, for the sake of maintaining the facade matching

their colored contacts and chiseled fangs, they took the twenty-one minutes needed to walk the distance.

There was little argument when Kaius ended their skirmish in the snow. He was too distracted by the sweet-scented cake and the woman who left with a wave and a cheerful smile on her face which lifted her soft cheeks and crinkled the corners of her eyes. Knowing the training session was pointless, he walked into the house without a word, Boy following him as he strode to the bathroom and grabbed the fang clips from the medicine cabinet. While he blinked his contacts into place, Boy snipped his own teeth and glared at his lens case, popping them in with more agitation than Kai had ever seen him demonstrate.

"Boy?" He frowned as they approached the small house with the music pulsing into the street. "Do you think she'll be angry? It is her night off. Perhaps we should head back."

His sire leaned against the familiar SUV and crossed his arms, leveling him with a flat glare.

They shouldn't be there.

In the far reaches of his mind, he knew this wasn't him, knew that brash impulsiveness was something he balked at. While they ran, flashes of intense meetings and collaborations with his hauntmates crossed his mind. He envisioned detailed notes with maps and contingency plans for missions he couldn't quite place, his recollections proving he was not one to jump without assessing the dangers first.

And the disconnect weighed heavy on him.

Boy's phone buzzed incessantly once they hit the town limits, Nichol's tracking system working overtime to document every mile of their unnecessary mission.

The longer they remained in town, the more insistent the texts became.

Bending down to check his hair in the SUV's side mirror, he attempted to smooth the rogue pieces disheveled from their run to town, his unbeating heart nearly seizing when Harper's voice broke through the night.

"Hey! Get away from that car!"

For a moment, he debated running, turning tail, and taking off down the street to make it back to their farmhouse before she returned.

But the urge to see her took hold and he straightened, stepping under the streetlamp while Boy remained tight to the shadows of the SUV. "Hi, Harper."

He could see her delicate brows knotting as she squinted into the darkness. "Kaius? Is everything okay?"

"We're good," he replied, nodding toward Boy, and receiving an unimpressed glare in return. "We…I was curious about…" His head dropped a fraction as he realized how weak and wrong his excuses would sound to her, how pathetic they sounded to himself.

She bounced down the sidewalk on her tiptoes, her bare feet hopping along the dry patches of cement. "Oh my goodness, of course you were." Drawing up tight to him, she examined his eyes and reached up to tap his chin, smiling when he bared his clipped teeth. "Boy? Are you all human'd up, too?" Met with a flash of blunt fangs, she linked her arms through theirs and hopped along the path. "I don't know why I didn't think to ask if you two would like to come. Probably because I wasn't all that keen on being here myself, so why would I subject you guys to this noisy, drunken disaster of a party?"

Resisting the urge to carry her over the cold pavement, he opened his senses to hear the music pounding through the walls of the house, pinpointing a conversation about anti-vampire laws and the growing division in Canada's political stance. "Are you sure our presence won't be a concern?"

"Just follow my lead and stay tight to me," she stated, throwing the door wide open. "And stay away from the brunette with the green shirt. She's looking for a meal and you two are definitely the tastiest steaks in the place now." Linking her fingers in his, she reached her other arm back and grabbed Boy's hand. "Let's introduce you to the birthday boy."

****

Harper bit back a smirk when Austin's brows shot up at the sight of her newfound companions flanking her as she entered the crowded living room. It didn't take great powers of observation to notice the heads turning their way while they squeezed through the room. The men blatantly sized them up while the women did the same with slightly more subtlety.

"Austin, these are my friends, Kai and...Theo?" she announced, stumbling over how to introduce Boy, and cringing internally when his nose wrinkled. "I'm bringing the cakes out in a minute, so don't run off on me."

Austin pushed himself to his feet and set his beer bottle on the end table, extending his hand. "New friends of Harper's?" he asked, shaking Kaius's first before addressing Boy. "Don't think I've seen you around here before. You two work up north or something?"

She knew Kai picked up the increase in her heart rate when he grabbed her hand again and skimmed his thumb along her wrist. He replied without hesitation, his mannerisms and language pulled from the movies they watched every evening. "We're just passing through on our way down to Cali. Theo and I are trying to break into the comics industry."

Hoping she was able to hide the rolling of her eyes, she jumped onto the story. "Kaius writes and draws some pretty cool stuff, and Theo is the colorist. I'll show it to you once it's not in the copyright submission stage anymore."

Looking mildly impressed, Austin looked up at Boy. "What's a colorist do?"

Kaius stepped between them, a perfect expression of exasperation on his face. "He goes over my drawings with ink and colors them in."

"So, like, you trace?" Austin clarified, and Harper exhaled.

"Yeah, he does," Kaius continued, lowering his voice. "He's dealing with some self-worth stuff right now, so he's not being very social."

Tugging both their hands, she led them away from Austin, calling out promises to light the candles right away. "Really, Kai?" she whispered while she removed the plastic wrap from the cakes. "Comics?"

He blinked a few times and grinned, showing off his straight teeth. "I panicked and went with the most modern story I knew."

Swatting him out of the way, she opened the cutlery drawer and grabbed a packet of candles and a lighter. "You two go find a seat in the living room and practice your story on some of the guys in there. I'll be out in a minute." She rose up on her toes and whispered into his ear. A small spark traveled through her blood when he steadied her with a strong arm around her waist. "If anyone asks about drinking, you're driving, and *Theo* is a body purest who avoids all alcohol and anything that isn't a whole food."

He paused just long enough to nuzzle her cheek with his, scenting her before leading Boy out of the room. His brief absence gave her a few moments to collect herself while she lit the candles and inserted periodic comments into the conversations around her. She called out for a complete darkening of the house. The flames flickered while she walked and led the guests in song.

Austin made a production of blowing out the candles, leaning over the coffee table to kiss her cheek and give her a tight one-armed hug. "Thanks, Harpy." He nodded toward Boy and Kai, smirking when both gave him a tight-lipped smile. "Two? Really? You know Candace is going to be all over whichever one isn't tied to you."

Kneeling to slice the first cake, she laughed. "Oh, please. They're just friends. Though I did warn them about Candace before they came in." Glancing over her shoulder at the woman, she sat back on her heels. "Seriously? She's not even waiting to see if either of them is with me before she starts unbuttoning her shirt?"

Snorting, Austin sat back down and passed her a stack of paper plates. "Go stake your territory. I'll feed the vultures."

CHAPTER NINETEEN

Kaius popped the engine into drive and eased onto the road, blinking his brown contacts into place a few times before inching his hand over the armrest to wrap around Harper's cold fingers. "I apologize for not thinking ahead enough to warm up the engine prior to our departure."

She leaned back in her seat and closed her eyes. "I'm just glad that's over for another year. And there were enough witnesses to Austin's promises to clean the rest of the house up I'm pretty certain he actually will." Opening one eye, she looked over at him. "I'm so sorry you had to sit through that conversation. I'd been hoping everyone would remember parties aren't the place for political chest-pounding."

"Cultures and societies across the globe have always feared our existence. Little can be said that Boy or I haven't heard before in one language or another." He brought the back of her hand to his lips and stopped, frowning into his rearview mirror, and lowering her arm. "I dare say most of my recovered memories center on shielding, defending, or ensuring my existence in the face of humans."

She glanced over her shoulder and met faint disproval on Boy's face as he monitored the placement of Kaius's hand on hers. "It doesn't make it okay."

"Which is something I would like to address."

Turning onto the gravel road that led to the farmhouse, he shifted in his seat. "While Austin and a few of the others dismissed your arguments without animosity, there were a few people significantly less tolerant of your words." Scanning the darkness for signs of wildlife, he forced the tension in his shoulders to loosen while images of the sneers and hardened eyes of several guests looped in his head. "Leaving yourself open to retaliation is unwise in this climate."

Her lips pursed, and she stared out the window. "Whatever. They're wrong."

Leaning closer to her, he shrugged. "Sitting silently while the discussion waged on against you was difficult enough, but had one of them chosen to act on the anger they were experiencing, Boy and I would have had little choice but to intervene. And in doing so, outing you and ourselves."

The defiance in her stature deflated, and she released his fingers to run her hands through her hair. "I wasn't even thinking about that. I was so focused on correcting all those ridiculous lies they keep spreading, it never occurred to me anyone might actually become aggressive about it. Though I suppose it should have."

He pulled up in front of the house, waiting for Boy to get out and do a perimeter patrol before he turned off the engine. He joined his sire, scenting the air for anything unrecognized while Harper opened the front door and gave both of them a look.

"I won't tell Nichol you two left the house unlocked," she stated, unzipping her boots, and setting them aside. "This time."

At the mention of the miserable vampire's name, Boy pulled his phone from his pocket and descended the ladder, his hair falling into his eyes as he responded to the litany of ignored texts.

Closing the curtains, Harper turned to him and slid her cell onto the coffee table. "I'll let Boy smooth this over before I respond, but when I do, what am I supposed to say? I took you two to a birthday party stacked with anti-vampers and women who groped you every chance they had?"

He crossed the room, ignoring the buzzing cell while he tracked the minutes left before sunrise. Scooping her hands up in his, he stepped in close. "You didn't bring us there. We disobeyed protocol and arrived without invitation. As for the groping, I'll admit it was unpleasant, but perhaps that's because the hands on me tonight weren't the ones I was craving." There was a quickening of her heart as he brought her hands to his chest and gently splayed her fingers. "May I?"

Licking her lips, she inhaled. "May you what?"

"Kiss you?" he murmured, releasing her hands to graze his fingers along her throat. "Preferably before sunrise and before Boy puts a definitive end to this opportunity?"

With a smile, she rose onto her toes, her nails digging lightly into his shirt. "You may."

Had there been more time, he would have taken the time to savor the moment, to study every nuance his mind might miss before his lips met hers.

But dawn was ticking closer, and Boy was sending a steady pulse through his head every ten seconds like clockwork. It was a cautionary warning his disobedience would be punished, that what he was about to do was breaking yet another protocol.

And while he knew instinctively he once existed and

thrived on rules and order, he also knew he didn't care one iota for who he once was.

****

Harper's heart was thumping hard enough to kickstart Kaius's back up by the time his lips finally brushed against hers, her anticipation only amping when he refused to deepen the kiss. She swayed into him, sliding her hands up his chest and clasping them around his neck to pull him closer while he continued to tease her with the gentlest of kisses until he nibbled on her bottom lip and trailed his tongue along her jaw to her ear.

"I should get into the basement before I ignite," he whispered, simultaneously sending a flutter and a cold rush through her veins.

Stepping back and looking anywhere but at him, she wrapped her arms around herself. "Of course. Right." She bit her lip and glanced up. "Go before I have to add 'vamp-fryer' to my resumé."

"It might get you a good job in this county," he joked, planting a final kiss on her forehead before he strode over to the hatch and climbed down the ladder. "Good night, Harper."

The first faint light brightened the small living room as he disappeared into the basement, leaving her alone to watch the texts from Nichol pop up on her phone. Slumping into the sofa, she picked it up and read through the messages, wondering if she could get away with responding at dusk.

The buzzing of an incoming call answered her question.

"Hi, Nichol." She greeted, reclining back to get comfortable. "I was just about to text you."

"Boy filled me in on all relevant information," he

replied tersely. "I just sent you an amended contract. It outlines the shift in your duties as it pertains to Kaius's current and evolving state."

Pulling her phone from her ear, she tapped the message open and scanned the file, the last of her evening's excitement draining. "The payment is very generous."

"Kaius's revitalization has occurred at a speed we had not anticipated and while I understand our initial contract secured your services for upwards of four more weeks, we no longer feel he requires the level of care you provide." A woman's voice whispered in the background, growing more insistent until she could hear a door close. "I hope you find our offer fair given the shortened time period."

Full pay.

A glowing, if not fictionalized, reference letter.

And a bonus to be paid upon Boy's acknowledgment she had indeed vacated the property in precisely twenty-four hours.

Running her thumb over her bottom lip, she closed her eyes. "I know you feel he's recovered his strength and those tests show his mind is firing on all cylinders, but he's still piecing together a lot of his past, and—"

"And Boy is far more qualified than you are to address any questions or concerns that arise," Nichol interjected. "I expect the signed contract returned within the hour. Termination is non-negotiable."

The phone went silent, and she swiped it alive, rereading the email once more before adding her electronic signature and returning it, glaring at Nichol's number before firing off a text.

—*Have you told Kai about this?*—

Nichol took his time responding, the minutes ticking by until her cell buzzed.

—*Kaius's priority is returning to his leadership position within the haunt. How that happens is my decision, on my terms. Not his, not yours. Thank you for the prompt contract return.*—

Summarily dismissed, she threw her arm over her eyes and tried to get some sleep.

CHAPTER TWENTY

Kaius paced the cement floor of his cell, listening to the water rushing through the pipes above him and counting the seconds until sunset.

Seven hundred, twenty-nine.

He rose with the taste of Harper's lips on his. The sensation of her body pressed against him kept him awake long into the morning hours while Boy sat against the door to the cage, his eyes open but unseeing while he rested.

Though disconcerting to have his sire watch him even in sleep, there was a strange familiarity to it. If he pulled his mind from Harper long enough, he could bring up images of Boy guarding him inside caves and dungeons, mansions, and hovels.

Filthy bastard beast and his vile pet.

Khthonios's voice broke his reverie and his steps faltered.

Visions of the raven-haired Khthonios filled his head during his rest for the past three days. Her black eyes looked down at him with a humored disgust as he knelt at her feet, his own blood trailing down his spine and dripping off his chin.

Disobedient little mongrel, aren't you?

Focusing on his fingers, on the feeling of Harper's skin, he tried to push the invasion from his thoughts, to keep fragmented those pieces of his memories swirling

147

together to show him exactly what kind of vampire he was.

Weak.

Traitorous.

Owned.

Flayings and de-fangings. Sunlight and chainings. Retributions for his failures, for his refusal to side with Khthonios over his own haunt. All balanced with her gentle hand on the back of his neck in those moments he was weak enough to do her bidding.

Always on his knees.

Always at her heel.

Boy's hand gripped his chin, his fingers digging into his jawbone and forcing him back to the moment. He stilled, his fangs laying long enough over his bottom lip to nick Boy's hand as he shook his head, a reminder to Kaius to lock Khthonios and her poison from his mind.

It was only when Boy seemed satisfied he had regained full composure that he released him and stalked to the cage door, not bothering to look back as he strode across the basement floor and climbed the ladder. Harper's soft voice greeted Boy, a hint of confusion in her words when the front door opened and slammed shut with enough force to send vibrations through the old beams of the house.

Kaius squared his shoulders and climbed into the kitchen, frowning at the baggage stacked beside the door. "What—"

"I made the executive decision that you and I are having a movie marathon tonight. My laptop is fully charged, cued up on the first film, and I'm ready for some serious chilling." Stepping between him and the pile, Harper patted his chest with a smile and held her coffee mug up to him. "If you manage to ask under twenty questions during my movie choice, I'll consider letting you pick the next one."

Following her to the living room, he sprawled out on the sofa and nudged the curtains open, watching Boy shimmy up a tree. "What's going on with him?"

She angled the computer and joined him on the small couch, propping a pillow against his leg before leaning against it. "He said something about needing to have some time on his own."

They were twenty minutes into the movie when he jiggled her with his knee. "Boy said he needed time on his own? Boy, who doesn't speak, said that?"

Her nose wrinkled as she pursed her lips. "Maybe he didn't say it in those exact words, but close enough." One arm wrapped around his calf, and she settled into him again, obviously unwilling to further the conversation.

Dropping the subject, he did his best to focus on the plot amid the feeling of her body against his, the constant change in her expressions as the characters spoke, and the periodic shifting as she nestled up closer to him until she was laying across his chest, grinning at the on-screen antics of the actors.

When the end credits rolled, she moved to sit up, and he protested, holding her tight to him when her movements brought a wash of cold air over his heated skin.

Wiggling against his loose grip, she pushed herself up onto her elbows, the bones digging into his ribs. "The app will start a random movie if you don't pick something to watch, so you better act now or you'll lose your chance."

Skimming his thumb along her spine to her neck, he

wrapped a long strand of brown hair around his finger and let it unravel, watching it fall across her shoulder. "I'll take the loss on the film selection if it means we stay just like this for the rest of the night."

Her eyes flicked to the window and then her phone before she looked at him and gave him a lopsided grin. "Just like this?" she murmured, lowering her lips to his and grazing them soft enough to make him question if they made contact at all. "Or is this, okay?"

"This," he replied, arching up to kiss her with more insistence, "is okay. This too."

He gripped her and hiked her higher onto his chest, bringing her level with him as she smiled against him, her eyes closing when he nipped at her bottom lip and slid his tongue into her mouth.

The fluidity of women always amazed him, the way their bodies molded against another's as though unconstrained by bones and muscle. Despite his limber agility in his sparring and training, he felt awkward and rigid beneath her as he ran his hand along the smooth arch of her back while she pressed into him. Even the gentle shift in her legs to straddle him was graceful, the passion in her kiss unbroken as she maneuvered lithely on the small sofa.

He slid one hand under the hem of her shirt, desperate to feel her bare skin.

"Boy."

Opening one eye to assess the closed door, he frowned. "What about him?"

She covered his hand with hers and nudged it down to her hip. "I would really rather he not walk in on your hand up my shirt."

Zeroing in on his sire's movements outside, he

pinpointed his location. "He's tree-hopping. I doubt he'll be coming inside anytime soon."

Her eyes narrowed, and she pursed her lips. "You'll warn me if he does?"

"I swear it."

Apparently satisfied with his guarantee, she tugged a blanket off the back of the sofa and snapped it out above them, draping it over her shoulders before she leaned down and kissed him softly. "Is there any chance this could bring on some wild flashback?"

He reached up and tucked her hair behind her ears, committing the black flecks in her brown eyes to memory. "There's no corner of my mind that isn't occupied by you right now. So no, Harper. No chance at all."

****

Harper splashed cold water on her face, eyes closing when she heard Kaius's footsteps approach, and his knuckles rap lightly on the door.

"Dawn's two minutes away," he said softly. "I'll see you in a few hours."

Taking a deep breath, she got to her feet and forced her expression to relax while she opened the door, unable to resist smiling when he grinned at her with enough elation to make her reconsider breaking Nichol's order. "One more smooch and then you get that butt downstairs," she commanded, rising up on her toes as he wrapped his arms around her and kissed her leisurely. It was a far cry from the frenzied make-out session they indulged in for the past four hours, a make-out session that ended with Boy's arrival and a resigned sigh from Kaius. "Now go before you fry."

With a final peck on her forehead, he jogged down

the hall to the kitchen hatch and snatched his jeans from the floor on his way, the sound of his feet hitting the basement cement thumping through the house as the first light broke.

On cue, her phone buzzed on the coffee table.

Scanning the bathroom for anything she forgot, she padded across the hardwood, tugged her socks out from between the sofa cushions, and picked up her cell to read the message.

—Final payment will be deposited upon confirmation of your departure from the premises.—

With a glare, she fired back.

—Keep it—

She shoved the phone into her back pocket and snapped the laptop closed, winding the cord around her hand as she looked around the place one last time.

The sofa had a definite dip where they snapped a supporting board.

The fingerprints on the windows would be easy to clean.

The table definitely needed its legs tightened.

And the vamps didn't need the extra kitchen chair that had collapsed on them an hour earlier, almost staking Kai in the process

Unzipping her suitcase, she placed her computer and cord on top of her clothes and zipped it back up, easing her coat off its hanger and slipping it on as her phone buzzed again.

—Leave the keys in the SUV and Boy will ensure it is removed from your property by midnight.—

She tugged her boots on and hooked her bags on her arm, set the old lock on the door, and closed it tight.

CHAPTER TWENTY-ONE

Kaius sat at the table, his gaze moving between the camera, the maps, and the satellite images on the new laptop screen while he listened intently to Nichol's detailed assessment of the changes he was considering to Denver's perimeter patrol. "If the surrounding communities are eager to become included within the sanctuary borders, encompassing the west to the mountains would provide a natural barrier. It would reduce sentinel posts to the few roads extending through and allow you more flexibility in the defense lines to the north and south."

Scribbling a few notes, Nichol nodded and rocked back in his chair. "Deviant attacks from the east have increased with the warmer temperatures, so a limited western line would benefit us on that as well. I'll have Mickey and Jagger begin negotiations with the community leaders and update you as we make progress." Placing his pen in line with the others, he picked up his phone and fired off a message. "Tensions are heating up among the haunts within the city limits. Too many fangs, not enough territory."

"I trust you can handle it."

Nichol tossed his pen on the table, and it skidded to the floor. "Here's the problem we—I—am facing. Your name without your presence can only carry us so far. With the dust of the evacuation settling, it's your name, not mine, on the tongues of every vamp and human in this city. They're starting to believe the FANG talk of some phantom godliness with you as the poster boy. It's setting a dangerous tone, Kaius, and we need your boots on the ground to dispel the stories before they evolve into something we can't quash." Before he could respond, Nichol ran his hands through his hair. "I don't like it, Kai. We've started something here that's spreading to other cities. Other countries. Whispers of vampire strongholds throughout Europe, Australia, and Asia are filtering through Mickey and Jagger's sources and every goddamn one of them is tied to your name."

He didn't need his memories to know the danger false idolatry could pose. "What do you need me to do?"

Slouching back in his chair, Nichol stared past the camera. "I don't know, Kai. But I know this: the longer you're gone, the higher you rise among those buying into the FANG tales. And they'll turn on us when they find they're wrong." He cleared his throat and straightened. "I'm forwarding you and Boy a sparring program Jagg put in place for those UV flashlights I shipped to you last week."

The weight of Nichol's words hung around his neck. "We'll begin training tonight and I'll report before dawn," he confirmed before logging off and opening his email to read over the fighting regime Jagg implemented for the haunt.

For *his* haunt.

His haunt, who was carrying the burden of his absence. His weakened condition silenced their tongues in the face of whispered rumors dangerous enough to cause a permanent rift in both vampire and human societies.

Pushing himself to his feet, he steadied the wobbling table before joining Boy outside. The sparring ring was already dug into the mess of mud and slush covering the yard and coating their boots. Splatters of drying sludge and muck speckled the deck and SUV. Boy stood in the center of the ring, a dozen flashlights dangling from ropes wrapped around eight feet of rusted pipe protruding from the ground.

"I believe I recall using this method with maces," he grumbled, tossing his shirt onto the porch steps, and toeing off his boots as he glared at the lights Boy was turning on one by one. "And I believe I recall despising it."

With a shrug, Boy hefted the pipe out of the earth and spun it. The UV rays sliced over his arms when they picked up velocity. Looking pointedly at the small sparring ring, Boy jarred the pipe, disturbing the predictable rotation of the lights as Kaius stepped into place and the first burns slashed his chest.

In the limits of the defined perimeter, it was easy to focus his mind on eliminating the threat piece by piece, to narrow his attention on the beams blackening his skin and haloing his vision. Predicting Boy's next movements, calculating the sway of each light, and countering the instinctual urge to retreat from the UV rays required intense concentration that pushed all other thoughts from his head.

In the ring, there were no visions of Khthonios standing at the edge of the tree line, her black eyes watching him with revulsion. No memories of the accusation in Rhys's dark eyes every time he abandoned his haunt for his creator. Or the exhaustion in Nichol's.

He could shove aside Dominic's confusion and

Jagger's unspoken disappointment. Even the guilt of Mikhail's empathic overloads was ghosted away while he knocked the first flashlights from their ropes and they dropped into the mud, scorching his bare feet.

A tangle of beams bore into the threads of his filthy jeans.

Filthy jeans he would strip off and drop into the washing machine with the artificial floral detergent left behind one hundred, sixty hours ago. A scent that filled the house and clouded his head every time the laundry was done.

The rusted metal pole swung toward him, narrowly missing his cheekbone as he caught sight of the trajectory, and swerved away only to have one of the remaining flashlights catch him across the back of his skull.

He had a duty. Responsibilities waiting for him. A haunt holding down the fort until he stepped up and returned to his position as leader.

A bastard bloodline leading the lambs to the slaughter.

Khthonios's voice whispered into his ear as he caught hold of the pole long enough to rip one light from the rope before Boy doubled back, bringing the steel down on his shoulder and shattering his collarbone.

They surpassed sparring for technique two nights prior, with Boy now pushing Kaius to fight blind, fight injured, fight dirty. His sire took no mercy, held nothing back as the pole reared up and slashed toward his legs, narrowly missing his kneecaps when Kai slid back on the muck, exposing his belly to the light in Boy's hand.

I never imagined vampires would be ticklish.

Her smile flashed through his head as Boy dropped

the metal pole and held the UV beams steady on his stomach. Jumping to his feet, he squared his shoulders and met the assault, allowing his mind to drift to the playfulness in her brown eyes while her fingers skimmed his ribs.

The memory of her heat pressed against him temporarily drowned out the stench of his burning skin and numbed the pain when the rays broke through and worked their destruction on his organs. He remained motionless, withstanding the assault until Nichol's voice barked through his consciousness.

Her function in your recovery is no longer required or practical. It now rests in your hands to reclaim your position and the obligations tethered to the Kaius name.

Raising his hands in defeat, he bowed his head and dropped to one knee. When Boy didn't move for several minutes, he looked up to see his sire studying him, eyes narrowed as he pulled out his cell and tapped out a message, passing Kai the phone.

Go. I will inform Nichol you are spending the evening working on your tracking skills.

****

Harper startled as a sharp knock pierced the quiet of her little house. Glancing at the time, she set her book down and tiptoed to the door, grabbing Austin's hockey stick while she flipped the deadbolt. She cracked the door open and swung it wide when she saw Kaius standing on her porch, his hands shoved deep into his pockets.

"Kai? Is everything okay?" Her heart jumped into her throat as she moved aside to allow him in, and she scanned the dark street before she closed and locked the door.

He tilted his head for a moment, something he did frequently when he assessed his surroundings. When he remained silent, his eyes averted, she took a step closer to him, the surprise of seeing him replaced by an increased concern. "Kaius? Does Boy know you're here?"

Nodding, he swallowed, his shoulders hunched. "My apologies for interrupting your evening. Boy and I were sparring and I…" Trailing off, he shrugged and looked down at her. "And I wanted to see you again."

The vampiric stillness she became accustomed to during her time with Kaius and Boy was gone as Kai shifted his weight, his eyes blinking against the brown contact lenses disguising the slight ovaling of his blue irises. She smiled up at him and grabbed his hand, leading him into her living room. "I'm so glad you're here. I was just finishing up a chapter in my book and was going to toss on a movie." Sitting, she patted the seat beside her, knowing he could probably hear the thumping of her heart but appreciating his lack of acknowledgment. "I narrowed it down to two, so you need to make the final decision."

The tension in his body visibly decreased as he sat on the sofa beside her, his fingers still intertwined with hers. "Are you sure you don't mind? I considered calling when I hit the town limits, but Nichol has yet to deem me ready for my own communication device."

Wrinkling her nose at the mention of the cantankerous vampire, she passed him the remote and spread a blanket over them, warmth flooding her veins when he draped his arm behind her and relaxed into the couch. "I'm just happy you came by," she reassured him, hoping he felt the truth in her words. "How has everything been going? Boy isn't beating on you too badly, is he?"

"No, the beatings have maintained an appropriate level of damage." He grinned, his expression no longer holding the reserved guardedness he had when he arrived. When her brows knotted, he ran his thumb lightly between her eyes. "No need to worry. Vamps have remarkable recovery speed."

"And he's okay with you being here? What about Nichol? I won't have an irate vamp banging down my door anytime soon, right?"

He busied himself with the movie selection, refusing to answer as the opening credit ran.

"Kaius?" she pressed, squeezing his knee gently. "Does Nichol know you're here?"

"Boy informed him I'm spending the evening focusing on my tracking skills," he stated slowly, a smirk on his face. "The details of who or what I was tracking were neither requested nor required."

CHAPTER TWENTY-TWO

Kaius numbered the handwritten pages and placed them in a neat pile before sliding them under the others, his history slowly unfolding century by century through Boy's slanted scrawl.

Every move and countermove.

Each weighted decision and repercussion.

Decades of obedience.

Seconds of defiance.

All laid out in a succinct timeline of his deception and betrayal of the vampires he sired.

Khthonios owned him for over two thousand years, keeping him tethered to her as a pawn in the sadistic games she loved to play. He was nothing more than her foot soldier, serving as guard for her weaker, corrupt spawn, like Dovidas and Chen, who indulged in depravity and relished in sinking into the worst of their impulses and desires.

The fates of her few spawn who retained a grain of morality after their turnings were handed over to him, the task of their executions bestowed with flippant commands from ruby lips curled into a sneer so often reserved for Kaius and his bastard bloodline.

Pitiful mongrels, every one of them.

Her whispered taunting pierced his thoughts day and night. His mind filled with hushed reminders he failed to shield his haunt from the twisted games she favored, failed to build his strength enough to become a worthy opponent, failed to stand alongside his hauntmates.

And he would fail them again when she returned to settle the score.

He tracked a coyote through the window as it trotted through the yard, its eyes gleaming in the light of the half-moon until it crept into the unmoving pines. His sire's chair scraped across the knotted hardwood and Boy padded barefoot across the floor to his side, crossing his arms and regarding him with a cocked brow. The two stared each other down for a moment before Boy relented and swung the door open, gesturing to the SUV parked alongside the house.

A wave of anticipation coursed through his veins, and he jogged over to the kitchen counter, snatched the keys, and shoved Khthonios and his future to the back of his mind. "You sure? What will you tell Nichol tonight?"

Boy had to be running low on excuses by now, a week's worth of unsanctioned visits to Harper's house making Kai unavailable whenever Nichol called in.

His sire shrugged and stepped aside, his expression a mixture of exasperation and resignation.

Jumping the railing, he popped the locks on the car and got in, revving the engine a few times before backing out of their property with a quick wave.

He knew his freedom would come to an end soon enough. His evening romps into town would soon be replaced by the looming obligations of haunt existence. He would be hunched over spreadsheets and maps in the basement with his creator long into the morning hours instead of at Harper's side.

There was no question his time with her was fleeting. The rush of warmth through his mind every time he looked at her would not be considered while he examined and shored up alliances with haunts he was slowly remembering. But at the moment—on the highway into town while he opened his contact lens case with one hand and popped the brown tints in—he could shove the clock aside and focus on the next five hours.

She was standing in the doorway when he pulled up, a long black sweater wrapped tight around her willowy form and tall black boots on her feet. Swinging her purse over her shoulder as she closed and locked her front door, skipped to the SUV, and got in, her warm brown eyes bright.

"So your dad let you take the car?" she teased, leaning over to kiss his cheek as she buckled her seat belt. "What time's your curfew?"

Stretching his arm across the back of her seat, he grinned. "Home before the street lights go off." When she reached up and ran her thumb lightly over his fang, he cringed. "Oops. The clippers are in the glovebox."

"I wasn't expecting to see you pull up." She smiled while he angled the rearview mirror and used the reflection to snip the tips of his fangs. "Since you're in the driver's seat now, you choose our destination."

Pulling onto the road, he took a left turn back to the highway. "If you're hungry, we could go to the restaurant Nichol sent us to a while back. It doesn't quite have the ambience appropriate for a proper courtship, but I'm afraid our choices are somewhat limited at 2 a.m."

She bopped his shoulder with her forehead and laughed. "A proper courtship, eh? Sometimes I forget you're a billion years old, and other times you remind me in the cutest way ever."

Rolling his eyes as he turned on the radio, he

chuckled. "Ancient vampires aren't usually referred to as cute. Lethal. Dangerous. Manipulative. Maybe dashing or charismatic. But cute?"

"You're cute," she stated, running her fingers along the nape of his neck. "And since I'm the non-vamp around here, I get to choose the adjectives this human will use."

"Can't argue with that logic," he agreed, exiting onto the side road that led to the restaurant. "But while we're on the vampire subject, if we encounter any issues tonight, or any night for that matter, your entire job is to get out as fast as possible. I can handle whatever comes at me, but it will be significantly easier if I know your safety isn't compromised." He caught sight of a UV bulb lighting up the front stoop of a farmhouse. "More so."

"Got it," she replied solemnly. "Get out, get away, and contact Nichol."

Pulling into the parking lot, he found a spot on the far end and killed the engine. "Did he ensure you retained his contact information? I was under the impression he wiped your phone once he terminated your contract."

The subject of the contract hardened her eyes instantly, her lips drawing into a tight line. "I don't have any phone numbers, but I have email addresses if I need them." She avoided looking at him as he walked around the car and held his arm out to her. "I've refused to accept the last deposit he sent when he fired me. It feels wrong and insulting."

Surprised at her declaration, he slowed their approach to the doors. "There's nothing wrong with accepting payment for a completed task."

"There is when that payment was nothing more than

a bribe to stay away from you," she grumbled, glancing down at their linked hands. "Besides, he'll cancel it the moment he realizes you've been disobeying him, and I haven't stopped you."

Scoffing, he opened the door. "Nichol may call the shots right now, but eventually he'll be answering to me again. If he's as smart as I believe him to be, he'll tread carefully and pick his battles with foresight."

****

Harper held tight to Kaius's forearm while they stood at the till and he passed the cashier a wad of bills, waving off the change.

"Are we going to head back to my place for a bit?" she asked, bracing herself for the crisp spring air to hit her as they left the warmth of the restaurant.

Running his tongue along his blunt teeth, he escorted her to the car and opened her door. "I can think of no other place I'd rather be tonight." He got in the SUV and started it up, blinking to right his contacts and stretching his arm along the back of her seat. "Is Austin still away for work?"

Nodding, she tugged her phone from her pocket and checked her messages over. "He'll be around for the weekend, but then he's on site in Grand Prairie for the week." Biting her lip, she snuggled a little closer. "So I guess that makes tonight the last time I'll see you until Monday?"

She wasn't certain, but she would swear Kaius's foot was heavier on the gas than usual on their way back.

They'd spent the week huddled in her living room, alternating between watching movies and having long, hushed talks in the dim glow of the television screen. She knew he was developing a preference for darker, stranger

B-movies, but he happily sat through her favorite romantic comedies. He wasn't fond of the smell of anything containing preservatives, but was inordinately interested in the aged cheeses she often indulged in during their 3 a.m. discussions. She knew he was worried about the anti-vamp signs on her neighbor's yard, but wasn't keen on bringing up the sentiments shared by her roommate.

And she knew he was gaining confidence in his memories, but was struggling to attach any emotion to them.

I can recall several moments of deception, of elation, of uncertainty, but I experience no recollection of how I felt in those moments. Merely the emotions I experience while reliving them, and the two remain separated by an unyielding wall.

While he maintained more stoicism than usual during their evening out—his attention torn between their conversation and their surroundings—the time they spent alone was a rollercoaster of expressions easily read. His blue eyes lightened and darkened with his moods, his laugh lines deepening when he was happy. Even his posture would shift as they talked, leaning forward when he was excited, relaxing back when he was content, and slouching whenever he broached a personal question he was uncertain he should ask.

Whoever said vampires were unreadable spent no time with Kaius.

The wall between his memories and his emotions bothered him. The dim light of the television amplified the creases of worry on his forehead whenever he spoke about it, eased only when she trailed her thumb over them and snuggled in closer.

His shift into what he deemed 'proper courtship' was a source of amusement to her. It was a far cry from the intense make-out session at his house before she'd crept out into the sunlight. He made no move on her outside of a gentle kiss on his way out the door every morning before dawn, the hunger in his eyes telling her precisely how much control he was exhibiting when he walked away.

Pulling up tight to the curb, he turned off the engine and got out, jogging around the car to open her door before she did. He escorted her to her door, his eyes narrowing at the UV lights lining the garage of the neighbor's house.

"I have the urge to leave a note informing those individuals no vampire is interested in stealing their snowmobiles," he stated, holding her purse while she unlocked the door and following her inside. "I also have the urge to straighten their Christmas lights, but it's unrelated."

Laughing, she grabbed his hand and led him to the sofa, waiting until he sat before she stretched out across him, her head on his lap. "Your turn to pick tonight." She reminded him, passing over the remote.

Settling on a nature documentary, he pulled the afghan from the back of the sofa and draped it over her arms, his fingers twirling her hair while penguins waddled across the screen.

"Harper?"

"Yeah?" she murmured, completely relaxed by the gentle caressing of her cheek and temples.

"Do you think this moment will embed in my memory with emotion, or will it become colorless and muted like the others?"

Wrapping one arm around his thigh, she nuzzled in tighter. "I don't know. But if it makes you feel better, I'll keep it in my mind as it is, and you can always borrow the memory from me whenever you want it."

CHAPTER TWENTY-THREE

Kaius released the blade and followed its path until it embedded deep into the hilt of Boy's, splitting the wooden handle of the practice knife. "That's four in a row," he stated, holding his hand out for the car keys. "Am I free?"

His sire skulked up to the tree serving as their makeshift enemy and yanked both blades apart. He examined the broken one for a moment before shoving them into his back pocket and pulling out the keys to the SUV.

Scraping the mud from his boots, he looped the keyring onto his thumb. "Any thoughts on where Harper and I could go on a Monday night? Maybe to a motion picture?" he asked as he opened the car door and grabbed the clippers from the front seat, grinning when Boy merely leveled him with a flat stare. "It's early enough that I can probably make it into the city to pick up flowers first."

He was acutely aware of Boy watching him while he snipped his fangs and popped his brown contacts in, the intensity of his sire's study becoming unnerving. "I'll ensure I'm monitoring my surroundings at all times," he promised, knowing every moment of his perceived freedom hinged on his ability to remain undetected by local human watchdogs. "See you at dawn."

When Boy made no move to interfere with his plans,

he backed out of the muddied property and tore onto the highway, thrumming with the anticipation of seeing Harper for the first time in three nights.

The monotony of the financial holding's reviews Nichol subjected him to all weekend was made bearable by the brief moments he allowed his mind to wander to the woman who occupied a far more prominent place in his head than was likely wise.

While Nichol laid out the meticulously curated empire Kaius had established, it wasn't the power, money, or reputation he noticed, but the contingencies. Bank accounts in seventy-eight countries. Three hundred bolt holes strategically placed across four continents. Allies established along ports with connections to others hunkered in remote locations. And all attached to a litany of escape plans from various locations across Europe, Asia, and the Americas.

With the perusal of the scanned files Nichol sent through the computer, his recollection of his mindset throughout his existence became clearer.

Survival above all else.

Detailed maps filled his screen hour after hour, each color-coded and cross-referenced for easy access to information about safe houses, alliances, and routes. Notes on maps redrawn over the centuries were dated, tweaked to include satellite data unavailable during their initial creation. Ancient ally lists included haunt branches and contact information. Faded ink was written over to ensure the names were not lost to age.

His entire existence was laid out as nothing more than a plot to ensure the survival of his line when his inevitable end arrived.

It was that realization which caused yet another

argument with his second-in-command.

"I was against the idea of sanctuary, wasn't I?" he demanded when Nichol's attention was pulled from their discussion to respond to an email from a haunt in India seeking the Kaius name's blessing to begin the establishment of their own fortress.

Nic's hazel eyes ovaled. "You walked away from us. Your opinion was invalid."

"You should have remained under the radar, manipulated the situation to the benefit of our species with the stealth I taught you," he snarled. "Didn't you see we needed to keep in our place? We are outnumbered, Nichol. One misstep now and they'll crush us. From both sides."

The screen had gone blank. Nichol's blackened eyes disappearing with a curse.

Shaking the argument from his head, he circled the parking lot of the store, noting the three UV lights at the entrance and zeroing in on the dead zone on the eastern corner. With a quick check to ensure his eyes and teeth were humanized, he shoved a wad of bills into his back pocket and strode through the safe zone into the glaring fluorescent of the supercenter. The din of music and voices competed with the rumbling of rickety cartwheels until he filtered through the assault to his senses.

He slowed his speed, taking in the rush of humanity moving throughout the store in the late evening hours. Men in worn work boots filled black baskets and wove past couples strolling through the produce. The cry of a baby pierced his skull alongside the desperate whispers of the mother doing little to calm the fretting infant while other women pushed their carts past her, flashing understanding smiles while their own young dragged their feet behind them.

Young who, in his time, would have been heads of their own households.

The meager selection of the floral department provided few options. Scenting the different bouquets for signs of rot, he settled on a simple collection of daffodils and walked over to the open cashiers, choosing the longer line when he noticed the shortest was occupied by two men in Species Purifier hats.

The young woman ahead of him glanced back, her eyes raking over him before she caught sight of the flowers he placed on the conveyor.

"For your girlfriend?" she asked, smiling up at him while the cashier ran her purchases through. "She's a lucky lady."

Nodding, he pulled his money from his pocket, a wave of self-consciousness hitting him when the woman's eyes dropped to his bare biceps and lingered. "She's not lucky. She's spectacular. Intelligent, compassionate, stunning. I'm grateful for every minute she spends with me."

When his unintentional proclamation met with a squeal, he took a small step back and blinked a few times to ensure his contacts remained in position, acutely aware it wasn't his eyes the woman was focused on.

"That's just the sweetest thing I've ever heard," she gushed, passing her credit card to the cashier and side-eyeing his chest. "You two must make the cutest couple."

****

Harper crossed her arms and leaned against her kitchen counter, barely able to hold back her laughter while Kaius recounted his shopping experience. "Ogled you, did she? Want me to track her down and beat her up?"

His expression was serious as he shook his head. "She meant no harm. It was merely disconcerting to be appraised so thoroughly despite my obvious attachment to another. I was unprepared for the situation. Most who size me up with such concentration are usually attempting to discover a weakness before an attack."

"Oh, she definitely wanted to attack you." She laughed, grazing her fingers over the soft petals of the daffodils once more before she grabbed his hand and led him outside to the SUV. "Has your human interaction really been that limited?" she asked as she got into the passenger side, and he closed her door wordlessly. She waited until he revved the engine and pulled onto the road before pushing the subject. "Kaius?"

He adjusted the rearview mirror. "Haunts often have a selection of humans on site to serve various roles," he replied slowly, his word choices blatantly purposeful. "I know my younger hauntmates are more comfortable with public settings than Nichol, Boy, and I are, though. They can mimic basic human traits like blinking and breathing with less thought than those of us who have been removed from those experiences for longer."

"Back up a second," she stated. "A selection of humans? You mean like Simone, Molly, and Audra?"

Hitting the highway into the city, his jaw tensed. "No. I have no recollection of human partners existing within my haunt until recently. And if my memories are accurate, I had little interaction with any of the women my hauntmates have become united with due to extenuating circumstances." He leaned a fraction closer to the driver side door, putting an extra inch of distance between them. "You're aware of Rhys?"

Nodding, she allowed her hair to fall forward enough to cover the pinking of her cheeks.

"He ran the Tender training and trading for our haunt," Kai continued, attention locked on the road. "For centuries, he curated courtesans specifically for vampire society. While we moved away from independently acquiring women several decades ago, his role was only terminated within the past two years."

Frowning, she tilted her head and studied him. "So the news was right? Vampires were trafficking humans?"

He hesitated before nodding. "It was not a choice made lightly. But yes, I was the one who made the strategic decision to address shortfalls within our community in a way that would limit the potential for exposure. Once our haunt was established in North America, Boy was also in charge of our bloodslave quarters and ran the collection and distribution of blood to haunts experiencing shortages due to injury, age, or location."

The lack of emotion in his voice threw her, putting her on edge. "None of that is anything I hadn't heard rumors or news about," she replied, leaning against her own door. "Obviously, I don't agree with any of it, but I can wrap my mind around the rationale behind it, given the whole underground society thing." When he didn't respond, his face void of emotion, she tightened her hold on her purse. "Kaius? Are you okay?"

Blinking a few times, he shrugged. "My decisions resulted in the imprisonment and deaths of hundreds over the centuries. Yet even now, I have no sense of remorse or guilt. I can recognize the impact the loss of those human lives had on their families and loved ones, but have no regret over the choices I made for the survival of my haunt or my species." Glancing over at her, he gave her a tight-lipped smile and slowed as they approached an intersection. "Would you like to return home?"

"No," she exhaled, reaching over to squeeze his hand as he gripped the steering wheel. "I don't know much about vampires outside of what I've read online, but from what I know of you, and what I saw with Nichol, I'm going to guess no decision you've made over the years was done without a lot of thought. And I would also guess you weren't one for randomly slaughtering entire villages of innocents."

"Attacks like that have historically been considered unwise for vampires," he stated, sounding more like Nichol than she'd heard before. "Reducing the human population during my younger years would have been counterproductive to my nutritional requirements, and mass murder in later years would draw far more attention to a region than was prudent for maintaining a secretive existence." The words hung heavy in the air as he drove to the movie theater and pulled into the parking lot. "Perhaps we should reconsider this tonight."

Crossing her arms, she examined him. "Kai?"

"Yes?"

"Have you ever had a pet?"

He frowned and blinked. "No."

"If you were to get one, what would you want?" she pressed, watching his face closely. "Pretend someone appeared right now and threatened to stake you unless you adopted an animal. What would you choose?"

His expression morphed, the locked-down hardened look softening into one of perplexed contemplation.

"While that scenario seems improbable, I would select a cat." When she motioned for him to continue, he smiled and nodded, solidifying his decision. "I've often lived on the outskirts of cities where feral cats roamed, and I enjoyed their presence. I spent many nights observing them, watching them train their young to track and hunt, noting the patience the mothers had for their litter. And I find both their fluidity and the softness of their fur quite relaxing. So yes, if faced with the threat of staking, I would get a cat."

Content with the lilt of warmth in his voice that had been absent earlier, she set her purse at her feet and relaxed against his shoulder. "We'll do the movie tomorrow night. Let's just drive and talk until the sun comes up."

CHAPTER TWENTY-FOUR

Traitorous little mongrel, aren't you?

Kaius shot to his feet in the dark cell, crouching in preparation of attack until a small pulse of warning rippled through his mind and Boy turned on the light, illuminating the room.

Crawl back on your knees, pathetic animal.

He scanned his surroundings, backing into the corner to ensure nothing could come at him from behind while the voice continued to whisper.

The woman doesn't care for you. She pities you.

His sire's gentle blasts eased as Khthonios withdrew from his head. Boy remained out of reach to give him time to regain control over his mind.

"She's watching us, isn't she?" he growled when his thoughts finally silenced. Pacing the floor, he kicked aside the blue mats serving as their beds. "These aren't memories I'm hearing. It's her."

Boy maintained his position in the far corner. His vacant gaze locked on the darkness of the basement visible through the open door.

Coming to a halt in front of his sire, he forced Boy's attention to him. "What does she want with me? Her blood is no longer in my veins. She has no tie to my existence. No investment in me. No ownership. So what are her intentions and how do I end this?"

Boy's head dropped a fraction, his long hair falling

into his eyes before he slunk past him, pushing the unlocked cage door open and leading him into the other room where they'd established a makeshift workstation they could access during daylight hours. He sat down at the laptop, examining it for a moment before pressing the power button and watching the screen light up.

He paced the floor behind his sire, his thoughts becoming darker with every step.

He knew his history, knew what he'd done under the thumb of Khthonios. He knew he caused death and destruction brought about solely through her word, that he had been her weapon and her lapdog. He could pull the memories up at will, could watch Khthonios's games unfold, could hear his own words which brought about a two-thousand-year race to the battlefield. A threat spoken in a moment of rage as her heel dug deep into his bloodied chest.

Your blood may keep me at your feet, but it will be my blood that brings you to your knees.

Boy opened an empty document and tapped the keys, his large fingers struggling to maintain any speed while he typed and deleted, motioning for Kai to come to his side.

My blood is that of Khthonios. Therefore, you carry hers through me. As your haunt does through you.

"But the only one directly carrying her blood anymore is you," he argued as he sat on the cement floor and draped his arms over his knees. "She's powerful enough in her own right to have no need for me, so why? Why continue to seek me out?"

Reining in his impatience while his sire responded, he sifted through his memories for any hint of weakness in the female vampire.

Though her siring of you was brought about by my failure, you were her greatest achievement, a perfect specimen of vampirism. But it was the lingering scent of my blood in you that brought about her ire, reminding her you were tainted. Your existence would have been one of luxury and ease had I brought you to her first for turning instead of defying her order to remain isolated from all others. You were tethered to her rage for my disobedience and deficiencies.

Boy's shoulders hunched as he continued to type with methodical movements until he sat back and angled the screen.

You proved the strength of your bloodline through the curation of a haunt capable of withstanding her attacks. But in doing so, you also proved your worthiness as her partner. And I believe she is now beginning her courtship.

****

Harper opened the door to Kaius and pressed her finger over her lips to silence him as she listened to Austin's frustrated rant. She closed her eyes to zero in on his words and not on the responses already forming in her head. "I can be there within an hour, okay?" she reassured him, lolling her head against the wall. "And I get to say this once. I told you so."

"Thanks, Harpy." Austin sighed. "And yeah, you earned the right to say it. I'll even let you say it once more after you get me the hell out of here."

The line went dead, and she slid her phone into her purse. "Hey, baby," she ground out, her brows knotted while she hunted through her bag for her keys. "I'm afraid I've been summoned to the police station downtown to bail Austin out." Looking up at him, she clenched her teeth. "He and his dumbass friends were arrested west of here for trespassing and spray-painting anti-vamp slogans on a farmhouse. Oh, and public drunkenness."

Kaius stepped in tight to her without a word and wrapped his arms around her, his chin resting on her head.

"I should leave him there," she murmured into his chest, the tension in her shoulders releasing when he merely tightened his hold on her. "I told him this would happen."

They stood there for a few minutes in silence until she eased out of his grasp and ran her hands through her hair. "Okay. I'm good. This will probably take a few hours, so movie night will need to be postponed."

Following her out the door, Kai waited at her side as she locked up before he finally spoke. "Let me drive you," he offered as they walked to the street. "I'm not comfortable with you going downtown at this hour."

"You'd never make it past the UV lights around the station," she grumbled, unlocking her car. "And trust me when I say you do not want to see the side of me I'm going to be unleashing once I get Austin's sorry butt in the car. And whoever else he ends up convincing me to bail out. Bail out with vampire funds, I should add."

He knelt beside her when she sat in the driver seat, blocking her from closing the door. "If it's too risky for me to go inside with you, I'll wait in the car. But I would prefer you not be on your own this evening. You don't know the state of inebriation Austin, or his friends are in."

"Fair point," she conceded, unable to hide her smile when he hopped to his feet and jogged around the car, folding his long legs into the cramped passenger seat. "Make sure to put that seat back as far as it will go. They don't deserve legroom on the way home."

****

Kaius tracked every movement along the quiet street, scanning the rooftops for signs of a violently amorous female vampire, while he waited for Harper to walk back to the car.

She'd been inside the heavily lit police station for almost two hours and without a phone of his own, he was left in the dark as to how the bailing process was progressing.

"I do not want to hear it." Her voice carried on the night air, her steady footsteps to the east competing against the lumbering thumping of three others. "So help me, Austin. If any of you push it with me right now, I'll leave you on the street."

The bubbling anger in her voice had him straightening up as he turned toward the direction of the footsteps, his frustration easing once he set eyes on her.

"Hey," Austin slurred, waving at him. "That's the guy from my birthday. The comic guy." Undeterred by Harper's laser glare, he elbowed his two buddies. "No wonder she's pissed. We interrupted her first date in like, Harp? When did you and Asher break up?"

Asher?

Harper stopped cold and spun around to face her roommate. "Try me, Austin. Just try me right now."

Austin appeared as stunned as Kaius was with the cold fury in her voice. All softness and warmth was replaced by an iciness silencing every male in the vicinity as Austin and his two friends squeezed into the back seat.

They were on the highway before drunken stupidity opened the mouth of one of the passengers, his Species Purifier shirt stained with dirt and paint.

"What'd I tell you?" He attempted to whisper. "Fucking cops have been bought off."

Kaius placed his hand on Harper's knee, willing her to let it go until the two of them were alone and she could unleash without repercussion.

Austin leaned in to his buddy. "I know, right? Half the guys in there are probably blowing the vamps for side-coin."

Harper's eyes narrowed, hardening when she adjusted her rearview mirror and the other guy chimed in. "And did you see the chick at the fingerprinting? Fucking whore tried to cover fang scars with some cheap-ass tattoo. She was probably tag-teaming those freaks in the station before they all crawled back into the sewers where they belong."

The car slowed on the highway and Kaius leaned over, bringing his lips as close as he could to her ear. "Ignore it. Let's get them home and you and I can go for a drive."

She didn't respond, but her foot lifted off the brake while the men behind them continued their musings about the depth of vampire corruption in the police department. His blood boiled as their focus zeroed in on the female officers with disdain.

He angled his position to maintain a visual on them, using the side mirrors and window reflections to ensure none of them made a stupid move that would result in a full-on slaughter.

Because the darker Harper's mood went, the redder his vision was turning.

Every sense was on high alert, his mind and body primed to fight and feed. His logical side was the only thing keeping him in check throughout their disgusting positing about women who chose vampires over human men, the predator in him rising with the tension in Harper's body.

Pulling in front of a house on the south side of town, she threw the car into park and stared straight ahead. "Out."

Austin's friends vacated the backseat with muttered thanks for the ride. When Austin didn't move, she turned around.

"You, too. If you so much as breathe near my house in the next twelve hours, I will not only call the cops on you, I'll tell them precisely who was there during your last little farmhouse attack. Am I clear?"

Her roommate's jaw dropped before he slowly undid his seatbelt. "Come on, Harper. Be reasonable." Met with nothing but stony silence, he got out. "I'll call you tomorrow, okay?"

The door closed, and she tore onto the road toward her home.

He held his silence while she led him inside and slammed the door before locking it and throwing her purse onto the counter.

"That's it, isn't it?" she finally snarled, shoving the kitchen chairs in tight to the table. "I'm supposed to just sit there and take it while they spew the most disgusting, repulsive lies? Smile and nod to avoid being called a problem while they get to call me a slut and a whore?"

He held position in the entranceway, giving her space to lash out against the counter and furniture. "They weren't speaking of you," he said softly. "They were speaking of strangers, people with whom they have no ties or relationship."

"And that makes it better?" She seethed. "If I'd exposed us right then and there, you think they would change their minds? That they would suddenly see *me* and not some vamp slut spreading her legs for the devil?"

Hearing the words from her mouth—from the lips he kissed and the voice that filled his dark nights with light—he tightened his grip on the door frame, choosing to remain silent while he fought back the desire to track down Austin and his friends.

Because he wasn't certain any interaction with the men would remain verbal. And he hadn't eaten in two nights.

Harper hopped onto the counter, her head in her hands. "This is who Austin is now, isn't it? And if he knew about us…maybe he'd think twice before spray-painting my home or burning it to the ground, but he'd still do it, wouldn't he?"

Crossing the floor, he wrapped his arms around her. "I would like to think he wouldn't."

"But you wouldn't put money on it, would you?" She sighed, leaning back on her hands, and looking up at him. "How do you let it roll off you? The things they were saying. How are you not affected?"

He smirked and shrugged. "I have a strong poker face. The words of humans have rarely, if ever, impacted me. But tonight, I was far closer to draining all three of them than I care to admit." Tilting her chin up, he kissed her softly. "They have no idea they owe their continued existence to you and your easily stainable fabric car seats."

One arm draped across his back, and he wedged

himself between her knees, nuzzling the crook of her neck as she arched into him, pressing her body against his.

"A little scare wouldn't have killed them," she countered, trailing her fingers lightly down his back and sending electricity through his veins. "Maybe next time?"

Straightening up, he cupped her face in his hands. "I'll make you a deal. When you and I walk away from this place for good, I'll have a pleasant little chat with each of them on the way out of town." Catching his slip of the tongue, he corrected himself. "If. If you and I walk away. Deal?"

Her eyes lit up, and she bit her lip with a nod. "Deal. Are you staying for a bit?"

Peering through her window into the empty street, he nodded. "You go put the second season of that zombie series on and I'll do a quick tour of the perimeter."

He was halfway around the yard when Khthonios's voice slithered through his mind.

It's bad business to make deals before all offers are presented, Kaius.

CHAPTER TWENTY-FIVE

Kaius flipped between the color-coded maps of Denver and the surrounding towns and compared them to the recent surge in Deviants staggering over the mountain passes.

"Maintain the established human-vamp Deviant task force on the north and south routes and pull half of those patrolling the west. Double the financial relocation compensation for anyone remaining in the region to reduce casualties and complications, and anticipate another wave from the Midwest," he recommended, glancing at the clock on the screen. "Anything else?"

Nichol's hazel eyes narrowed. "We need to discuss your return and reintegration into the haunt. Our alliances are questioning your whereabouts publicly, and it's becoming an issue I cannot hold off for much longer."

Distracted, he stood and smoothed down his black shirt. "I have to run a course Boy set out for me, so maybe write up your thoughts on it and we can discuss it another time."

His second stilled. "Inform Harper I require her to accept her final payment before I can reconcile and close out the account I used during your initial recovery phase."

The screen went black, and Kai froze.

Nichol knew.

Opening the video link, he tapped on the haunt number, knowing he was cutting it close to his promised pickup time but unable to walk away.

"What."

Crossing his arms over his chest, he leaned back in his chair. "How long have you known?"

"You're surrounded by my drones, Kaius. I've known since the first night Boy released you to visit her."

His temper spiked. "You've been tracking my movements."

"I've been monitoring the situation, yes," Nichol stated. "Harper's existence and knowledge poses a direct risk to you and Boy, and your association with her outside of the confines of the property has opened up the possibility of discovery and retaliation from anti-vamp factions in the region."

Tampering down the low growl building in his chest, he stared his second down. "Harper poses no threat, as you should know, since you're the one who vetted her."

Nichol broke the stare down first, his gaze falling to his keyboard. "Kai, I've been your right hand for centuries. My responsibility to ensure the survival of my hauntmates extends to you. Started with you."

"And it was I who taught you all you know."

Nic's jaw twitched. "You're in uncharted territory here, Kaius. I can understand her nature has an appeal to you in your condition, but she doesn't fit in well with our current priorities. That said, should your relationship with her become unstable or threatened, I have contingency plans ready to evacuate you and Boy. I'm aware emotional attachments are not always mitigated easily through financial compensation or logistical discussions. I am also aware you have a date, and we can discuss this another time."

****

Harper's thumb hesitated over the deposit button for a moment. "I don't need the money," she stated. "Your haunt more than compensated me for my time already."

"And as I said earlier, your refusal to deposit it has created a stressor for Nichol because he has an account he's unable to balance and closeout," Kaius reiterated with a smirk, glancing in his rearview mirror as he sped onto the highway. "Would it make you feel better to know I had a look at all the haunt accounts, and I suspect we spend more on shampoo and conditioner in a year than the amount Nichol attempted to bribe you with?"

Groaning, she tapped the button and watched her bank account balance skyrocket. "Stop using the word 'bribe'. It feels sleazy enough as it is, being paid to stay away from you and then not following through."

"Then let's refer to it as an incentive and I'll inform Nichol you found my companionship worth more than his meager offering."

Leaning against him, she wrapped her arm around his and traced the defined muscles running the length of his forearm. "You wouldn't be wholly incorrect. Did he seem angry?"

Shaking his head, he kissed the top of her head. "Not with you. But I suspect he's keeping the information close to the chest. I doubt the others are aware." He paused. "I'd very much like to see the rest of my haunt again soon."

"Do you miss them?"

His forehead creased and she reached up to smooth the lines out as he nodded. "With the exception of the

187

night I reverted into Deviancy, my memories have become completely unified again. And while I still lack an emotional connection to any of my recollections of my hauntmates, I know I was tightly bound to them."

Smiling, she watched the lights of the oncoming cars as they passed. "Are you excited to return?"

He slowed when they reached the turnoff to the theater and signaled while he pulled into the parking lot. "I have yet to decide if I will."

They walked hand in hand into the busy theater, casually slipping through the narrow pathway unlit by the UV lights surrounding the exterior. The cashier barely looked up into Kaius's brown contact lenses as he paid, sliding their tickets across the counter with mumbled instructions to head toward the right.

Arms loaded with popcorn, bottles of water, and a purse full of candy, they settled into their seats in the back row, allowing Kai the opportunity to monitor the premises as needed.

"The reviews on this haven't been great," she warned when the lights dimmed, and the first ad blasted onto the screen. "Yikes, that's loud."

Wrinkling his nose, he nodded and draped his arm over her shoulder. "I don't believe I've seen a color film in the theater," he whispered into her ear, his tongue flicking her lobe. "If memory serves, my experience with a black and white movie was a date with Nichol. And he was more interested in the technology involved than in the plot line."

"Hey, Mr. Older Than Dirt," she hushed back. "You better keep that rogue tongue in check during this, or we're going to get kicked out."

When his response was a kiss in the same spot, she

snuggled up against him and settled into two hours of escapism, broken only by the odd wandering hand feigning interest in the popcorn bag on her lap.

****

Kaius pocketed his contact lens case and scanned the neighborhood rooftops before following Harper into her home, his gaze lingering for a moment on a shadow three houses down. "Has Austin made contact since last night?"

She slid her purse onto the counter and toed off her shoes. "He swung by to grab a few things while I was sleeping earlier. Left a note letting me know he's giving me a few days to cool off." Giving him a look that told him precisely what she thought of it, she shrugged her jacket off and draped it over a chair. "I'm not ready to speak to him."

He was halfway to the living room when she grabbed his hand and gently tugged him down the hall to her room. "Are you tired? I can head off if you like."

Leading him into her space, she closed the door and leaned against it, her heart rate rising. He opened his senses, unable to pinpoint the threat sending her pulse into overdrive until she pushed off the door and grasped the hem of her shirt, pulling it over her head and dropping it to the floor.

"You're not tired, are you?" he stated, aware he was staring at her black satin bra but unable to look away.

"No, Kaius, I'm not tired." She laughed as she walked over to him and trailed her fingers down to the hem of his shirt. "A little nervous, but not tired."

When she pushed his tee up his chest and her cold hand made contact with his skin, he swallowed, yanked the shirt over his head, and tossed it onto the bed.

"Nervous?"

She kept her gaze on his chest, her fingers splayed across it as she traced the muscled plane. "Well, yeah. I mean, the possibility of rejection aside, it's always a little scary with someone new, isn't it?"

Unable to keep his hands to himself any longer, he smoothed her hair off her shoulders and bent down to kiss her, the desire he kept locked down tight over the past few weeks barreling to the forefront of his mind. His fangs lengthened as her tongue swiped across his and he pulled back instinctively before he sliced her, covering his mouth with his hand.

"Kaius?"

She looked up at him, eyes wide with concern and a vulnerability that nearly buckled his knees.

Dropping his hand, he ran his tongue along the lengthened canines. "It's been a few centuries since these elongated for anything outside of bloodlust." He stilled when she reached up and brushed her finger along one. "I don't want to hurt you."

"I'm tough," she whispered as she rose onto her toes and replaced her finger with her tongue, the sensation a direct line to the almost painful erection straining against his jeans. "Are you…the biting…"

"The two aren't mutually inclusive," he groaned, pulling her closer while she moved her lips along his jaw. "A non-issue tonight."

The gentle teasing of her tongue along his throat tested the increasingly short cord of control he was clinging to while he popped the button of her jeans and slid them off her hips, the view of her bare backside in her boudoir mirror stunning him for a moment.

Toeing her jeans off, she stepped back and bit her

lip, shying away from his gaze.

"I'm sorry," he murmured, shaking out of the stupefied silence her thong had thrown him into. "I'm merely memorizing every inch of you so I can embed this memory for eternity."

Her cheeks pinked, her arms crossing over her stomach. Frowning, he unwrapped the hold she had on herself and knelt before her, trailing his hands down her ribs to the swell of her hips. Her heartbeat thumped in his ears, her breathing becoming shallower when he hooked his fingers in the band of her thong and inched it down her legs, his attention wholly consumed by the smoothness of her skin under his touch. Indulging in the sensation, he ran his hands along her thighs and calves, committing the feeling deep into the farthest reaches of his memory.

"Kaius?"

Her voice wavered, and he looked up the length of her body, suddenly very aware of his position at her feet. "No other woman has brought me to my knees voluntarily. Ever." He stood slowly and clasped his hands around hers, bringing them to the band of his jeans and stilling when her nimble fingers popped the button in a single motion. She eased the zipper down and relieved some of the intense pressure keeping him grounded.

When her cold hand slipped under his boxers and gripped, he inhaled sharply and she released him, jumping back. "Oh god, Kai! I'm so sorry. My hands are always so cold and—"

Silencing her with his lips, he brought her hand back to where it was, shuddering when the ice of her fingers cooled the unbearable heat of his erection. "Ever put a cold compress on a burn?" he murmured, pressing against her hold and almost whimpering when she pumped him with excruciating slowness. He could hear himself panting from the effort to maintain control. The sound was as foreign to him as the rising urge he had to mark her was, to lay claim to her as only the most primitive of his species did.

"You sure you're, okay?"

Not trusting his voice, he cleared his throat. "You've made an ancient vampire breathe," he growled as he unhooked her bra and tugged it off her shoulders. "So yes, I'm sure I'm okay." He cupped one breast and froze as the barrage of sensations overwhelmed his head. "Harper?"

"Yeah?" she breathed, tightening her grip on him.

The thrum of her heartbeat only added to the surges blasting his senses, from the scent of her arousal to the taste of her peach lip gloss.

Slipping out of her hold, he shoved his hands through his hair and squeezed his eyes shut to eliminate the temptation of her warm body. "I'm not," he exhaled, centering himself. "I don't have a strong grasp of my control right now."

Her thumbs brushed along his forehead and temples. "I don't want you in control."

"And I don't want to hurt you. Or scare you."

He opened his eyes and watched her walk past him to the bed. She reclined back, slinking into the middle of the mattress as she crooked a finger at him and bit her lip, her heart racing. "Please?"

****

Any modesty Harper had was torn from her when her back arched off the bed, one hand fisted in Kaius's

192

hair and the other clinging to her headboard as though it would keep her anchored against the orgasm threatening to crest hot on the heels of her last. Her knees trembled and fought Kaius's hold while her body warred between sinking into the overpowering sensation building in her every nerve and pushing back against it. When the pressure of his tongue increased again, all rational thought flew from her mind, her incoherent moans sounding miles away until she came down from the peak.

She dug her heels into the bed, pulling at his short hair when he refused to let up.

"I can't," she whimpered, her body betraying her by pressing against his hand, encouraging his fingers to stretch her farther. "God, Kaius, I…ohgodrightthere."

Whatever magic spot he found deep inside her had her thrashing beneath him moments later. Her vision blurred in and out of focus as he crawled up the length of her body, his fangs grazing along her skin while he kept up the deliciously torturous motion of his hand.

The blue of his eyes was almost completely gone, little more than a faint rim around the blackened oval irises. The transformation into predator was instantaneous once she beckoned him to her bed. The gentle nuzzling of her skin every few minutes the only reminder Kaius was still very much in there.

Another wave slammed through her, and she cried out, clinging to his biceps as she rode out the tremors. Her skin was damp, the chill of the room sending a shudder through her.

Kaius tilted his head and studied her, scanning her body before he reached across the bed and tossed the blanket over them.

Mouthing a thank-you, she cupped his chin, her

muscles too exhausted and relaxed to do much more as he reached between them and gripped himself, his black eyes still monitoring her every reaction. When she took a deep breath and nodded, he pushed inside her, stilling to allow her body to adjust to his size before he went farther. She could feel a faint shaking in his arms as he buried himself to the hilt and held position until she arched against him, encouraging him to seek his own release.

As his hips moved leisurely, a low growl rumbled from his chest, making her smile when her mind immediately likened the sound to a contented lion. The sudden shift from riding a continuous high for well over three hours to the languid connection of their bodies lulled her as he continued to move inside her. His head was buried in the crook of her neck while her breathing leveled out and her mind cleared, her hands exploring his muscled back as it flexed above her.

How long he maintained the rhythm, she couldn't say. Twenty minutes, an hour... It wasn't until her toes curled, she realized he'd been building her toward another peak. His unhurried movements merely primed her for something far more intense than she'd ever known. Her thighs tightened around him, and he pushed himself back onto his haunches, pulling her hips along with his in a move so swift and smooth, she didn't realize he'd shifted position until his tempo increased and the slow build ramped to a frenetic pace.

The low growl continued unabated as her moans joined in. Her attempts to speak resulted in nothing more than the rasped chanting of his name as he continued to thrust into her. A slight shift of his hips hit something inside and sent her body into overload. An almost unbearable pleasure ripped through her in waves, dipping only long enough for her to catch her breath before he drove her right back toward the cliff again.

"Kaius," she whimpered as she exposed her throat and braced herself for the exquisite torture she knew was moments away. "Please?"

The thread holding the last of his control snapped and he slammed into her faster and harder, sending her over the edge for a final time. His fangs sunk into her skin, his entire body going rigid as his orgasm tore through him with an animalistic snarl. Unhooking his fangs from her neck, he collapsed onto her, holding his weight with his forearms as he dropped his forehead to her shoulder and gasped for air.

The minutes ticked by as they lay there, their senses coming back online one by one until he pushed himself up and looked down at her, his blue eyes wary as he scanned her body.

"Are you okay? Are you injured? Did I scare you?"

She licked her lips and smiled lazily, the euphoria of the past few hours still seeping through her veins. "I'm never walking again. Scared is the opposite of what I'm feeling right now, and I'm very, very okay in that completely-sated-and-exhausted way."

Sliding off her, he stretched out on his side and pulled her tightly against him, running his finger over his bite marks and adjusting the blanket to keep her covered and warm before she drifted off.

CHAPTER TWENTY-SIX

Kaius stumbled back as Boy's fist made contact with his ribs in what should have been an easy dodge.

"Sorry." He pushed the two broken bones back into place. "Okay. Go."

His sire came at him again and he ducked out of the first hit, turning straight into the second, which sent him skidding on his ass across the dirt.

Leaping to his feet, he crouched in preparation of the next round, straightening when Boy remained in place, arms crossed and a look of exasperation on his usually expressionless face.

Wiping his hands on his filthy cargos, he grit his teeth. "I know. I'm just a bit distracted."

One brow lifted and he amended his statement.

"I'm really distracted."

There was no denying it. He'd barreled through the front door with mere seconds to spare as the sun rose that morning, jumping down the hatch into the basement as the first UV rays brushed against the nape of his neck. With Harper's scent covering his clothes and skin, he spent the day sitting in the corner of the cell, staring at the cement floor, and cycling through the images and sensations burned into his mind.

The parting of her lips as she arched against him, his name the only coherent word spoken.

The strength of her grasp on his biceps that would

loosen in a flash, as though she feared her small hands would damage him.

The way her body molded to his when she fell into a deep sleep, holding his arm tight around her and scrunching her face when he eased from her grip to ensure he made it home before the sun rose.

His sire's left hook couldn't compete.

Boy continued to watch him, likely tracking the swells of emotions the memories of Harper stirred.

"Nichol wants to discuss my reintegration into the haunt," he stated, unnerved by the intensity of Boy's assessment.

Tugging his phone from his pocket, Boy brought it in tight and tapped out a message, handing it over as they walked inside.

—Do you desire reintegration?—

Frowning, he pulled his dirty boots off and set them aside, stripping out of his filthy cargos and dropping them into the washing machine as he grabbed a fresh pair from the dryer. "What else would I do?" he scoffed, trading his tee shirt for a black button-down. "Start fresh? Build a haunt from the ground up? Abandon the vampires loyal to me for centuries?"

Boy stood by the door while Kaius grabbed the keys to the SUV and slung his jacket over his shoulder, glancing down at his sire's phone and pausing as he read the last message.

—Stay with her—

The words hung in the forefront of his mind as he drove to the small town where Harper's little home sat. The porch light would be on in anticipation of his arrival, the lamps of the living room giving off a faint glow through the gauzy blue kitchen curtains. He'd knock and listen for her bare feet to skip across the old hardwood floors, sliding to a stop moments before the lock would click and the door would swing open, her nose scrunching as she smiled up at him. She'd step aside as he entered, glancing outside with a glare at her neighbor's house before she'd lock them in for the night, her delicate fingers wrapping around his while she led him inside.

There would be no injury reports. No intricate alliances to negotiate. No favors to call in.

No one's life would dangle across his every decision. No bloodlines jeopardized by a tactical choice made after sifting through thousands of pieces of intel.

Nichol had proven himself a leader, demonstrated his strength of character through one of the most turbulent periods in vampire history. He carried the North American vamps through the worst of the storms, created a sanctuary where the injured could heal, the lost could find their footing, and the strongest could be mobilized.

He pulled up to Harper's home and turned off the engine, staring at the yellow glow of her porch light.

Staying wasn't an option thirty minutes ago.

Now it was all he wanted.

****

Harper stretched out across Kaius on the sofa, shifting in place until she found the most comfortable spot on his chest. "That okay?"

"Now that you've removed your elbow from my groin, yes." He wrapped the throw across her back and tucked it under her arms. "So what does this potential job entail?"

Reaching over to the coffee table, she picked up her

phone and opened the advertisement, angling it toward him. "They're looking for people willing to take part-time hours but be on call for large-scale emergencies and the potential for advancement is high. I figured since I don't need to worry about making ends meet every month, I can take a job like this and work my way into my ultimate goal of being the Queen Bee."

He chuckled, and his chest rumbled. "Queen Bee?"

"The boss," she clarified with a grin. "The head honcho. The big cheese."

Flicking through the TV channels, he stopped on a medical drama and draped his arm across her back. "So you like being the one calling the shots, do you?"

"You're damn right I do."

Sinking into the cool comfort of his body, she zoned out to the storyline, worn from spending most of the day arguing with Austin via text and calls. After the physically exhausting night she had being pillaged by the vampire snuggling her now, the hours she spent verbally sparring with her roommate left her emotionally drained.

"Your heart rate is rising," Kaius said softly, twirling her hair around his fingers and letting it fall rhythmically.

Burrowing a smidgeon closer into him, she huffed. "Austin and I had it out today and I can't stop thinking about it. I hung up on him right before you got here and I'm just…I don't know. I can't pull him out of this, and I know it. But he keeps getting deeper into the Purifier movement and I…" She trailed off, unable to find the words.

"And you're lying on top of a vampire right now?" he offered, grazing his thumb over her temple.

"Pretty much." She craned her neck to look at him.

"You're old. You've seen a lot. Do you think he'll come around? Or that this ridiculous division will end? What's the historic precedent?"

Another low laugh rumbled through him. "You enjoy reminding me of my age, don't you?" When she nodded, he rolled his eyes. "Historically, politics and religion have been the greatest dividers of humanity. They have torn apart marriages, friendships, and bloodlines, creating rifts lasting for generations." He wrapped his arms a little tighter around her. "Vampire society hasn't been immune from this either. Some of my own bloodline sought to align with the Purifiers, and many of my species eagerly watched while Rhys burned in the Deepfryer, so it would be remiss for me to say humans are the sole cause of the global discord."

Shoving the memories of Rhys's live-broadcast Deepfrying aside, she sat back and straddled him, smoothing her hands along the hard planes of his chest and biting her lip when his hips shifted beneath her. "Have you ever wanted to escape to a deserted island? Just let everyone sort their stuff out and hope you can return in a decade or two and find world peace?"

"It's something I'm looking into."

****

Kaius set the lock on the doorknob and eased it shut behind him. He paused to listen for Harper's steady resting heart rate before he jogged over to the SUV and got in, revving the engine a few times before he started toward the acreage.

Escape to a deserted island.

Although he allowed himself to indulge in the thought for a while, he knew it was nothing more than a fanciful whim.

Even if he did run through the locations of his bolt holes in case any fit the bill.

Harper had plans, had the desire to be more than the companion of a vampire who could never exist in her reality, who would never be more than a secret whispered in the night. Her compassionate heart needed more than him to care for, thrived on being the secure port for those seeking help.

To entertain the fantasy as anything other than the escapist dream it was would be akin to proclaiming her desires inconsequential. And in doing so, it would erase the core of what he saw in her, what he craved.

He entered his house under the weight of the decisions bearing down on him, passing Boy in the basement with little more than a nod on his way to the cell where he could stretch out on the thin mat, free from distraction.

His mind was cycling through his options for the eleventh time, when Khthonios's voice broke through the loop.

We could be partners, you and I.

Inching onto his elbows, he leaned forward to peer through the doorway, reassuring himself Boy remained occupied with the blood donor rotation. Reclining back, he closed his eyes again, reigning his core in tightly to avoid alerting his sire as he reached his mind out toward the whispers in his head.

I bring nothing to a union you cannot attain on your own.

He could feel Khthonios's satisfaction pulse through him as she replied, her voice clearer.

You bring more than you know. The respect of your name, the fear of mine, the power behind us. We could become gods on earth.

Opening his senses to track his sire, he stilled.

I do not desire worship.

Khthonios's low laugh wormed through his skull.

Perhaps not. But you do desire to have it all. And only I can grant it.

CHAPTER TWENTY-SEVEN

Harper screeched, jumping to the right and covering her mouth as she spun around the deserted park. Giggling, she scanned the darkness for the vampire who groped her. "Come out, come out, wherever you are."

Her ponytail flipped over her eyes and her hand shot out behind her to feel nothing but a wisp of cool air brushing against her skin as Kaius ghosted away.

Inching closer to the dim lamplight illuminating the playground, she squinted at a shadow beneath the slide. "I spy with my little eye, a vamp too big to fit under there," she sang, groaning when lips skimmed the nape of her neck. "Or not." His hands slid along her hips, and she turned to look up at him, smirking at his disheveled hair. "I'm mildly impressed."

A single brow lifted, and he stepped back, crossing his arms. "Mildly?"

"Well, yeah," she hummed, pursing her lips in challenge. "I mean, you're fast, yes. But superheroes have more than speed going for them."

Glancing around, he gave her a quick kiss on the forehead and sauntered over to the parking lot, lifted the front end of her car with one hand, and lowered it gently back.

With a flourish, he bowed to her slow clap. "Is m'lady appeased?"

"Moderately," she called over, laughing when he

lolled his head back. "What else do you have, big boy?"

Grinning, he knelt down to pick something up, then jogged along the trees lining the park until he found a stick. Running over to her, he held out the stick and a large rock. "Want to see me play ball?"

"Why not?" She smiled as she sat on the grass and wrapped her blue sweater tight around herself. "Need me to pitch?"

Walking to the small ball diamond in the corner of the park, he shook his head, tossed the rock up, and slammed it through the air with a crack as the stick snapped in half. Her eyes tracked the rock while it descended and fell into his open palm on the other side of the field. Before she could applaud, he chucked it to first base.

And caught it.

On to second base and third.

By the time he tried to put himself out at home plate, she was clapping furiously.

"Bravo." She laughed as he jogged back to her, slid across the grass, and struck a pose at her side. "Okay. I'm appeased. Now how on earth did you discover you had that entertainingly useless talent?"

Grabbing her by the waist, he rolled onto his back, bringing her on top of him. "Mikhail used to try it when he needed to burn some energy up and no one was available to spar. But he never made it past the second base catch."

"And you had to prove it could be done?" she teased, shaking her hair out when he tugged the elastic from her ponytail.

He smiled and reached up to tuck her hair behind her ears. "Jagger incorporated the activity into our sparring regime shortly after. I mastered it to provide a demonstration of the skills required." Arching his head up to kiss her, he grinned against her lips. "And to remind them who was, as you say, top dog."

She pushed herself onto her elbows and looked down at him. "Are you worried about going back?"

"Who said I'm going back?"

"You have to," she stated, resting her forehead against his. "Kaius belongs with the Kaius haunt."

He wrapped his arms a little tighter around her. "Fine. I'll change my name to Kevin and the issue will be settled."

Tilting her head, she frowned. "Are you really considering not returning? They need you there. The movement needs you there." When his jaw tensed, she sat back, straddling his hips and splaying her hands on his chest. "When I watch the news, everything vampire related references the Kaius haunt. And whenever I think back to the night Boy re-vamped you, the thing that stands out the most is how hopeful your haunt looked, how much they tried to appear unaffected and how badly they failed at it."

All good humor was gone from his face, his eyes darkening. "Nichol has proven himself a solid, capable leader."

She knew she was pushing a sensitive subject, but was unable to stop herself. As much as she wanted to remain there in the park and in that moment forever, she knew he was meant for more. Needed for more. "If you ask me, he seemed to be stressed to the max last time I saw him on video. I think Nichol is trying to make up for being the reason you were in the Deviant situation in the first place."

****

"Kaius, dear, are you ready?"

He kept his eyes on the blackened sky, unable to meet the stares of his hauntmates as he crossed the field and stood at attention.

"I see the guard dog is still tethered to you." She sneered, her disdain for Boy's presence evident in the revulsion coating her words. "Kaius. Come. Introduce me to your spawn. I want to see what your bastard blood has sired."

Echoes of shock and betrayal coursed through the mental links he held with his eldest hauntmates, centuries of unequivocal camaraderie obliterated in a flash as Khthonios drew blood from Nichol and Rhys.

Such lovely lambs, *his sire whispered into his mind while she kicked Boy's legs into position and yanked his hair, her eyes lingering on Boy's throat.* You always did attract the most beautiful of gems.

He lowered his head in deference to her until his allegiance to his hauntmates overtook sound judgment. "Nichol answers to me," *he ground out, stepping in front of his second to draw her ire away from the younger vampire.*

His feet left the ground, her fingers drawing blood as she lifted him into the air. "And you answer to me."

Such a display of defiance, *she laughed into his head.* Let's see how you manage to balance both sides now that your haunt knows you've misled them for centuries.

He didn't need her words to bury the dagger farther into his gut. Nichol's thread was a whirl of anger and confusion against a peculiar haze muting the growing determination flooding his line.

From Rhys, a pure resentment rose, overtaking all else as a wall Kaius could almost touch rose in the core of his wildest child.

He watched his hauntmates retreat to their corner of the field, knowing Nichol would rally, would hold the others centered while they established their plan of attack. His second-in-command would do what he had to in order to protect the haunt, would step up in his place with a loyalty Kaius didn't deserve.

If he fell at the hands of Nichol that night, it would be an honorable end.

Khthonios's voice slithered into his mind. I'll enjoy seeing your bastard blood stain the earth. Almost as much as I'll enjoy watching your faithful mutt choose between your existence and his.

As a hardened resolve rippled through Nichol and Rhys's threads, he faced the field, tearing across the perimeter at his sire's command. When Nichol drew Khthonios's attention, he slowed, willing his hauntmates to gain the upper hand against Dovidas and Chen and trusting their strength and experience would carry them above the insurgence of powerful blood coursing through the pampered, unskilled Khthonios vamps.

Chen and Dovidas were weak without her, vampires who lived under the protection of the strongest of their species, defended by her obedient servant.

And then Rhys stumbled.

Every cell in his body bellowed in rage as Khthonios weakened his hauntmates through the manipulation of their blood. Of his blood. His sire's commands wretched his skull apart and he scanned the field.

Nichol would know to take out Chen, to remove the strongest threat before turning his attention to Dovidas.

Boy retained the upper hand against the ancient vampire, his attention torn between Khthonios, Chen, and Kaius. A steeled concentration replaced the emptiness of his blue eyes which flickered with rage whenever they landed on the female vampire who watched Boy with an unsettling intrigue.

And Kaius knew well the dangers of receiving the interest of Khthonios.

The tremor of Chen's final death surged through him while he moved closer to his second oldest, his stomach knotting as he tracked Rhys's movements and noted the lingering weakness of a vampire who survived Deepfryers, tombs, cells, and dungeons.

He would face the wrath of his sire before he would allow Rhys to be brought down by the likes of Dovidas.

"Don't you dare let my baby fall, you useless bastard."

Khthonios's words rang in his ears, and he tackled Rhys to the ground, intending to shield him should she enter the fray. But it wasn't Dovidas's image Khthonios inadvertently pushed into his head while her voice called out in alarm.

It was, if he wasn't mistaken, a younger version of Boy.

He reared up, bringing Rhys to his feet and baring his own back to his sire until Nichol's crossbow trained on him. Kaius held position while Dovidas was felled by a wooden bolt whispering from the Stojanovski tree line. He feigned resistance when Boy's arms wrapped tight around his and exposed his chest to his eldest, willing Nichol to release the bolt before Khthonios inserted herself into the fight.

His trust in Nichol's aim remained steadfast as Nic

drew back, aligning the bolt with Kaius's abdomen.

Higher, *he pushed toward his eldest, knowing he lacked the telepathic abilities of his sire but desperate to end the battle while his hauntmates remained alive and undamaged.*

Nichol's impeccable aim of the crossbow faltered, and Kaius stilled, tracking the bolt's trajectory until it embedded deep into his chest and ended Khthonios's reign over him and his haunt once and for all.

****

"Come on, Boy. Pick up," Harper whimpered, tucking her hand under Kaius's neck as his back arched off the grass and the convulsions continued unabated. Met with voicemail, she dialed Boy's number again and scanned the deserted park. She crouched over Kai's thrashing body while a petite, raven-haired woman strode across the field toward them, her dark eyes locked on Kaius.

She spread herself over him, shielding him from the woman's amused gaze. "Lady, I have help coming," she ground out, her fear for Kaius coming out as anger. "Just go, okay?"

Hands on her hips, the woman shook her head and chuckled. "Oh, you precious little kitten. I am the help." Flashing her fangs, she knelt and grasped Kaius's jaw, shoving Harper aside and restraining Kai with her knee as she examined his teeth. "He's always had the most sublime curve to these, hasn't he? A perfect specimen in theory."

Without hesitation, Harper moved to pull her off Kai and was met by a hand on her chest which sent her skidding across the grass on her backside.

"Settle, human." The vampire laughed. "I have no

intention of damaging him." She tilted his chin to the side and ran a nail along his jugular, smirking when he snarled through the low growl reverberating in his chest. "I dislike damaged goods."

Harper's eyes widened as the vampire straddled Kaius and brought her wrist to her lips, tore open her own skin and held the dripping wound over his mouth as she repeated the action with his, her tongue flicking out to capture his blood. "You're Calliope, aren't you?"

"Calliope?" the woman exclaimed, sounding almost delighted. "Oh, you truly are sweet for something so shockingly common. No, dear, I'm no muse. I'm much farther up the food chain." She extended a perfectly manicured hand, angled for kissing, not shaking. "Khthonios."

When her offer was ignored, she glanced down at Kaius, licking her lips as a sound caught her attention. She rose to her feet, her heeled foot pushing off Kai's ribcage. "You're too late, street rat."

Boy skulked out of the shadows of the precisely spaced trees, his fangs glimmering under the yellow streetlight. He stalked toward them and caught Harper's eye, lobbing his phone her way while he stepped up toe-to-toe with Khthonios.

Scrambling to the light of the cell, she snatched it up and inched closer to Kaius where he now lay motionless.

The tiny brunette vampire stood her ground against the enormous blond male, his eyes blackened with rage, hers alit with a terrifying excitement.

Turning the phone over to see the muted screen, she met with Nichol's hardened gaze, his finger over his lips before he pointed behind her. She angled the phone to Khthonios, monitoring it while she continued to creep closer to Kaius, her presence long forgotten by the vampires sizing each other up.

"The amalgamation of his existences is once again complete," Khthonios announced, a coquettish tilt to her head. "Vampire and Deviant. Your blood and mine." When Boy bared his fangs in response, she swayed to him a fraction. "There is nothing his haunt can offer him I cannot provide." Boy's gaze moved to Harper and Khthonios scoffed. "I could perhaps be convinced to allow an arrangement until the human's death. It isn't his body I'm interested in."

Realizing she was the human, Harper clutched Kaius's hand and crouched at his side, wondering just how far she could drag him should the standoff between Khthonios and Boy become physical.

The female vampire slithered closer to Boy, pressing against him. "He spent fifteen centuries curating a haunt capable of domination, proving his worth in spite of his bastardized bloodline. At my side, he will become a god, worshipped by millions until his replacement proves himself worthy enough to take the throne."

Harper huddled closer to Kaius, placing her hand over his mouth when she felt the first twitches of his muscle under her fingers.

Something unspoken passed between the old vampires and a blur of movement ghosted over Harper and Kai, stilling on the grass a dozen feet away. Khthonios's small hand grasped Boy's throat, his fist pressed tight to her breastbone.

"I could end you now," Khthonios murmured, her blackened irises locked on his.

Boy lifted a single brow in challenge.

Harper heard a surprised grunt come from the phone

as Kaius jumped to his feet, hauling her up with him. Khthonios smiled and released Boy, squaring her shoulders as she walked away. "You'll want for nothing at my side, Kaius. As I'll want for nothing more at yours."

CHAPTER TWENTY-EIGHT

Harper nodded at Boy while he stood guard at the bathroom door, the rush of shower water a gentle hum. She poured a cup of coffee and returned to the rickety table in Kaius and Boy's kitchen. The hot liquid dripped over the edge of the mug as the tremor in her hands persisted. "Sorry, Nichol. What did you need me to do?"

The vampire's hazel eyes were weighted, his lips drawn into a tight line. "I'm emailing you detailed instructions to get your phone back on our system. All contact information should automatically update once you complete the reboot, and we won't experience another break in communication like this again." He turned away from the screen and nodded at someone before facing the camera again. "I apologize for my error in judgment. It was ill-advised and lacked foresight."

She didn't need the words to know how bad Nichol felt for leaving her and Kaius without a failsafe net of contacts. Remorse tinged his clipped responses to her explanation of what went down in the park, and his silence when Kaius succinctly detailed his end of it spoke volumes.

"It's done and we're all okay," she reassured him for the umpteenth time. "Once Kai's out of the shower, I'll give you guys some time to discuss things."

Nichol motioned for Boy to join them, his voice dropping to barely a whisper. "Mikhail was driving to the eastern perimeter when Kaius came back online. The impact resulted in a collision which left two humans hospitalized with minor injuries and multiple witnesses to Mickey's inability to channel the sudden overdose he experienced with Kai's completed rejuvenation.

"Jagger and Bianca are containing the social media damage as much as they can, but the video footage we've bought or pulled offline will likely be used by our opponents in the political arena." He frowned and lifted his phone, muttering as he typed out a quick message.

"Louis was first on the scene and is apparently being hailed a hero for getting control of the Kaius haunt vamp who, and I quote this reporter, snapped."

She glanced over at Boy, her nerves spiking when she caught his solemn expression. "Is Mickey okay?"

"He's recuperating from the physical damages at Louis and Jonathan's in the city until Rhys can pick him up and transport him here. Audra is awaiting his return and has remained in phone contact with him since he regained consciousness." Nichol sat back and crossed his arms. "The limited reports I've received from Mick—combined with Kaius's own words earlier—indicate there has been a full recovery."

Taking a sip of her coffee, she nodded slowly. "That's good news, right?"

"For us, yes," the old vampire replied. "His memories and core have reconciled, as Boy can attest. It would appear it began prior to the influx of Khthonios's blood, but was completed with her intervention."

Guilt flooded her. "I mentioned the night he was changed. That you were the one to do it. I'm so sorry."

Nichol pursed his lips for a moment. "There's no need to apologize. Kaius understands the safety of the haunt comes before that of the individual members. It was, after all, him who passed that edict down to me."

Boy skulked back to the bathroom as the shower turned off, his back to her as she scooted closer to the laptop. "Will he be okay? He didn't seem like himself on the way back here."

Not himself was an understatement.

Completely detached and borderline robotic was more apt.

Nichol's jaw clenched, the faint movement of his grinding molars visible through the screen. "He may have appeared different to you, but to us, he's himself for the first time since I staked him."

****

Kaius scanned the video footage Nichol linked to the laptop, noting the number of spectators surrounding Mikhail while he snarled and lashed out, his movements lacking the precision and control of a Kaius haunt male. "Individual nondisclosure agreements with substantial payouts should counter any offers coming in from outside parties, but Jagger should continue to push Louis's involvement while Bianca leaks intel regarding Mickey's condition. Can we attribute it to a negative reaction to feeding off a vegan or some other dietary concern? Nothing that will cause alarm."

"I'll fire off the orders now."

While his second spun around to face his other computer, Kaius glanced over at Harper. "Perhaps it would be a good time for you to return home. If Boy escorts you now, he'll be back before dawn."

She'd been sitting silently at his side since he emerged from his shower and replied to her inquiry about his state with a simple, *I'm well, thank you.* Her dark eyes tracked him intently while he and Nichol got down to business immediately, addressing the most public issues prior to what would likely be a long, hard assessment of Khthonios's intentions and the ramifications her presence entailed. With Mickey's condition stable and one of the two injured humans already released from the hospital, containment of his inopportune rejuvenation was his top concern, having already assessed Harper for injury on the way back to the acreage.

Eight scratches, three bruises.

While something buried deep in his core reared up and raged at the damage to her frail human body, logic dictated she was, in fact, fine despite of the danger he placed her in with his presence.

She glanced between Nichol and Boy and nodded, rising from her seat before kneeling at his side and looking up at him. "Are you sure you're, okay?"

"I sustained no injuries," he reassured her, turning back to the screen. "Is it possible for your drone to monitor Harper's home? While I don't anticipate Khthonios will attempt to make contact, I would like eyes on the property until we deem the possibility no longer in play."

The door shut quietly at his back while Nichol flipped open another laptop and moved his fingers across the screen. "I'm entering the coordinates now. Your app should begin feeding the video within the next minute or two."

He became acutely aware of the absence of a heartbeat as the SUV moved Harper and Boy out of range. Opening the drone app, he watched the static flit across the laptop until a greyscale image of the vehicle traveling down the highway appeared. Resisting the urge to touch the tiny car, he minimized the screen and crossed his arms. "Bring the others in."

****

Kaius leaned against the cement wall of the cell, staring absently at Boy while he rested.

Did she make it home okay?

The thought had been looping through his head for hours. But the words caught on his tongue.

He knew Harper was safe in her home. Boy would not have left her otherwise.

And the drone footage playing on the computer beside him confirmed it.

Still, he had an illogical desire to ask, to hear what he knew was true.

Except there was no time to entertain irrational ideas.

He could feel remnants of the shift within him. He could catalog with complete accuracy every surge of elation, each burst of determination he experienced while Harper lay atop him, and he contemplated a future without his haunt.

A future that did not—and would not—exist.

The reconnection with his hauntmates solidified it. The relief and anticipation coursing through their lines and into his mind was a concrete reminder of his responsibilities, of the obligation he had to return to his position as head of the haunt leading vampire survival in North America.

In a few hours, he would contact haunts across the globe to reassure them of his presence and leadership. Favors would be traded for information, money transferred in a show of good faith. Alliances would be reassessed against the losses sustained during the evacuation into Denver and tentative bonds would be formed with young haunt leaders stepping into roles they were ill-prepared to take. Letters would be written to those vampires who avoided modern technology, his personal seal already en route from Nichol's stash in the haunt's communication room.

With the reestablishment of his presence in vampire society underway, he would spend the next few nights working alongside Boy and Nichol to compile intel on Khthonios, creating a roadmap to her intentions for him.

You'll want for nothing at my side, Kaius. As I'll want for nothing more at yours.

Nothing more.

Whatever it was she desired belonged to him and until he figured it out, they would be at a disadvantage in the ever-evolving game that was Khthonios's eternal entertainment.

Adjusting his position on the thin mattress, he relaxed back and watched the aerial footage of Harper's house, half of him hoping she'd walk into the sun so he could catch a grainy glimpse of her, the other half knowing the woman could no longer be anything more to him than a capricious desire.

CHAPTER TWENTY-NINE

Kaius leaned back in his chair and tested the strength of the old wooden legs while Nichol brought the meeting to order, the haunt's camera feed placed along the far wall of the communication room to ensure Kaius could see everyone in attendance.

He felt a palpable buzz of excitement despite their distance. The faces he recognized regarded him with confidence, while the two new ones remained far more wary.

"Perhaps," he interjected when Rhys and Dominic kicked at each other's chairs, "we should start with introductions."

Mickey leaned closer to the camera, all signs of the injuries he sustained six nights ago gone. "Mikhail Kaius, director of human-vamp relations and resident video game king."

"Like hell you are," Nichol barked. "Sit down and shut up." Grabbing the hand of a woman Kaius recalled rotating through the haunt years ago, Nic's eyes softened for a moment before returning to their usual annoyed glare. "Simone leads the human wing of the vamp-force training alongside Jagger and has the burden of being my connected female."

The woman squeezed his hand and Kaius felt a rush of contentment filter through from his cantankerous eldest. It was an emotion he had no recollection of throughout Nichol's fifteen centuries. "Good to see you again, Kai."

Before he could reply, Nichol cleared his throat and motioned to Louis and a dark-haired vampire at his side. "Jonathan Minks, co-leader of the Minks-Forbes haunt. He and Louis are raising a passel of orphan brats and doing a surprisingly good job."

"Minks," he echoed, straightening in his seat. "It is an honor to have you at our table. Your sire was a strong and respected ally."

The male bowed his head in acknowledgment while Louis stretched his arm across the back of his partner's chair and addressed him. "That passel of brats is currently unsupervised in the common room, so if I duck out of here at any point, Kai, I apologize in advance, and we'll pay for any damage those damn kids do while they're here."

"They are all in their first decade, correct?" When Louis and Jonathan nodded in unison, exasperation on both faces, he chuckled. "Enjoy the next twenty years. After that, they morph into the vamps you see around you."

Dominic smirked and his connected female Molly grinned.

"And you two," he continued. "I understand there's a ceremony in the near future?"

Rhys and Jagger launched into a detailed description of a pre-wedding celebration of Dominic's bachelorhood while Audra negated the plans. Half listening to the petty argument as he tracked the drone circling Harper's home. He rocked back in his seat again, savoring the camaraderie of his growing haunt and pushing away the resentment it carried.

****

Kaius sat on the porch and watched Boy shimmy up a tree, balancing precariously on an upper limb while one of Nichol's drones flitted around him. The tiny flying robot was speedy and precise in its movements, but it was no match for the ancient vampire stalking it. Darting within a hair's width of Boy's fingers, the drone was captured and examined before being tossed back into the air. Nichol's voice snarling through his phone speaker to indicate his displeasure with Boy's new game.

"That's a thirty-thousand-dollar machine you just frisbee'd," Nic barked. "Not to mention the amount of time I spent tweaking the hardware. Holy fuck, Boy, stop batting those damn things around. You aren't a cat."

Smirking, Kaius leaned back on his hands while Boy inched higher and stretched across to another pine within swiping distance of a drone perched on an upper limb.

"I suspect Boy doesn't care much for the expense," he stated as his sire teetered on a branch trembling under his weight.

There was an audible grunt of annoyance from the cell phone. "Have you spoken with Harper since your recovery? I have no record of you visiting her."

Straightening, he shook his head. "I haven't. Why? Is there an issue? She has access to my contact information, correct? Is Boy's presence required at her home?"

"I was merely making an observation about the lack of time you've spent with her recently when compared to previous weeks." His second leveled him with a flat stare. "Have you placed yourself in the doghouse? I can forward my research and files regarding the navigating of modern women and their relationship expectations."

Glancing over at Boy, he took his phone off the speaker function, brought it close to his ear, and lowered his voice. "My position doesn't allow for indulgences. And I believe it's wiser to maintain my focus on appeasing Khthonios for everyone's safety."

"Appeasing Khthonios," Nichol echoed. "Haunt consensus deemed Khthonios's offer to you unacceptable, and we're prepared for the shit-storm your refusal will bring on."

"Refusal isn't an option. But negotiation may be once I determine what it is she's after."

Nichol sat back in his chair and shoved his hands through his auburn hair. "I thought we discussed this. She wants your reputation and the power that reputation holds in the human realm."

They had discussed the issue at length. The haunt agreed that while Khthonios believed the idea of a sanctuary city akin to cornering rats in a cage, she likely noticed the increased support and fortification the stronghold had attained over the past year.

It would be a perfect base for a vampire keen on securing power within the species and loyalty to the Kaius haunt by both vamps and humans would be instrumental.

Watching while Boy sprang through the air and snagged another drone zipping by, he draped one arm over his knee and stared at the dark sky. "She can take all that at any time. She wants more."

"Yeah, well, you aren't on the auction block," Nichol retorted.

Don't you dare let my baby fall, you useless bastard.

The words had looped over and over in his mind, coupled with the image of what looked like Boy's face before the strength and build of manhood angled and defined his features.

But despite hours of prodding and questioning, all he was able to glean from the plethora of Boy's responses was Khthonios truly despised him and wholly believed Boy to be nothing more than an animal chained to her through blood and blood alone.

"Regardless," he murmured when his sire loped toward the adjoining pasture. "Exposing Harper as a potential target of negotiation would place both her and myself in a precarious position."

"Khthonios isn't an idiot." He looked over at the screen and Nichol snorted. "You think she doesn't know Harper is a weakness for you? We all know, Kai. At least I do. The others have an inkling, but with everything else going on, your relationship status has not made the official nightly agendas. Until it does, they will not make decisions based on assumptions."

Grimacing when he caught sight of Boy hopping onto the back of one of the cows, he put his phone back on speaker so he could scan the news headlines, eight of the top ten revolving around the FANG movement and its agenda. "Khthonios seeks godliness."

Nichol's image in the bottom corner of the screen stilled. "She said that?"

"She speaks to me telepathically," he murmured, reading the articles over one by one. "Aligning with me—with us—and proving herself more powerful would elevate her among both species."

His second ran his tongue over one fang. "Do we offer her the crown and bow out of the race?"

"Bow out and plan her takedown from below?" he mused. "Shall I pose the option?"

Nichol nodded slowly. "We'll think on it and explore the possibility at dawn." He cleared his throat and leaned closer to the camera. "I apologize for overstepping Kai, but I discussed your attachment to Harper with Audra."

"There was nothing to discuss," he grunted, his shoulders tensing at the mention of her name. "I was negligent in my duties when I pursued her. It was not clear to me before, but I'm now able to step back from the situation and assess the risks involved."

Placing his phone in front of the camera, Nichol allowed Kaius to read a text on the screen. "Mickey registered a spike from you eleven seconds ago." Setting it down again, he lifted a brow. "Audra pointed out having Simone at my side has not weakened me, has perhaps strengthened me as she forces me to achieve some balance. She also mentioned my position on your relationship with Harper may have been influenced by the influx of other factors and stressors arising during that time."

Snapping the line to Mikhail shut, he scanned a news article comparing the Species Purifiers with the FANG movement, extolling the virtues of both sides with a flippant disregard for the dangers the extreme positions created. "While I appreciate your blessing, my obligations lie with my haunt. Once Khthonios is eliminated as a threat, I'll be returning to Denver immediately." *Or remaining at her side to ensure the haunt's survival.*

"Audra mentioned self-care is an important facet of stable, capable leadership," Nichol continued, reading off a notepad in his hand. "She also reminded me our haunt struggles with recognizing and validating the importance of emotional connections outside of our bloodline, and this deficiency often culminates in brutish behaviors and impulsive actions akin to those of an unwieldy child." His expression morphed into one of solemn wisdom. "This makes our refusal to acknowledge our draw to a partner more dangerous than the perceived weakness keeping us from doing so."

Smirking at the coaching Audra had done with his second, he leaned back on his elbows and looked up at the sky, serpentine promises flitting through his mind. "Keep me updated throughout the evening, and I'll log in at dawn to discuss our plan for Khthonios."

He waited until Boy's shadow moved farther into the darkness, hidden among the cattle.

Khthonios?

Her presence whispered through his head. *Are you ready to come to me?*

Ensuring there was no spike of adrenaline to draw Boy's attention, he sat up and gazed into the tree line. *I'm ready to hear your offer.*

Meet me at the park. I desire a stroll.

Swiping his new phone to life, he opened the app controlling the drones circling the property. Overriding a few commands, he closed it out and stood, taking a final glance at the field to ensure Boy was distracted before he ran off toward the highway.

****

Khthonios sat perched atop a slide when he arrived, her black hair woven into an intricate braid hanging over her delicate shoulder and blending into the sleek catsuit she favored. She was motionless, a statue against the harsh yellow light illuminating the children's play area.

"What do you stand to gain from our alliance?" he

called, refusing to cross the sand and close the gap between them.

She cocked her head. "I see we've forgotten our manners." She leapt from the slide, landed silently beside him, and linked her arm with his. "A walk, Kaius. I have no desire to discuss our union from an impersonal distance."

His skin crawled under her touch, memories of the damage those gentle fingers could do embedded deep in his core. "And I have no desire to draw these negotiations out longer than necessary." He led her to the paved path looping the park. "Your intentions, Khthonios."

"Perhaps we should start with my offer." She smiled up at him, her dark eyes black in the dim light. "I place the world at your feet. The strength and power to manipulate and control our species as it rises to the top of the food chain. To stand at my side while the new religion forms and spreads." She licked her lips, running her tongue over one fang. "Our likenesses gracing halls and alters, songs written in praise. Led by your haunt, we would be unstoppable. Unrivaled."

Her words were punctuated with images she pushed into his mind, visions of human bodies lining the path to ornate thrones of onyx, ancient vampires powerful in their own right, kneeling before her as he stood at her side. "World domination has never held appeal for me."

"No," she murmured, tightening her grip on his forearm. "But survival has."

"And making myself a bigger target than I already am for those seeking to eliminate our species is counterintuitive to my goal."

Her laugh was light. A disarming melody for those

who knew nothing of the lethal vampire strolling beside him. "Force will meet resistance, my dear. A few slaughters and others will rethink their opposition."

"Our numbers have fallen in recent years."

"Which will make the army we build together even more powerful in the face of weakened resistance on the vampire front."

He led her around a divot in the pavement, taking care to avoid the gopher holes peppering the field. "Why now? You had the power to force my alliance for centuries."

"I didn't deem it necessary until now."

They closed the loop, and he stopped, unhooking his arm from hers. "You've offered nothing I crave."

She placed her hands on her narrow hips and pursed her lips into a knowing smirk. "What you crave will be the first we take. She will be tethered to you for eternity if you so desire."

"I have no need for a concubine."

"And I have no need for your soul or your body," she purred. "We will be consorts in name only. Your sweet little human can live out her existence holding the honor of being the preferred mistress of a tangible, immortal god."

Pressing on, he stepped closer to her and looked down, knowing his height was nothing more than an illusion in their imbalance of power. "You would wield the human to keep me compliant."

"I give my word I would not toy with her."

"If I refuse your offer?"

Her coy expression didn't falter, but the natural power emanating from her darkened. "I will present it again under more persuasive circumstances." She straightened her spine. "Do you refuse?"

"I do."

Delicate brows lifted. "Until we meet again, future consort."

In a flash, he was alone in the park.

Pulling his phone from his pocket, he swiped it to life and tapped on Harper's contact info, his thumb hovering over her number before he thought better of it. Gripping the cell tight, he trekked home.

CHAPTER THIRTY

Harper smiled at the bartender and dropped a few dollars into his tip jar before she carried the plates of nachos over to the table. Placing them down, she yanked hers closer to her seat when Austin dove into his with the fervor of a starving man.

"Slow down and chew or you're going to choke," she warned, scooping up some salsa before he polished off his and went for hers.

Waving her off, he downed half his beer in a single gulp. "Yes, Mom." When she stuck her tongue out at him, he grinned. "I miss you, Harpy."

"Yeah, yeah," she grumbled, nudging her cup of sour cream toward him. "How's the new apartment? Are you and Ethan working out as roommates?"

He shrugged, his mouth full. "Nowhere near as clean as your place." Swallowing, he swiped the jalapenos off her nachos. "Ethan sucks at picking up after himself, and it's already at that point where there's no way I'm bringing a chick home unless I know he's got an out-of-town gig. But we're surviving." Giving her an eager smile, he glanced down at her meal. "How's it going with the comic guy?"

Appetite gone, she pushed her plate to him and shoved aside the creeping hurt that slipped through her every time something reminded her of Kaius's total freeze-out. "I don't want to talk about it."

"Fair enough." Diving into the second helping of nachos, he took a long drink of his beer. "Probably a good thing you aren't getting involved with a guy from the States."

She slumped back in her seat. "I said I don't want to talk about it."

"I'm not talking about it," he countered. "Just saying it would never have worked out anyway because you'd never be able to get clearance into the country. Better to end it now before it got serious, right?"

Unable to hide her souring expression, she crossed her arms. "Whatever. I have a totally clean record."

"Not according to the laws they passed last week. One look at your social media and you'll be screwed."

The Preferred Population Support Law passed through all levels of the American government without hesitation, the majority held by the anti-vamp politicians who were ramming their bills through as fast as possible before the impending election. Providing border security the ability to turn away those they deemed supporters of vampire existence was one in a string of laws enacted to quash the rising numbers of vocal proponents of the pro-vampire movement.

"Not your business, Austin," she stated, placing her wallet in her purse, and checking her phone.

He tossed his napkin on the empty plate. "Just looking out for you, Harper. I know we have our different opinions and shit, but that doesn't mean I want to see you get yourself in trouble. Besides, that guy looked like…ah, hell. Like that guy." Leaning forward, he dropped his voice to a whisper. "Ex at six o'clock."

She didn't need to turn around as Austin swung a chair out with a wary greeting and an offer to join them.

She knew the fit of the shirt in her peripheral, the cargo pants hanging low on slim hips. Her memory went on alert when the familiar cologne wafted over her, a brand she knew Nichol shipped in from Italy.

Kaius stood at her side, muttering a thanks-but-no-thanks to Austin, and she took a deep breath. Looking over at him, she felt her heart hammering in her chest and knew he would sense it, too. "Hey. Um, how's it going?"

He held his head at a strange angle, his strong back hunched. "May I have a word?"

She quickly understood the visit on his behalf was unplanned. His speech was almost indecipherable as he hid his unclipped fangs. "Yes. Yes, of course." She rose, leaning across the table enough to block his ovaled irises from Austin. "Text me next time you're in town, okay?"

Austin smirked and lifted his glass to her while she ushered Kaius out the door and under the overhang of the bar's pitched roof.

"I apologize for interrupting your evening," Kai opened as he scanned the back alley. "I'll be quick."

Wrapping her arms around herself to resist the urge to touch him, she shook her head. "It's fine. Is everything okay? How's Boy?"

He shoved his hands into his back pockets, snatching them out and straightening his posture as the uncertainty in his eyes shifted into the detached control she saw in them before Boy drove her home over a week ago. "Has Khthonios made contact with you?"

"No. I haven't seen her since the park."

His gaze remained just past her shoulder, his face angled to remain in the shadows. "And you? You're well?"

"I'm good." She tried to move into his line of sight and failed. "I miss you."

Brows knotting, he glanced at a truck pulling into the parking lot before finally looking her in the eyes. "I've never heard those words outside of my hauntmates. And even then, it's always been said in jest."

She risked a step closer to him, relieved when he didn't move away. "No joking here. I've been worried about you. And Boy."

"There's no reason to be concerned over our safety. I assure you, we're well-equipped to deal with any challenge we encounter."

Biting back a smile, she tightened her hold on herself. "I have no doubt about that."

They fell into an awkward silence until he shifted his weight and clasped his hands behind his back, head cocked while he listened to sounds of the night she couldn't hear. "I dislike this return to my established existence."

"I'm sure you'll get the hang of it again soon," she replied quietly, the reassuring words bitter on her tongue and reminding her she was nothing more than an infinitesimal blip on his limitless lifeline. "In a month or two, it'll feel as though you never left."

The blue of his eyes darkened. "Perhaps that's what I find most bothersome. Whether I accept Khthonios's proposal or not, survival alone will once again become paramount. And I've lived long enough with living as my only ambition."

"Hold up," she said, raising her hand. "Her proposal? Your ex-maker wants to marry you?"

There was a slight twitch of his nose. "A politically motivated union to consolidate power," he corrected, his attention drawn by another truck inching through the parking lot. "Not uncommon among royalty across dynasties, but yes, by modern standards, the disgust in your tone is justified." As the truck pulled onto the road, he looked down at her. "The idea doesn't sit well with me either, even if she did attempt to coerce my acceptance by offering you up to me."

"As what, your dinner?" she scoffed, unable to think past the thought of Kaius marrying Khthonios. Marrying anyone, for that matter.

"As my mistress."

She blinked, her hand dropping to her side as she took in his statement. "She can't do that. She doesn't have the right."

"Khthonios cares nothing for human standards of rights and freedoms," he replied, lips drawn tight over his fangs. "I refused her offer, but she will return with another. Something she feels I cannot turn down so easily."

The words knocked her in the chest, and her lungs stilled under the sting of the hit.

Turn down so easily.

She knew the moment Boy dropped her at her doorstep that Kaius's life had shifted, and she no longer held a place in his world. The mute male escorted her home, his empty eyes holding a glimmer of sorrow when she took a deep breath and wished him a good night and a safe drive home.

The nights of silence that followed anchored it.

But a small part of her had been lying in wait for Kaius to put the final nail in the coffin, to hear it from him.

And she wasn't prepared.

"Harper?"

Swallowing, she squared her shoulders and gave him a cheerful smile. "I'm sure you'll make the decision that's best for you. Now, I should probably get home and—"

"You're angry."

"I'm not angry," she retorted louder than intended. "I have things to do tomorrow and—"

"And you're angry," he reiterated. "I received that exact smile in the cage after we argued about Austin." When she didn't respond with anything more than a glare, he narrowed his eyes. "You're displeased with Khthonios's proposal."

"Of course I am. And stop using that word," she huffed, crossing her arms, and widening her stance to cover for the tremor in her body brought on by her refusal to cry in front of him. "She had no right to use me in her offer."

"Precisely why I refused the propo—offer. I have no desire to tether you to me in a subservient position, leaving you vulnerable to her whims." He mimicked her stance, his gaze on the wall behind her. "Khthonios lacks the ability to understand your physical presence is not the trophy she believes it to be. She's incapable of comprehending how it differs from being the recipient of freely given affections. The idea of forcing your allegiance turned my stomach in a way I hadn't yet experienced as a vampire. I would prefer my memories of my time with you not be sullied by centuries of resentment, loathing, and that artificial smile framed by none of the laugh lines I love to see when you're truly happy."

In a strange way, his explanation was worse than the

initial hit.

She could walk away from someone who didn't want her, and have a good, long cry before placing the nights spent together into a little box to be remembered years from now. It wouldn't be easy in the moment while she recovered from the initial impact, but her mind and heart would vilify him until she could step back and appreciate the relationship for what it was.

But this wasn't an ending brought about by arguments and choices. It was one of circumstances she didn't want to accept.

One Kaius apparently didn't want to accept, either.

She took a deep breath and licked her lips, hoping her voice wasn't as shaky as her heart. "So what happens now? Are you heading home until Khthonios decides her next move?"

"Not tonight," he replied, his gaze on her mouth. "Tonight, I'm selfishly seeking a reminder of who I am when I'm not bound to Khthonios. When I'm not maneuvering through the delicacies of vampire or human politics, not sought out for judgments and decrees. The sense of wholeness I experience with you is addicting and I find myself distracted by a subconscious search for it when you aren't around. Tonight, I want to remember what it's like to be known and seen for who I am without my name."

"And then you'll be gone," she replied, finishing what he left unspoken. When he didn't respond, she ran her fingers through her hair and squeezed her eyes shut. "I'm sorry, but I can't. Not tonight. Not again." Shoving her hand into her purse, she tugged her car keys free. "You have unlimited of nights ahead of you, but for every one I spend crying over someone, my life's clock ticks down." She gripped her keys tight, unable to look at him. "I already know I'm going to cry over this, over us, but if we have one more night? It's going to be that much harder and take that much longer to move on."

CHAPTER THIRTY-ONE

Kaius nodded absently to Nichol's detailed explanation of the route he and Boy would be taking back to Denver, his mind occupied by Harper's words spoken before she drove away from him three nights ago.

My life's clock ticks down.

The frailty of her humanity had never crossed his mind, never haunted his thoughts. Now, it wormed its way into every memory he had of her.

The urgency with which she devoured the books on her coffee table.

The heartfelt sadness in her eyes when she spoke of a friend who passed years ago.

The smile of pure happiness moments before she took the first bite of a slice of cake.

For her, the past three months would never be recovered. Her lifeline would continue to wind on death's spool while his remained static and unmoving against the passage of weeks and years.

A century from now, while his hauntmates and sire remained preserved in the frozen time of immortality, Harper would be nothing more than a memory in the deepest recesses of his mind. There would be no long hair to twirl, no soft skin to nuzzle, no brown eyes lighting up when he knocked at her door.

"So while we can get the SUV over the border using some of our underground guys, you two will go on foot for a good eighty miles on this route," Nichol stated as a map flashed onto the laptop screen. "Best case scenario, eighty. Worst, you're walking closer to two hundred along mountain paths. Absolute worst, you'll be doing the two hundred with all the gear from the vehicle strapped to your back."

The talking stopped for a long moment, and Kai looked into the camera. "Summon the others."

Nichol's hazel eyes narrowed before he nodded tersely and lifted his phone, tapping a message out. "Rhys is out of range unless we want to wait until dawn, but Mick, Jagg, and Dominic are still on site." He set the cell down and leaned back in his chair. "Do I get a briefing before they arrive?"

Releasing a spike of frustration Boy would feel from wherever he was topside, he pushed his chair away from the table and rested his elbows on his knees, listening to the heavy footsteps tromping through the kitchen above. "I've kept many things from this haunt for centuries. This changes now."

Boy jumped through the hatch and stalked over to him, scanning him over before his eyes moved to the computer screen where Jagger and Mikhail were making their appearance, Dominic hot on their heels.

Ensuring his lips were in clear view of the camera, he greeted his hauntmates, satisfaction rippling through him when they flanked Nichol and sat, their chairs a fraction behind the default leader.

A cohesive unit.

"I will debrief Rhys after he and Bianca wrap up the interview they're doing in support of the presidential challenger's position on vampire-human relations," Nichol informed him, glancing at his brothers.

"Dominic, we slated you and Louis for the segment on philanthropy in the community next Monday."

When Dom responded with a groan, Kaius cleared his throat. "I won't take much of your evening." He straightened up. "Khthonios has suggested she and I amalgamate and form a unified front. She seeks to build off the emerging religious undertones of the FANG group and believes our haunt is the key to a smooth transition into her desired status of goddess."

Jagger's ice eyes hardened. "Have you agreed?"

"Her first offer was unpalatable. However, she'll return with one I may not be able to turn down. And I would like both your opinions and your non-negotiables should I be required to decide at a time that doesn't lend itself for consultation."

The males looked to Nichol.

"What was the first offer?" his second asked, reaching over to his desk to grab a pen and notepad.

"Power, worshippers, and Harper."

Mick's eyes widened. "Harper? The medic?"

"Yes."

"Why the hell would she offer that?" Dominic scoffed. "We don't get sick. What good would a medic do you now that the re-vamping was a success?"

Mickey swatted his younger brother. "You really are obtuse, you know that?" Facing the camera, he ran his hands through his hair. "That's hard to pass on, Kaius. Isn't it?"

"I've no interest in taking a mistress forcibly bound to me," he replied, channeling indifference to cover for the spike of longing rising in his chest and spreading through his veins. "However, having refused Khthonios, I believe she will wait until I'm in a weaker position

239

before she presents again."

Nodding slowly, Jagger pulled his chair closer to the table. "Then let's address your weaknesses and go from there."

Boy crouched at his side, attention flitting between him and the screen.

"Us," Mick stated. "If she attacks Denver or comes for us, she'll have something to hold over you."

Nichol snorted. "According to humans, female vampires don't exist. Khthonios is smart enough not to bloody her hands if she wants to emerge as a deity. She won't risk an attack on the sanctuary region."

Humming softly, Jagg frowned. "And holding us hostage would damage her plan as well. If Kaius dug his heels in, she'd be forced to eliminate us one by one, thereby damaging her public perception. Especially since we have enough ties to the media to make it a real nightmare for her."

With a loud exhale, Dominic flopped back in his chair. "What else? Seriously, you don't like anything else enough for her to target."

"Except the medic," Nichol interjected.

"Yeah, right," Dom chuckled. "Like Kai would take on the scariest female vamp in history for a woman." The room went silent, all attention on the haunt's youngest until the light came on in his turquoise eyes. "Oh, fuck. Really?"

Crossing his arms, he gave a single terse nod. "Yes. And Khthonios is aware of my attachment to Harper, despite the unpleasant termination of our relationship."

His hauntmates visibly cringed, and Mickey shifted in his seat. "Jeez, Kai. That sucks. Sorry."

"Kaius has a document outlining possible post-breakup scenarios I assembled a few weeks ago," Nichol grumbled, the discussion making him uncomfortable enough to project the feeling through his line into Kaius's head. "Unfortunately, the possibility of Khthonios's involvement wasn't a consideration at the time, so most of the strategies won't apply. However, several of those from the 'Doghouse' file I forwarded may assist the situation."

Ignoring the snickers from Mickey and Dominic, Kaius redirected the conversation back to the task at hand. "As I was saying, Harper would be a complicating factor, so ensuring her safety is of utmost importance."

"Easy enough." Nichol spun his chair and faced his other computer, pulling up maps and opening an internet search tab. "We evacuate her into Denver and proceed from there. I can have her on the move within the hour."

The tension in Kaius's body reduced slightly as Nichol prepared a series of calculations and contingencies, the others swiping their phones to life without a word to assist in the planning.

None mentioned Kaius's inability to see the path himself.

"There's a strong possibility she'll oppose this," he warned them when Nichol slid across the room to check out Jagger's phone for potential hotels. "Harper's been anxious about a local job prospect and her friend support network is centralized around the region."

Nic stopped and turned to the camera. "Harper's no fool. Let her know her choices are to go along with this and deal with an upheaval that may be temporary, or to be responsible for the possible decimation of dozens—if not thousands—of humans and vampires across North America. And in my opinion, that's a conservative estimate of what Khthonios will do if she feels slighted. Publicity will mean nothing to her if she can't cash in on your name, so there will be nothing swaying her to play nice if her actions do not result in you at her side."

Kaius opened his phone contact list and tapped on her number, frowning when it went to voicemail. "Harper? It's me. Kaius. Kaius Khthonios." Dominic grinned at him, and he angled away from the screen. "Please make contact with me or Nichol as soon as you receive this message. Again, this is Kaius Khthonios with an urgent message for Harper Strauss."

Facing the laptop again, he caught Mickey running his hands through his hair. "Kaius, man. No one listens to voice messages anymore. You should text h—"

"Maybe," Nichol interrupted, irises ovaling, "you should find her."

CHAPTER THIRTY-TWO

Harper gripped her knee and leaned forward to catch her breath, holding a hand out to Austin as he crossed the field toward her. "Give me a second," she panted, straightening, and pushing her hair out of her eyes. "Okay. I'm ready."

"For what?" he asked, looking back at the large group assembling at the other end of the field.

"To drag you the hell away from here."

His lips drew into a thin line. "You shouldn't be here. This has nothing to do with you."

"*You* shouldn't be here," she hissed as a howl of excitement rose from the group. "What the hell are you thinking? If things go bad here, and I guarantee it will, everyone's going to know you were with this group of lunatics, thanks to your post online."

He shifted his weight on his feet, a growing agitation on his face. "Get the fuck out of here, Harper. If this vamp comes through here and shit hits the fan, it's going to get very real, very fast."

"Real," she snarled. "Austin, use your damn head. Why would a vampire reach out to a group like this? To talk? Think with your thinking brain."

He stepped closer to her, forcing her to look up at him while he blocked her view of the growing mob. "Can't you just get over it? For god's sake, Harper, no one asked you to come here, and no one wants you and your save-the-vamps bullshit here."

A muffled voice called into the crowd, spurring a disgusting chant growing in volume until the rumbling of dozens of truck engines was drowned out. More and more supporters were arriving by the minute, the beams of their headlights illuminating the growth of the spring-planted field and casting an unnatural glow into the moonless night.

There was only one vampire in the region she could think of who would contact the local Species Purifier chapter, and that vamp wasn't hoping for a peaceful discussion.

"Austin, you need to listen," she pled, shrinking back instinctively at his imposing presence. "This vampire you think you're going to take down? She's stronger than you can imagine."

He snorted. "She? There are no lady vamps, Harper. And what's one bloodsucker going to do against this many people? We have Purifiers from all over northern Alberta. Probably two hundred strong, and it's not even midnight yet." As though remembering himself, he inhaled and stepped back. "Just go, Harpy."

"I'd rather you stay, *Harpy*," a familiar voice sang behind her. "In fact, I insist."

Her heart stuttered in her chest.

Swallowing, she turned around to see a slim figure leaning against her car five hundred feet away. Her face was shadowed by the halogen truck lights skimming the new canola growth but there was no mistaking the terrifying—and stunning—vampire.

Austin stood at her side and crossed his arms. "Nah, she needs to head home. But the rest of us are convening over there."

Khthonios stalked fluidly across the broken ground. "Does Kaius know you have another suitor?"

"Suitor? Like a boyfriend?" Austin echoed, his stance relaxing while the diminutive woman came closer. "Oh, no, lady. We aren't a thing."

Harper gripped Austin's upper arm and squeezed hard, hoping he would take the hint and shut up. "Does Kaius know you're here?"

The female vampire laughed, her fangs glinting in the artificial light. "No, but I do hope he figures it out soon."

She knew the moment Austin caught the elongated canines. He tensed under her hold and his mouth opened to call out for the others, snapping shut when Khthonios was on him in a blink, the palm of her hand pushing his chin up with an audible crack of his teeth.

"Shhhhhh," she whispered, running her tongue along one fang. "We don't want to spoil my grand entrance." Lifting onto her toes, she nuzzled his exposed neck and inhaled, smirking against his throat when Austin grunted, and a trickle of blood inched down his lip. "Let's give your little clan over there a show, shall we?"

Harper reached for her phone, panic taking root when she realized it was safely charging on the passenger seat of her car. "Khthonios?" she opened, keeping her voice low and her eyes on the vampire's nails digging deep into Austin's skin. "Maybe you and I could talk or something. A woman-to-woman thing."

Dark eyes met hers, the mirth in them sending a bolt of fear through her. "Your words don't interest me."

"But maybe we could make a plan," she rambled, her mind whirling in a hundred different directions against the hollers and fervor of the mob across the way. Her gaze moved to the blade hilts visible over Khthonios's shoulders. "I mean, you want Kaius, right? Maybe I can help or something."

Something.

Anything to buy a few more seconds, to keep the ancient vampire's attention from the group raring up for the hunt.

Khthonios paused long enough for a glimmer of hope to rise in Harper's chest before the vampire spun Austin around and placed one hand along the center of his back. "If you do anything to displease me, my hand goes through your spine, and I'll use you as my personal puppet. Now walk."

****

Kaius swerved to the side of the gravel road and threw the SUV into park, pulling up the drone app while he listened to Nichol's frustrated mutterings through the speaker.

"Surveillance is always the last fucking thing you pack," his second grumbled. "You were the one who taught me that, Kai."

One by one, he scanned the aerial footage of the airborne drones.

Nichol was right, but he couldn't think about it now. Not when he was searching for Harper. Or Khthonios.

Or both.

It was the barked commands of his second keeping him focused while Harper remained unreachable. Instructions to unpack the drones, to calibrate them until they launched into the dark sky and swept the fields. Orders to do a visual check of her home for a scent before expanding the search once he and Boy were met with a dark house void of heartbeats.

In his increasing desperation, he got back onto the road and continued northward, reaching out to Khthonios for the dozenth time.

I'm ready to negotiate.

The minutes ticked by. Boy texted updates from his southwestern tour while Nic continued to rant about the clarity of the drone footage without the moon to provide light.

Hello, future consort.

Throwing up a mental wall between his line to Khthonios and his internal thoughts, he fired off a text to Nichol and Boy, warning them he'd made contact.

I'll come to you, he offered. *Tell me where.*

The thread went silent again, snapped shut on her end until she returned, her voice pitching higher in excitement inside his head.

You're about to miss my grand entrance. Perhaps your little human and her marionette will survive long enough to tell you about it.

The physical task of transcribing the words to Nichol and Boy kept him detached just enough to allow him to hold onto a shred of cool logic while his core raged against the threat.

Hold off on your entrance and I'll make it with you. Where are you?

She laughed at his question.

Surely the Kaius haunt can find me. I promise to behave until you arrive.

With that, she withdrew from his mind.

"Take the second right coming up," Nichol barked through the speaker. "The Purifier group Austin associates received a vamp sighting on an acreage eleven miles northeast of you. The online group is fourteen hundred in number, but I would put my money on one-fifth showing up this time of night, judging by the comments beneath the original post and the images already posted to all the group accounts." As he sped up toward the crossroad, Nichol's computers buzzed and beeped in the background. "I've pinged Boy with the location, but he's at least thirty minutes away at top speed, Kai."

The message was clear. He was on his own against Khthonios and the Purifiers.

It would take him ten minutes to get there, leaving him fighting solo for twenty until Boy arrived on site. Khthonios was amping for a battle, and if he ran with Nichol's numbers, there would be approximately three hundred humans on site, huddled tight together in naive unity before the slaughter began.

And slaughter she would.

"This is Khthonios's next offer," he stated, one eye on the road as he reached over to pop the glovebox open. He snatched all the small blades he could and set them on the passenger seat. "Taking her godhood by force. She's found the perfect way to shred the reputation of our haunt if I don't agree, and cornered Harper as a bonus in the process."

"The live streaming," Nichol grunted. "Fuck. I can try to interrupt the footage through a back channel on the main site, but to cover all avenues would take time we don't have." There was a frantic clicking of computer keys, and his voice became muffled. "Jagger, you and Mick keep bouncing between those tabs and try to get me a body count. Rhys, park your ass in front of my main monitor and take over the drones. And call Lis and Audra in here. I need eyes on all social media tracking posts and trending hashtags associated with this clusterfuck."

He sped up along the dirt road, his rear tires spinning out and kicking up a burst of dust. "I'm two minutes out. Endgame?"

"Endgame is survival," Nichol stated. "For you, Boy, Harper, and at least half the Purifiers for marketing purposes if possible. Khthonios, on the other hand, needs to be brought down."

Cresting a small hill, he met with a field lit up by hundreds of headlights in the distance. "Is everyone listening?" he queried, squinting into the crowd as he descended. A murmur of acknowledgment rumbled through the phone's speaker. "Despite his bravado, Nichol is well aware the likelihood of success is negligible at best. Should aligning with Khthonios become the only viable option, Harper is to be evacuated and relocated to a secure site through what is left of our underground. Pull favors to make the transition as comfortable as possible for her."

"On it, boss," Rhys replied, his voice tight.

He parked the SUV, sliding the blades one by one into the pockets of his cargos. He grabbed his phone as he got out and popped the trunk, shrugging his blade sheath on and strapping it across his chest. "Nichol, in this eventuality, use your judgment in all future communication with me. Assume every word I speak comes from Khthonios and act accordingly. Until she is no longer, you are instructed to consider me the enemy." When there was no response, he slammed the trunk shut. "Have I made myself clear, Nicholai?"

"Crystal," his second growled. "I have one drone tracking Boy's progress and the other three doing a wide perimeter sweep of your location. Harper's car is parked to the southwest of your current position, but no visual of her. Boy should be on site in seventeen minutes, Kai, so you need to keep the death toll to a minimum until then."

His legs were weighted by the honed steel hidden in every article of clothing he wore. He walked toward the crowd. The excitement in their hollers was a good indicator Khthonios had yet to make her presence known.

"I'm pocketing the phone now," he murmured, scanning the clumps of trees lining the field for signs of movement while he scented the air. "Talk to you on the other side, gentlemen."

CHAPTER THIRTY-THREE

Harper remained motionless at Khthonios's side, taking in the increasing fervor of the group assembled in the clearing. The number had swelled over the past fifteen minutes, with a few latecomers still trickling in and joining the din of chants and raves called over distorted megaphones.

She didn't dare turn her head to assess Austin's condition, her last attempt having met with his accusing glare of betrayal and the back of Khthonios's hand across her cheek. Although her knowledge of the vampire's strength was limited, the fact her face was still intact with little more than a bruise meant Khthonios was holding back. And there was no way she was going to push her luck.

Khthonios sauntered around her and Austin, commenting on the originality of the mantras called into the night and identifying the different beer brands she could scent on the air.

Were she not well aware of the danger Khthonios posed, Harper could almost imagine her as a chipper, animated gothic pixie observing humankind from afar and eager to take part in their world.

Of course, reality was far more terrifying.

"So many phones out," the vampire smiled, smoothing her black braid over her shoulder before tossing it back with a flourish. "These pants have no pockets suitable for lipstick, so I suppose a touchup is out of the question." Turning to Harper, she pursed her lips and placed her hands on her hips. "Do I look ready to conquer?"

Drawing a deep breath that shook in her chest, she nodded.

Khthonios tapped Austin on the chin to remind him of his place before she resumed her appraisal of the crowd. "Harper, dear, you would be wise to remain close to me. I have no intentions of ending you unless Kaius becomes difficult. As he's prone to doing." Glancing over at Austin, she grinned, ensuring he had an unobstructed view of her fangs. "And you're here to ensure she stays in line. So I suggest both of you hope Kaius is feeling agreeable tonight." Her nose twitched, and she arched her head into the air. "It's time to make my entrance, humans. One on each side, try to keep up, and don't trip on this uneven ground. It'll ruin the moment."

Harper's heart hammered in her chest as she willed her reluctant body to move forward. Her desire to obey ratcheted up when Austin's hesitation was met with Khthonios snatching his hand into hers, the crushing of his bones audible over the din of the Purifier celebration.

"I believe the hill over there would be an ideal location from which to address the partygoers," Khthonios mused aloud as she surveyed the area, seeing details human eyes had no hope of catching. Harper squinted into the fields, her vision struggling to bounce between the light beams and the darkness of the night. Movements drawing her attention and lifting her hopes were quickly dashed as Purifiers dipped into the brush to relieve themselves while they waited on the arrival of the vampire expected at any moment.

"Stay two steps behind in deference," Khthonios ordered when they approached the peak. "And stop searching for an exit. I could decapitate you and be continuing my advance before anyone knew I'd moved."

Something deep in Harper's survival brain knew she wasn't exaggerating.

Slowing enough to fall back to the assigned position, she stopped cold behind Khthonios. Austin followed suit with his broken hand hanging awkwardly at his side.

The vampire looked over at her with a gleeful smile. "This will be entertaining, won't it?" Without waiting for confirmation, Khthonios strolled down the hill toward the horde gathered below them. She walked directly into the glaring spotlight provided by the trucks while music blasted from pounding speakers, until little by little, the crowd noticed her approach.

"No sign of the bloodsucker yet," one man called over, motioning for them to join his crew. "Coward may not even show."

The blood stains from the gaping holes in the chests of eight men barely formed by the time Harper realized Khthonios was no longer by her side, but instead standing among the bodies as they fell, one by one. Voices silenced in a wave until the music was the only sound carrying through the night.

Dropping the collection of hearts cradled against her, Khthonios wiped her bloodied hands on her pants and returned to the spot where Harper and Austin stood, stunned in terror.

"An anticlimactic introduction wasn't an option." She turned to the shocked crowd, and waved as royalty might, her smile wide to show off her long, slim fangs.

"Surprise, vermin."

There was a rumble of whispers rising through the crowd and Harper stared at them, willing those few who met her eyes to understand this was no regular vampire.

Khthonios lunged to the right, her arm outstretched milliseconds before a gunshot rang out. Pinching a bullet between her fingers, she brought it in for examination, her nose wrinkling as she chuckled and reached behind herself to pull a longsword from its sheath. "Study your enemy before the opportunity to attack presents itself," she advised, walking through the crowd, and nodding in appreciation when it parted, all eyes on her sword and the failed bullet. "And let's turn that music off, shall we? It interferes with my ability to communicate with words."

She craned her neck and changed direction, stopping in front of a middle-aged man who stood, rifle at the ready. "Put it down, fool," she scoffed, forcing the barrel of the gun down. When the man brought it back up, she rolled her head back in annoyance. "Rule two of combat, don't die on a hill you cannot hope to conquer."

She spun the man around and her hand punctured through his spine. Ensuring the majority of the crowd could see her handiwork, she lifted two organs into the air, allowing them to fall to the ground before the man's body followed. "This," she sighed, shaking her head, "is what happens when verbal communication breaks down. Now let's get those stereos turned off."

Harper's stomach lurched, and she bowed forward, gripping her knees to steady herself as the night air went quiet.

Khthonios strode out of the crowd and poked at a few of the dead with her sword while she passed by. "Is it not customary to genuflect before a goddess?" she enquired, planting the tip of the blade into the ground at her feet and smiling at Harper. "Demonstrate, mistress of Kaius."

Shaking, she lowered herself to one knee.

"Both."

Her breathing was ragged as she knelt, the position leaving her vulnerable to the vampire and the Purifiers who were linking the Kaius name to the infamous Denver haunt.

A shouted order to attack rang through the air. Khthonios jumped forward and swung her blade, slicing it cleanly across the kneecaps of a dozen Purifiers and smiling with satisfaction when the people fell to the dirt.

The others froze in spot. The attack was thwarted in a single slash.

"I'm sure those watching from home will understand my reaction," the vampire announced, kicking her heels across the earth. She kept her face in the headlights, ensuring the phones angled in her direction would pick up her best features. "A proper display of respect and homage is fundamental in the human-god dynamic. It makes us much more amicable and benevolent."

Her head swiveled to the left as a handful of people made a run across the open field. She was on them instantly and four bodies dropped to the ground in a heartbeat. "You. Were not. Dismissed."

Her rampage encircling the terrified crowd in a bloody slaughter as she created a barrier of bodies around the survivors.

Screams rang out through the night, the last person falling while Khthonios strode back to Harper and

Austin, her clothing soaked with blood. "Enough," she bellowed over the crowd, slamming her sword into the ground with finality when they went silent, save for dozens of muffled whimpers. "Tolerance was never a virtue I possessed. Isn't that right, Kaius?"

Harper exhaled, her posture faltering as Kai's voice thundered from behind the barrage of trucks strewn across the field. "You've made your point, Khthonios. There isn't a soul here you need. Stand down until the survivors vacate the area. You and I can finalize this negotiation once and for all."

"My reluctant believers." Khthonios laughed, tilting her head with a smirk. "Those who remain intact, at least. May I introduce Kaius Khthonios, leader of the Kaius haunt, and my future consort."

****

Kaius continued to stalk through the crowd, stretching his senses across the stench of fuel and motor oil over the ripple of hushed shock traveling through the horde.

"I said negotiate, not agree," he countered, tuning into the buzz of activity to his right. "Launching an attack on me now would be detrimental to your continued existence," he warned the group, glancing their way as he pulled his double-edge blades from his cargos. "One of us is the lesser evil. Take me out and there is no one to stand between you and her."

Harper's scent wafted over him, and he growled, scanning through the teeming mass for her while Khthonios's voice carried over the growing whispers.

"Your name is synonymous with death, Kaius," she sang. "I know it. The Species Purifiers know it. We've seen the footage, seen the destruction. Your mongrels have even caused the decimation of our kind, Kaius. How many did you lose during the great evacuation?"

Elbowing aside the few humans who stood in his way, he continued to follow Harper's scent and Khthonios's voice, refusing to be drawn into a verbal sparring that would distract him while the number of potential attackers at his back grew.

"The Kaius haunt needs a firm hand," Khthonios called out, no longer addressing him. "They've grown reckless, abusing their position of power within the vampire community."

Slipping past the last of the people cowering from the female vampire, he stepped over the bodies encircling the Purifiers. Fury coursed through his veins when he finally laid eyes on Harper, her heart thrumming in terror as she knelt before Khthonios.

"Get up," he snarled, unable to hide the rage in his voice at the sight of her position and the smirk of satisfaction on Khthonios's face. "Harper. Stand."

Harper's heart pounded in his ears, her dark eyes pleading with him to end this while she remained frozen in place.

"Where's your faithful mutt?" Khthonios asked, glancing behind him as she spun her sword in the dirt. "Should he not be tight to your heel, begging for your castoffs?"

He drew his steel, confident in the strength of the blade honed by his haunt's skilled metallurgist. "These humans behind me, those watching tonight's slaughter on their phones and computers, they know my name. And while many may spit it from their lips, none can deny I'm the strength behind the most powerful haunt on earth."

Khthonios's mouth curled into a snarl, and he pressed on, goading her further to pull her attention onto himself and away from Harper. "Every vampire across the globe knows who we are. The strongest seek our favor and alliance. But you? For centuries, only I and a handful of others knew of your existence." Running his tongue over one fang, he smiled. "And it was my haunt who took that handful out, wasn't it?"

CHAPTER THIRTY-FOUR

Harper shrieked when the first strike of Khthonios's sword met Kaius's and the clang of the metal pierced the horrified silence of the captive audience. Leaping up, she yanked Austin's arm, unbalancing him enough to snap him from the stupor he was in. His wide eyes locked on the death ringing the crowd while she led him away from the sparring vampires.

Blade to blade, the initial strikes were evenly matched. Shoving Austin into the mass of survivors, she watched Kai hold his own against the female vamp, his composed focus keeping him on par against her while she lashed out in a fury. Even to her untrained eye, Harper could identify the lack of precision in Khthonios's attacks. Her movements were wild and uncontrolled. Although Kai had yet to gain the upper hand, he retained the balance of power, his practiced swings and jabs a fraction slower than his opponent's but truer in their aim.

Austin grasped at her hand, his breathing ragged. "Come on," he hissed, gagging when his foot slid over a bloody mass in the dirt. "Harper."

"Go," she whispered, shaking loose from him. "You and the rest start running. Get as far from here as you can." Khthonios tore a second sword from her back, crossing both to block a decapitating strike and pushing against Kaius's weapon to send him stumbling back.

"Boy has to be on his way," she hushed to herself as Austin released her with a curse. "He can't hold her off forever."

The clanking of metal stopped for a moment while the vampires sized each other up, assessing the injuries they caused and those they incurred.

Khthonios was bleeding heavily from a deep gouge in her left arm. Kaius was noticeably favoring his right leg while the gash on his left thigh stained his cargos red.

"On your knees, mongrel," Khthonios snarled, dodging a hit that went wide before she parlayed forward with a double strike and caught Kaius's right shoulder. "Your bastard blood will sign the parchment tying you and everything you have to me." She punctuated her statement with a leap away from the fight and paused, licking Kai's blood from her sword. "It matters little if it's given willingly or not."

Harper caught the movements of dozens of people scattering into the tree lines but their race to freedom went unnoticed by the vampires battling amid the wheat.

Kaius shifted his weight from foot to foot, his blackened eyes locked on Khthonios's arms with the same studious concentration he often had when watching Boy's legs during sparring practice. "You can have me any time," he growled, his fingers sliding a small knife from his back pocket. "But I come to you only with my body and mind."

"There's no part of your body or mind I desire."

The blade had barely left his fingers when Khthonios snatched it from the air mid-leap and brought it to Kaius's throat as she knocked him to the ground.

****

Kaius pushed against Khthonios's hold with all his

strength, his muscles straining as the edge of the knife slid smoothly into his skin, grazing a vein. When the first trickles of blood ran cool down his neck, Harper's scream pierced his concentration and his grip fumbled, allowing the steel to slice gracelessly over his collarbone, the cut bone deep.

Boy was still two minutes away. Two minutes he didn't have.

Khthonios bared her fangs when gunshots rang out. She adjusted her position atop him, her slight frame holding him prone with her ancient strength until she faltered, the surprise flashing across her face shifting into a maniacal grin.

"Well, well, well." She laughed, her voice labored as she fought to keep the balance of power in the fight. "Blood manipulation, mongrel? When did this little trick manifest?"

With a grunt, he shoved her off him and jumped to his feet, thrown by Khthonios's sluggish movements when she stumbled up, her blade held loosely in her hand. "Perhaps you've become weakened by the number of bullets embedded in your body," he growled, unsure if her disorientation was a farce while he watched her shoulders for a tell giving away her next attack.

Her right shoulder twitched, and he dodged the lunge from her left. "Scratches," she scoffed, her words slurred as she backed up a step. "You fight dirty, mutt."

Snatching his sword from the dirt, he swung into her, blocked by an inelegant kick of her boot. It was a move wholly at odds with the finesse and ability of the ancient vampire.

Refusing to back off his weakened target, he lifted his weapon into the air, freezing when she held up a hand, her dark eyes glimmering with excitement. "Stand down," she whispered, trusting his honor as she turned her back to him and scanned the humans scrambling through the fields. Straightening her spine, she pushed the stray strands from her face, her eyes alight with excitement and something he couldn't identify as she reached out into the darkness. "Behold, a white horse."

Boy's blond hair stood out in the headlights of the remaining trucks, his movements as laborious as Khthonios's. The few humans who remained were crouched around the vehicles, their phones angled at the new arrival.

Khthonios smiled and dropped her sword, holding her arms out to prove herself weaponless. "A lame white horse," she called across the landscape while Boy loped closer. "I know too well the drain of manipulation. You cannot keep it going much longer without placing yourself in weakened peril."

Kaius crept toward Harper while Khthonios's attention was held by Boy. Her balance was unsteady as she sized up the vampire who had drawn nothing but scorn and disgust from her since his creation.

"Finally a true match," she murmured when he came to a stop several yards away, his blue eyes now blackened slits. "Have you come to defend your master or take his place?"

Stepping directly in front of Harper to block her from Khthonios's sight, Kaius reached back and felt for her hand while Boy stood motionless.

Khthonios closed her eyes. The visible shift in her returning strength caused him to widen his stance in preparation for another attack. He unhooked his fingers from Harper's to ensure he could hold the female vampire off long enough for Harper to join the people tearing over the hill, because once he was eliminated, Khthonios would have no reason to go after her. The game would be over.

It was a small comfort, but one he needed as he prepared to go down fighting.

And he was ready.

Over two thousand years of surviving were rewarded with a scant few weeks of happiness. It was those memories straightening his spine as Khthonios's lips turned up in a feral smile.

And it was in her smile that he realized it wasn't him she was hunting.

"Would you stand with me?" Khthonios purred as she tensed and stretched her muscles with complete control again before she advanced on Boy, circling him slowly. "Release yourself from the misplaced loyalty you've carried all these years for that bastard bloodline?"

Harper's fingers gripped Kaius's forearm, and she stepped in tight to him, unblinking, as she took in the same scene he was watching unfold.

"Do they still hide you? Keep you in the dark while they rise to prominence and power?" Khthonios leaned in and nuzzled his neck, oblivious to the revulsion in Boy's blue eyes. "Kaius and his spawn aren't like us. We're of pure blood. United. Finally equal in both power and skill."

I have no need for your soul or your body.

You'll want for nothing at my side, Kaius. As I'll want for nothing more at yours.

You bring more than you know.

The respect of your name, the fear of mine, the power behind us.

"Boy is the power behind us," he muttered, yanking his phone from his back pocket to see it was still lit up with Nichol's number listening in. Opening his texting app to avoid drawing Khthonios's attention, he tapped out a quick message.

It wasn't me she was after.

He fumbled with the app until Harper eased the phone from him, tapped a video icon, and angled it toward the vampire standoff.

Boy remained motionless, his long blond hair flicking in front of his eyes as the wind whipped up and died down. A swift blast of warning slammed through Kaius's head, and he tensed, steeling himself a split second before his sire spun around and took Khthonios down, catching her off-guard and flattening her in the dirt.

A surprised grin spread across her face, and she bucked Boy off, booting him in the gut and sending him skidding backward. "You believe you can best me?" She laughed as she jumped to her feet and snatched her sword from the ground. "I welcome the foreplay of true challenge, lover."

Kaius whistled while he sent his own weapon through the air to Boy, shoving Harper behind him when she moved to his side to get a better view of the fight.

"Go," he hissed at her as he yanked his keys from his cargos and pushed them into her hand. "Whichever vehicle you get to first, take it and get as far as you can. Nichol will direct you from there."

"No way," she whispered back, eyes wide when Khthonios's blade bounced off Boy's and he used the break in her momentum to swipe her feet out from under her. "Those people on the run saw me kneel before her.

My chances of survival are higher beside you right now."

Khthonios used her legs to capture and flip Boy over. His sword grazed her cheek as she snapped her fangs at the exposed skin of his forearm. Deflecting the bite, Boy went still and Khthonios wavered long enough for him to gain the upper hand, his fingers gripping her throat tight and drawing blood.

Khthonios's reaction was swift. Her struggle against the hold ended when she focused on Boy's face, and his arms weakened enough to drop her.

Kaius stepped forward as Boy stumbled.

Both ancients staggered back from each other, their eyes matching onyx ovals. Boy's shoulders slumped, his stance unsteady while Khthonios pierced the ground with her sword to maintain her balance.

"A sleeping tiger," she growled, wavering on her feet. "How long have you possessed this strength?" Met with silence from the mute vampire, she wrenched her sword from the earth with a weighted effort. "How. Long?"

Pushing his phone into Harper's hands, Kaius inched along the outskirts of Khthonios's peripheral, his eyes on her shoulders, while she heaved her weapon back.

"It was *me* you were meant to stand alongside," she snarled, her voice becoming shrill as she stalked closer to Boy. "You were created to fulfill your place at my side as *my* connected mate when you became wholly realized, not serve as the lapdog to an impure bloodline. *I* was the one who knew who you would become. The only one."

Boy held position. The drain on his strength while he kept Khthonios's at bay was apparent in the tension of his hunched posture.

Coming to a stop a sword's length from Boy, she turned her head slowly toward Kaius, a sneer of disgust and hatred on her face. "The loyalty you laid at the feet of that animal belonged to me. *Belongs* to me." Squaring her shoulders, she straightened with a laborious effort. "*You* belong to me."

Something in Boy's expression shifted, and Kaius drew the last of his blades from his pockets. "Boy," he said, his voice low. "Don't."

Ignoring his warning, Boy nodded and tilted his head, his arms at his sides as he exposed his jugular.

Khthonios's entire body relaxed a fraction, and she stepped close to him. Her grip on her sword tightened as she rose onto her toes and grazed her fangs over his throat. "I have your loyalty. Everything you are belongs to me," she confirmed, looking up at him when she was met with silence once again. "Do you seal your promise to stand as my connected mate in blood?"

A single nod and she stepped away, her fingers adjusting their hold on her weapon. "You betrayed me once, Boy. It will not happen again."

****

Harper screamed when Khthonios's sword sliced clean across Kaius's chest, and his blood splattered onto the ground. Nichol's hollers to run blasted from the phone in her hand. His voice was the only thing keeping her from Kaius's side as Boy stumbled forward, clutching his skull with one hand while he tackled Khthonios from behind.

With his arm wrapped tight around his gaping wound, Kaius lunged at Khthonios, his dagger embedding deep into her stomach while Boy fought to keep her exposed. The female vampire bucked and lashed out, her feral howls a stark contrast to the disarming poise with which she murdered dozens less than an hour earlier.

Unable to look away from the bloody fight, she backed up until her heel bumped up against a body and her stomach lurched.

"I saved this traitorous mutt for you," Khthonios snarled into the night, breaking free from Boy's arms, and elbowing him hard enough in the ribcage to send an audible crackle through the air. "*For. You!*" She scrambled toward her sword and buried her fangs into Kaius's throat when he reached it first.

He swung it awkwardly behind him, slashing Khthonios across the cheek and roaring in fury when she tore away from his neck, taking part of it with her.

The amount of blood pouring from the wound was terrifying. Kaius's skin was noticeably paling while he fended off another attack and Boy lurched into the battle, his shirt clinging to the concave indentation in his chest.

Harper could see Boy straining to weaken Khthonios mentally, as he had earlier, but it had little impact on the female vampire while he drained his own energy. She was rabid in her assault, charging Kai without care for the weapon in his hands. The injuries she sustained did nothing to slow her, her determination to end him consuming her.

"Boy is mine," she hissed, her fist making contact with Kaius's jaw while his sword sliced deep into her thigh. "He's now worthy of bondage to a queen."

"That's why you kept me at your heel?" Kai growled. "To ensure Boy remained tied to you through me until you believed him worthy of standing with you?"

He managed to get in a final strike before she

disarmed him, booting him across the field and leaping onto him, the tip of her sword piercing his chest. "I indulged your existence to keep my connected in line. You are no longer required."

CHAPTER THIRTY-FIVE

Kaius could feel the steel of Khthonios's blade slip deeper into his body, and he cursed the gods for allowing Harper to witness it when her desperate cry rang through the air and the sword pushed through him into the earth.

His useless lungs punctured, and he knew the Khthonios would make the necessary adjustment to the next strike to pierce his heart and reduce him to a pile of sludge. He braced himself for the hit, turning his face from Harper's view in case he revealed himself afraid in his last moment.

The sword once again cut into him, nicking his ribs before it dropped to the ground, and Khthonios's weight was lifted off him, her feet kicking against his gut as she was yanked away. He rolled over and pushed himself up, his vision pin-holing from blood loss.

A sharp pulse echoed through his head, and he snapped his attention to his right, zeroing in on Boy. He held Khthonios pinned tight to him, his fangs embedded deep in her jugular as she bucked and arched against the draining.

Another pulse and Kaius staggered forward, tugging one of Khthonios's arms free from Boy's iron grip and bringing it to his mouth.

The ancient vampire's blood hit him hard and his debilitating injuries healed at a speed far surpassing his own natural capabilities. Minuscule blasts of strength rippled through his muscles and his core urges surged forth. His senses involuntarily tracked every heartbeat in his radius. Homicidal thoughts wormed and circled. His control slipped more with every drop he consumed.

Releasing Khthonios's wrist, he backed away, pushing the palm of his hand against his forehead to center himself against the depravity seeping into him. "She's manipulating her blood," he grunted when the desire to disembowel the last of the humans on site swelled. "Boy."

Boy continued to feed off Khthonios. His blue eyes completely blackened as she stopped resisting and went limp, her glassy, satisfied stare boring into him.

"Boy," he snarled, keeping his gaze away from Harper for fear of what the ancient blood would crave from her. "Release her before her blood overpowers yours."

The vampire's fangs eased out of her throat for a moment. The blue of Boy's eyes flashed in acknowledgment before ovaling once again.

He scanned the ground and lunged for a dagger half-buried in the dirt. Mid-jump, his body turned on him and he collapsed gracelessly, disoriented.

"Kai!"

Harper cried out to him, and he fought to look her way, cursing inwardly when he couldn't. He heard her footsteps racing toward him and he bared his fangs, willing her to stay back. To get away from him. To run from Khthonios.

From Boy.

Her warm hand wrapped over his as she shoved his dagger against his palm and tried to close his fingers around the handle.

"Come on, Kai," she whispered, her voice shaking while she crouched behind his head and hoisted his shoulders up. "You need to get up. Something's wrong with Boy."

From his vantage point, he could see Boy standing in the field a dozen meters away, Khthonios's body still intact in his arms. Red rivulets dripped down his chin in the glow of the headlights while he stood motionless, his eyes locked behind Kaius.

Though she appeared unconscious, Khthonios's blood filled Boy's veins.

Her blood and the destruction it carried in its very makeup.

And it was through Boy that Khthonios controlled him once again.

Harper continued to clasp his fingers around the blade's handle, silently urging him to hold it under his own power. Boy's muscles twitched, his fangs lengthening as Khthonios stirred and he bit down on her throat once again, drawing in more of the contamination the ancient female carried. Small pulses broke through the dark thoughts still creeping through Kaius's head, beacons of warning and reassurance Boy was not wholly consumed yet.

Beacons.

Winding deep through his mind, he took a mental hold of Nichol's thread and sent a rhythmic pulse through to his second, counting on his eldest to catch the morse code before Boy became lost to Khthonios's pull.

Blade in heart. Harper.

He pushed the message through over and over, carefully easing the rest of his hauntmates online until his cell phone buzzed in Harper's pocket and she slid it out, cowering from Boy's intensity.

Her hands shook as she turned the screen to him, Jagger's contact info onscreen and a wall of texts, a list of clipped instructions.

How to hold the blade.

The angle of impact.

The strength required to puncture.

And the all-capitalized command to do it until Khthonios's body disintegrated.

She looked down at him and nodded, placing the phone beside him as she drew a deep breath.

****

Horizontal blade.

Grip tight but flexible.

In, out. In, out.

Harper clasped the knife in her hand and stood, watching Boy watch her while she crept closer to him.

He remained in place, one arm wrapped around Khthonios's limp body to keep her upright against him.

A rag doll.

A very dangerous, very much alive rag doll pulling the strings of the vampire staring her down.

There was a madness in Boy's eyes. His irises flickered between blue and black, much like Kaius's had done during the re-vamping. She advanced on him without a word, not bothering to hide the blade in her hand.

It wasn't Boy she was after, and she was certain some part of him knew it.

Her throat tightened when she got in arm's reach and Khthonios snapped her fangs at her. The movement appeared instinctual as the vampire remained limp.

Lifting the dagger, she stared at Boy, tracking the

shifting of his eye color until the blue held and he nodded.

The first puncture into Khthonios's body was met with the steel hitting bone. The blade refused to move deeper. Yanking it back, she lunged in again, screaming when an arm batted weakly at her, and the knife angled too low.

An eerie silence overtook her, and she looked up to see Boy's irises holding a steady onyx. Trembling, she inched away from him.

He took a step toward her.

And another.

A woman's voice called out through a phone behind her, drawing Boy's attention. While the woman spoke softly to Boy, the feral hunch of his back straightened, his free hand pushing his long hair from his face as the blue flickered in.

Harper inhaled and lined up her hit, throwing all her weight against the strike as Boy thrust Khthonios's body into her and the steel pushed cleanly through to her spine.

****

Kaius tore across the field, and wrapped his arms around Harper while she continued to scream, her skin slippery with the sludge coating her from head to toe.

"I have you," he murmured into her ear, monitoring Boy as he swayed on his feet, his arms locked in the position they'd been in when he pushed Khthonios against Harper's blade. "Shhhhhh. I have you."

He could hear Bianca Schumann's voice carrying soothing reassurances across the field from his phone lying face down in the dirt. The gentle tone spoke to something in Boy. Her quiet commands kept him in control of his mind long enough for Khthonios's hold over him to be brought to an end.

Harper's back remained flush to his chest as she quieted, gulping for air while the dagger stayed firmly in her grasp. "I killed someone," she rasped, her breathing speeding up again. "I killed someone. I'm not a killer. I'm not."

His stomach knotted at the rising panic in her shallow panting. "What you did was save hundreds. Thousands. This battlefield wasn't her first, nor would it have been her last." He focused on mimicking slow, steady breathing, allowing his chest to rise and fall against her until she unconsciously followed his lead. "The sirens are four minutes away."

Boy's gaze dropped to the ground, and he set to work collecting the weapons, shoving the smaller ones into his pockets before easing the swords into the holster strapped to Kaius's back. Scooping up the phone still transmitting Bianca's calming words, he loped over to them and waited.

Taking a deep breath, Harper nodded and stepped out of his arms. "You need to go."

"We need to go." Taking her hand in his, he led her toward the SUV, looking back long enough to see the phones of the remaining humans capturing their exit.

****

Harper clutched the damp towel in her lap, a shiver running through her despite the numerous blankets Kaius draped around her in the cool basement of the acreage. He looked up at her from his position on the floor, his attention pulled from the computer screen as he assessed her.

"You don't need to hear this." He reached toward her before placing his hand on the back of her chair. "We can get you settled into the bed over there and Boy and I will move into the cage room with the computer."

Shaking her head, she inched her hand out from under the pile of blankets and linked her pinky finger with his while Boy continued to pace the length of the basement room behind them.

Rhys muttered something to the other hauntmates sitting onscreen, and Nichol rolled his eyes. "Reports are rolling in faster than we can keep up," the cantankerous vampire grumbled. "Video footage has spread too fast and too far to contain and is being spun as we speak. Final body count is sitting at eighty-nine, ninety-one if we include the couple hit on the highway trying to flag down help."

Ninety-one.

Harper opened her mouth, closing it and squeezing her eyes shut when she realized she didn't want to know.

"Your friend was not on the list," Mikhail stated softly. "He is, in fact, one of the more vocal individuals being interviewed at the scene." As though knowing she would need the reassurance, he held his phone close to the camera, showing a muted news report with a closeup of Austin's bruised face. "He's claiming to be the closest friend of the goddess killer."

Blinking, she sat back in her seat and tightened the blankets around her shoulders. "The what?"

"Goddess killer," Nichol repeated. "An added complication to the media narrative, but one easily wielded in light of Boy's media-imposed status as the ruling god and Kaius's designation as Speaker of the Gods."

Kai scoffed beside her. "Says who?"

"Says the online communities across the globe,"

Rhys chimed in, bare feet appearing briefly on the communication room table before Nichol slapped them off. "I warned you all this fan fiction stuff was going to take on a life of its own. Now here we are, putting out press releases denying godhood and reassuring the general public Harper won't off Boy, invoke the wrath of an even higher being, and put the entire world into chaos."

"And speaking of chaos," Nichol interjected. "Another complication has arisen. Literally. Reports have been leaking in for twenty minutes now. We have another Deviant outbreak on our hands." Boy's barefooted steps stopped, and Nichol looked past her to him. "Yeah, big guy. Seems Khthonios only released a handful of her minions during the evacuation into Denver. Early numbers are sitting at five thousand globally, but we won't have an accurate estimate until a full night cycle has passed."

Every Deviant outbreak was international news, from the initial wave in St. Louis years prior to the recent influx unleashed during the massive vampire evacuation into the sanctuary city of Denver. Although vampires managed to distance themselves from the Deviants early on, rumblings on social media made the connection months ago, and those whispers were spreading like wildfire through an aged forest.

Boy crouched at her side and glared at the computer keyboard for a moment before opening a small chat window and typing methodically.

—*Plan?*—

"We've already sent out a kill notice to all vamps on file," Nichol replied to Boy's typed question. "Ten grand per documented takedown, twenty if we can use the footage in our marketing campaign."

Kaius nodded and sat up higher to ensure his entire face was visible to his hauntmates in Colorado. "With most vampires on the continent living in a centralized location, we need to address the issue from a different angle."

Jagger leaned into the camera, his light blue eyes almost white in the light as Nichol pushed away from the table and walked off. "I forwarded detailed instructions to every police and military department I could contact, as well as the FBI Vamp Division." He glanced over at someone off-screen and frowned. "We're going to sign off for now. Boy, you and Kaius need to rest in shifts until we put together a less physically demanding escape route for you three. Kai, Nichol wants you to keep the drone app open with the volume cranked in case of an alert. And Harper?"

With her thoughts still sifting through the haze of her mind, she blinked. "Yes?"

"Nichol says you did well. And Audra will contact you tomorrow evening."

The screen flickered as the connection was cut and she burrowed deeper into the blankets while Kaius and Boy got to their feet. Kai extended his hand to her, holding it steady until she took it.

Gathering her comforters in one arm, she shuffled to the mattress lying in the corner of the room and climbed on, keeping her fortress wrapped tight around her shoulders.

"Nichol is correct," he said quietly while Boy stalked over to the ladder leading topside and stood motionless, arms crossed and eyes staring straight ahead. "It may not feel like it, but you did well."

Closing her eyes, she turned her face into the pillow. "I'm a medic, not a murderer."

He sat beside her and the mattress dipping from his weight. "You're not a murderer. You're a goddess killer. Ninety-one lives may have been lost, but you saved the other two hundred and thirteen. Including Austin."

She took a deep breath. "What did Jagger mean about an escape route for the three of us? It's you and Boy who need to get out of here."

The room stilled, and she opened one eye to see Kaius staring at the cement wall.

"Kaius?"

His lips drew into a tight line over his fangs, and he draped his arms over his knees. "I'm afraid the coverage this event is receiving has made you a target from many sides now," he said slowly, refusing to look at her. "It's outed you as a sympathizer, so the Purifiers will have your face and name in every database they have. And with the added complication of visual confirmation of your role in Khthonios's demise, the FANG group will be gunning for you, too, since they've deemed you a goddess killer. While options to reestablish yourself in another city will be considered once the threat passes in five, possibly ten years, our immediate concern is relocating you to a secure environment."

"And by that, you mean Denver."

"And by that, I mean my home."

CHAPTER THIRTY-SIX

Kaius glanced at Harper in his rearview mirror as she lay curled up in the back seat of the SUV, her knees drawn up to her chest. "We'll be stopping for the day at a bolt hole just north of the border," he called over the rumbling of the tires on the gravel road. "At sunset, we'll continue on foot to Kinreed Coulee in Montana. Nichol arranged for a vehicle to be left there for us."

The steadiness of her heart rate gave him no indication if she heard him, or if she was awake or asleep.

It was the same state she was in when she woke at dusk, roused only out of necessity to make the most of the night sky. Her silence unnerved him, and his frequent texts to Audra did little to reassure him Harper was okay.

He didn't care if this was a normal response to trauma. Or that Harper's frequent sips of water were a good thing. He had no use for the platitudes Audra sent to his most urgent concerns. Or for the gentle reminders Harper's entire world had been upended and her reaction was common.

What he wanted was a plan and a guarantee. A fix. A list he could complete to repair everything he and Boy broke in those milliseconds it took for the dagger to end Khthonios.

"Nichol assured me this bunker is fully equipped and can accommodate up to eight," he continued, rambling like he'd done for hours to fill the quiet. "The owner is a young vampire with a penchant for silks and marble."

"How young?"

Encouraged by the interaction, he straightened up and adjusted the mirror to watch her eyes open, even if it was only to stare at the back of his seat. "Four hundred, give or take a decade." When his answer returned a small *scoff*, he smiled. "Age is relative."

Although she didn't respond again, his mood lifted while he scanned the dark road for the turnoff, slowing his approach when he spotted it. Even Boy appeared less tense. The slight drop in his shoulders was noticeable as they rounded the bend and their headlights lit up the drooping roof of an abandoned farmhouse.

Nichol's ringtone chimed through the quiet car and Harper sat up, tugging the cuffs of one of Kaius's shirts down over her fingers.

"I'm texting you the security code to the entrance now," he barked over the speaker. "It's good for eighteen hours."

Boy got out of the car and perused the terrain, leaving Kaius to pop the hatch of the SUV and grab their bags and supplies. "The cellar door, correct?" he confirmed, his phone tucked between his shoulder and ear. Balancing the cell and a box of equipment, he scuffed the dirt from a rusted keypad and entered the code. "We're in."

"Good. Get down there and secure the entrance," his second ordered. "I need your computer online."

Dropping into the bunker, he felt the walls for a switch, turned it on, and a pleasant soft white hue filling the space. With a quick look around to ensure there was no threat, he returned topside and extended his hand to assist Harper while Boy grabbed the last of their things and locked up the vehicle.

Harper eased the electronics box open and passed the laptop over without a word, glancing around the space with a gleam of curiosity in her dark eyes.

"Go look around," he urged her, powering the computer on. "The water heater will take a few minutes, but the shower should be functional soon."

The laptop's remote access fired up and a map of North America opened on his screen while Harper disappeared down the hall. "What am I looking at?"

"Deviant sightings," Nichol replied. "Notice anything?"

Examining the markers, he frowned. "The number has tripled since last night."

The red dots on the map shifted. "Notice anything now?"

Boy squatted beside him and shrugged.

"What about now?"

Exasperated, he tuned in to Harper's movements through the bedrooms. "Nichol. What are you getting at?"

The map zoomed in, a large green dot marking the house he and Boy called home for the past few months. The red ones moved, their trajectories marked by thin lines as the green spot shifted south. "If we tighten the area up, you can get a better view of what we're seeing," Nichol stated. The map narrowed its focus to encompass the green dot and those red ones within the screen as the simulation was run again.

He sat back on the leather sofa. "The Deviants are tracking us."

"Early intel, and only those reported or packs large

enough to be picked up by satellite, but yes, they're adjusting their paths to align with your location. Or, as I theorize, to align with Boy's location." Nichol glared at something off-screen. "He's the last pure carrier of the Khthonios bloodline. Without her control holding her little Deviant collection at bay, he may be the next in line."

Boy adjusted the laptop for a better look, his hair falling into his eyes as he bowed his head and pushed the screen back toward Kaius.

"The closest ones to you are a good three hundred miles away," Nichol continued. "Movement halts during daylight, so we have time to outrun the bastards, but this situation will need addressing in the immediate future."

Harper's soft footsteps came up behind him and Kaius nodded. "We'll discuss options before dusk tomorrow. Call me if anything pertinent arises."

"Will do, boss."

Boy brought the computer onto his lap, opened a document, and typed a quick message. He angled it enough for both him and Harper to read it before he got to his feet and slunk over to the entrance to stand guard.

****

Harper twirled her wet hair into a knot at the base of her neck and sat cross-legged on her bed while Kaius stood in the doorway and watched her.

Or, more aptly, monitored her.

"He won't really try to go off on his own, will he?" she asked, peeking past Kai's shoulders to see Boy's shadow motionless in the other room. "If there truly are thousands of those things, he can't possibly take them on by himself."

Kaius took a step into the bedroom, keeping tight to

the wall opposite her. "I can't recall a time Boy has made a declaration of intent. Especially one with the explicit instruction not to disobey as he did tonight." Crossing his arms, he leaned against the open door. "This may not be the time, but Audra has insisted she spend some time with you once we make Denver."

Focusing on the ornate detail of the area rug at his feet, she shrugged. "Like a debrief?"

"She runs several group therapy sessions for humans and vampires dealing with trauma. She was initially brought into the haunt to assist in Molly's recovery after her imprisonment in the home of one of Khthonios's other spawn, and has now established a successful treatment program." He licked his lips and cleared his throat. "Or so Nichol and Mikhail have reported."

Taking a deep breath, she looked up at him. "Am I a terrible person? I mean, I keep thinking about all those people she killed. How their families are affected. Their friends. But as much as I keep trying to feel guilty for murdering Khthonios, the one I really feel bad for is Boy." When his brows shot up, she shook her head and closed her eyes. "Monster or not, she was his mom, right? In vampire terms? Your mom, too, in a way."

There was a noticeable thumping toward her room and Boy appeared in the doorway, his blue eyes fixed on her with a flat stare.

"I believe Boy is trying to reassure you he and I both feel strongly that no, Khthonios was not a matronly figurehead for either of us," Kaius smirked as Boy nodded and returned to his post. "While her final death hit him hard physically, there is a freedom that comes with the elimination of your master. For that, he and I are eternally grateful to you."

She let the words loop and swirl in her mind, envisioning the recoil in Boy's body when Khthonios disintegrated in his hold.

And the relief flashing in his eyes moments later.

Kaius took a step away from the wall and hesitated. "I am truly sorry you were brought into this, Harper. Our haunt has a vampire skilled in hypnosis who may be of some service should you decide the memories of the past few months are too detrimental to hold."

Thinking back to her interview with Audra, Molly, and Simone a few scant months ago, she looked up at the ornately painted ceiling of the bunker and chuckled humorlessly. "You know, when Simone was insisting I learn how to defend myself with a handgun and Nichol was concerned about my lack of martial arts training, I thought they were overreacting."

"Nichol doesn't overreact. And I assume his partner lacks that characteristic as well."

Scooting back on the bed, she patted an open spot for him to sit at her side. "Yeah, well, I was going off what I saw of you. And even as a Deviant, you didn't scare me."

He appeared to be debating something internally, a sharp nod ending his silent deliberation as he strode over to her and sat, splaying his knees, and hunching forward. "When you and I arrive in Denver, we can examine your reintegration to society once Nichol and I deem the localized threat eliminated.

"You'll be provided the option for further training and education in your chosen field, with no obligation to practice your skills within the boundaries of Denver or for any member of vampire society. However, even if the broader risk is eliminated, I will insist Nichol remain abreast of your movements should you choose to relocate. I'll also be assigning allies to provide limited security sweeps an—"

"You're as wound as Nichol is now that you're full-on vamp, aren't you?" she asked, watching the tendons in his neck grow taut the more he spoke. "What about you? What happens to you once we get there?"

The question seemed to center him and he relaxed a fraction. "I'll relieve Nichol of many of the duties he's upheld for the past few decades. I'll resume Dominic's training and development, as I missed much over the years due to Khthonios's commands. Perhaps I'll venture from the city to solidify a few allies who have remained cloistered from society in recent centuries to ensure we have those ancients firmly on our side. Should Boy require assistance with this Deviant rising, that will, of course, take priority until the issue is resolved."

"Of course," she agreed, noting the shift in his eyes from wary to determined. "How about getting a cat? Is that on your list?"

He frowned and looked over at her. "A cat? Why? The haunt has no rodent problems I'm aware of."

His refusal to move past pure logistics hurt when she thought back to their hours of conversations about which movie had the most realistic portrayal of zombies, why egg-shaped chairs were ridiculous, and whose phone was superior.

Simple things.

Easy things.

Things that weren't attributed to a body count.

"If I have to live in the haunt for a while," she said quietly, leaning over to rest her chin on his shoulder, "I want a cat."

Swiping his phone to life, he fired off a text and stared at the screen for a moment before he nodded and turned it over in his hands. "I've informed Nichol of your wishes and he will place an order for one from an approved breeder within the week."

"Uh, no," she replied, butting her forehead against his arm. "You and I are going to go to a rescue shelter once we're settled, and we'll find a perfect kitty there." When he frowned, she smiled against his skin. "What kind of cats do you like? I like round, scrappy little ones with sharp claws and bitey teeth."

He went silent, his blue eyes darkening in contemplation before he rested his cheek on her head. "All teeth are bitey. But if I had to choose, I would select a sleek black and white shorthair. They hold a regality I admire."

CHAPTER THIRTY-SEVEN

Harper stood back while Kaius leaned in the driver side window of the black SUV they'd been traveling in since the border, Boy's blond head nodding while Kai whispered his final instructions. With a light tap of the roof, he joined her to watch the vehicle ease back onto the highway and the red taillights disappeared down the hill moments later.

"Where's he going to go?" she asked as Kai punched a code into the keypad beside the gates of the Kaius haunt compound. "Wouldn't he be safest here? Where he has backup and a fortified home?"

Hooking his pinky around hers, he led her toward a large garage, scanning the tree line running the perimeter of the property. "The danger to the local pro-vampire population is too great to risk an insurgence of thousands of Deviants. Nichol has calculated a few locations to minimize human contact and casualties while they make their way across the land, but I believe Boy will make his stand in an area he deems best."

She knew the thought of Boy venturing off alone to face the hordes weighed heavily on Kaius's mind. His growled one-sided argument with his mute sire lasted most of the two-night journey to Denver.

Deciding to place the unsettling thoughts aside for the moment, she followed him into the blue-lit garage, brows raising at the number of identical black SUVs lined up in a perfect row. "So you guys just have a fleet of these?"

"My hauntmates have less attachment to carbon-copy vehicles than ones they feel reflect their individual personalities, so it's just easier this way," he replied, a hint of exasperation in his voice. "Fewer fights over who changed whose stereo settings."

He opened a door and led her down a flight of steps into a dimly lit hall. Their footsteps echoed loudly on the dark hardwood as they made their way through a maze of hallways, which left her disoriented.

"Is it always so quiet here?" she hushed, inching closer to him with every step.

With an inelegant snort, he shook his head and leaned down to whisper in her ear. "They're messing with me. No doubt Nichol has been tracking our progress through video feeds since we stepped out of the SUV."

Suddenly aware of the uneven parting of her hair, she ran her hand through it, grasping his arm when he opened a door, and a flurry of activity erupted on the other side. Falling back to duck behind him, she peered over his shoulder as a stampede barreled through the doorway.

"Kaius, you old bastard," one called out seconds before Kai was tackled to the floor, the force sending her stumbling back against the door.

"Ah, jeez. Sorry, Harper," the young vampire Dominic hollered over his shoulder, cursing when another body jumped into the fray.

A tiny blonde woman with bright blue eyes grabbed her hand and tugged her into the room, wrapping her in a hug tight enough to push the air out of her lungs. "It is so good to finally meet you, sweetie." Before Harper could open her mouth, the petite blonde stepped back and cupped her chin. "We'll just give the boys a moment before we bring them back to civility. Let's get you settled over here until they've regained some sense of propriety."

The soft lilt of the woman's voice was familiar, a voice Harper remembered from the wheat field four nights ago. "You," she murmured, keeping one eye on the mess of bodies atop Kaius. "You kept Boy grounded against her."

With a delicate laugh leaving her feeling somewhat boorish, the stunning blonde smiled sweetly. "I merely reminded him of his worth." Releasing her face, she clasped her hand. "Bianca Schumann."

Jagger Kaius's mate.

Following the woman around the large table in the center of the room, she watched the scrum in the hallway die down as the imposing figure of Nichol Kaius stood over the mass of limbs, his arms crossed and hazel eyes unimpressed.

"Up," he barked, reaching down to yank Mikhail to his feet. Satisfaction crossed his harsh features when Kaius flipped off the remaining three vampires and leapt up, smoothing his shirt down.

Flashing Harper a grin that put her instantly at ease, Kai ushered the others into the room. "Okay, kids. I need a rundown of anything requiring attention within the next twenty-four hours, and then I'll be spending the rest of the night getting Harper settled."

"You get the boring details dealt with. I'll give Harper the tour," Bianca stated, her small fingers grazing Harper's back as she waved one arm out. "This is Nichol's communication room. What it lacks in aesthetic it makes up for in function."

As they slipped past the vampires, Bianca rose onto her toes to whisper into Kaius's ear, the quick shake of his head earning a hard stare before she strode from the room.

"I won't be long," Kai promised, giving her hand a light squeeze before he swung a chair around and turned his attention to his hauntmates. "Let's start with the Deviant situation and then move into southern perimeter patrol concerns."

****

Kaius stood outside his bunker, eyes locked on the closed door.

"It's not half-bad," Rhys stated behind him. "The whole mate thing. I'm getting used to the idea."

Shoving his hands into his back pockets, he glanced over at his wildest child. "Lis anchors you," he replied, keeping his voice low to avoid detection by the woman inhabiting his room.

"Anchors. Tolerates. Endures." Rhys smirked and ran his hands through his hair. "She's a fucking saint to stick with me."

"She sees in you what I do." He reached for the doorknob and hesitated. "It was an unsettling experience, coming into this wing of the haunt after Audra moved in."

"But?"

Shrugging, he released the knob and knocked, listening for the approach of soft footsteps. "But I find I'm rather content with Harper's presence."

"Content, hey? You're one smooth-talking guy, Kaius," Rhys snorted as he threw open the door to the bunker he shared with Lis and strode in, yanking his shirt over his head. "Let's take that new tongue ring for a spin, baby."

Blocking Rhys's line for the day became a top priority.

But all thoughts of Rhys, perimeter sweeps, and Deviant mobs evaporated when Harper opened the door and smiled up at him, her damp hair clinging to the fabric of one of his shirts.

"I hope this room's okay for me to use," she said, backing up to allow him in. "Bianca said it was the only one not in use or under renovation." Glancing down the hall, she shut the door tight. "Are you in this wing, too?"

The hem of his shirt brushed across her bare thighs, and he nodded. "We should have Nichol put in a clothing order for you at dusk. If you make a list, I'll ensure he gets it." Standing awkwardly across from his bed, he clasped his hands behind his back. "Is there anything you need in the meantime? Anything I can bring over from the kitchen? More pillows?"

She shook her head with the smile she often used whenever he or Boy appeared ill at ease. "Bianca took care of everything, thank you." When the silence stretched out, she took a deep breath. "Did you get caught up on everything you needed tonight?"

"Everything pertinent," he confirmed, rocking back on his heels. "I should let you rest. If you require anything during the day, anything at all, I'll be nearby."

She followed him to the door, smoothing his shirt over her legs as she licked her lips. "Oh. Okay. Thanks for checking on me."

His hand gripped the knob, the effort to turn it a mental feat of epic proportions. "Sleep well."

"Yeah. Thanks. You, too."

He waited until the door shut softly before walking the empty hall to the common room. Reclining on the longest sofa, he tucked his arms behind his head and waited out the daylight hours.

CHAPTER THIRTY-EIGHT

Kaius scanned the maps peppering the wall of the communication room, preferring the tangible use of pins and threads to the computer graphics Nichol favored. "I was under the impression we monitored all haunt phones through a GPS system. Can you not track Boy through that if he's electing to ignore communication?"

"I tasked Dominic with tracking his phone for the past three nights," Nichol grumbled as he angled his laptop screen and pointed to a green blip on the screen. "My error was in not detailing instructions to include a comparison between the phone's location and fucking logic." Zooming in, he sat back in his chair, arms crossed. "The phone has been traveling during the day and spending the nights in family-friendly campgrounds throughout Wyoming."

Watching the steady pulse of the stationary green dot, he mimicked Nichol's pose. "The current Deviant projection places Boy's route somewhere around northern Utah, moving west. If I had to put money on it, I'd say he's leading them into central Nevada. Low population, inhospitable territory, a few good defendable sight lines." He beckoned Harper in when she appeared in the doorway. "Can you send your drones out on recon?"

"The military presence in the area could be an issue," Nichol warned, already leaning forward to examine the options. "But if I can tweak a few things, we may get eyes on him once we pinpoint his location."

"Keep me updated." He placed his hand on the small of Harper's back to lead her from the room while he assessed her heart rate. "Is everything okay? Audra mentioned she expected you and Molly at the group session she was running this evening. Dominic and Mikhail are tasked with ensuring safe transport to and from the location and—"

"And you've been lying to me."

He froze mid-step. "Lying." Scanning through every limited conversation they'd had in the three nights since their arrival at the haunt, he frowned. "I've withheld a significant amount of information, yes, but I was unaware you had any interest in the lobbying we've been doing with the pro-vamp presidential candidate and her supporters."

Continuing down the hall, she entered the common room and stood in the doorway, arms crossed. "There isn't as much privacy in this room as there is in your bedroom, is there?" Glancing toward the sofas, she pursed her lips. "And I'm guessing none of those are long enough for you?"

Realizing he had indeed been caught, he clasped his hands behind his back and kept his distance. "I don't require as much rest as younger vampires. And I can sleep anywhere."

She tilted her head, her dark eyes narrowing like they did back at the farmhouse whenever she doubted his reassurances regarding the safety of a new training method. "Why didn't you just say something? I can move into one of the other empty rooms, Kai. There's no reason for you to be bumped out of your bed because you're stuck with me hanging around."

"Stuck," he echoed, taking a slow step toward her. "I am not *stuck* with you hanging around, Harper. My lack of foresight resulted in you being uprooted and moved from your home into an underground bunker where your freedom has become limited." Taking another step, he felt his fangs lengthen the longer the word looped in his mind. "*You* are stuck here. *You* are stuck with security escorts and video monitoring. *You* are stuck living among strangers while we continue on status quo."

When she responded with nothing more than the clenching of her jaw, he crossed the hall and stood directly before her. "You've known me at my weakest, Harper. You've seen me incapable of controlling my mind and impulses. You were there when I needed to be locked in a cage like a rabid animal. You dined while I fed off Boy. And not once did you react with revulsion or pity. You gave me answers when no one else would." Taking a chance, he cupped her chin, the first small intimacy in weeks sending a rush through his veins. "Sleeping on a quality sofa is nowhere near the atonement I should strive for. And I'm sorry it's all I have offered thus far."

"You have nothing to atone for, Kai." She sighed, subconsciously nuzzling his palm. "I'm just mad you weren't honest about it."

"Would it make you feel better to know I've been on quite the guilt trip these past three nights?"

With a frown and a nod, she inched closer to him. "A bit."

Emboldened by her proximity, he wrapped his arms around her shoulders and rested his chin on the top of her head. "So who told on me? Rhys?"

"Molly let it slip when she came to get me tonight." Her fingers ghosted over his hips with a brief hesitation before she slid his hands up his back. "She commented that the haunt leader's bunk was the smallest in the wing. It was totally accidental, but it confirmed what I already suspected based on the style of the clothes Bianca shoved to the back of the closet when she brought me there." They stood locked together in silence for a moment. "Why would Bianca put me in there, anyways? Is she angry with you?"

He chuckled, the tension he'd been holding since his return to the haunt lessening. "What do you know about Bianca Schumann?"

Releasing him, she stepped back, linked her pinky finger with his, and led him down the hall. "Not much. She and Jagger head up the resistance, and she likes to eat."

"That she does," he agreed. "She's also a Former Tender. Or was, prior to her renouncement of the title and incorporation into our haunt as an official hauntmate. She spent most of her life in vampire society and has a penchant for creating situations to achieve the outcomes she desires."

"So she aims to give you neck cramps?" Harper smiled as they reached what was now her room. She opened the door and walked in, pausing when he didn't follow. "Aren't you coming in? It still is your room. I'm just kind of borrowing it, I guess."

His room.

Her scent was on everything, from the bedding to the fabric of the sofa to the towels hanging neatly beside the shower.

He stepped inside and closed the door, a purple hairbrush on the nightstand catching his eye when he looked around the utilitarian space and compared it to the inviting comfort of her home. "It is my room, isn't it?" he muttered, noticing the lack of artwork for the first time. "Functional. Efficient." A small bottle of scented lotion provided the closest semblance to decor. "Impersonal."

The single chair he used countless times while he poured over maps and intel at the small table was draped with a blue sweater and placed by the couch, as though visitors were expected for tea and conversation. Tucking one foot under her, Harper sat on it and watched him scan the room over and over.

"Kai?"

Nodding slowly, he sank into the sofa, eyes still scouring the walls. "The rest of the haunt has changed. There are pillows in the common room with no purpose outside of their visual appeal. The gaming systems are stored in a decorative trunk instead of the crate we've used for decades. Paintings on the walls. Impracticality combined with want, not need." With a tight smile, he looked over at her. "There are also several blankets in there now. Many long enough for me."

There was a wariness about her as she spoke. "It's a living room though, right? I know you call it a common room, but it's basically the same thing. The wing where Bianca, Audra, and Molly are has one, too."

He licked his lips and rested his elbows on his knees. "They live in what used to be the Tender training quarters. It was the only wing containing items serving no purpose outside of an aesthetic appeal, and the stark contrast with the rest of the haunt created an intentional divide. One I never anticipated would be breached."

"Kaius. I can be out of here in ten mi—"

"I want it breached, Harper," he interrupted, running his hands through his hair as he stared at the coffee table he used solely as a flat surface to store accessible weapons. "I want it breached, and I want to breach it with you. I want to knock down the walls on this side and turn these two bunkers into something that gives me the same contentment I felt every time I entered your home." He stood and paced the floor. "I want more than one chair at this table. More than one towel in the bathroom. I want to argue over an area rug like Jagg and Bianca did, and I want to lose the argument. I want to waste time selecting a paint color, only to discover it looked better in the photo."

Skimming his fingers across the grey bedding, he paused before snatching it up and holding it out. "I want to sleep on sheets covered in pastels and delicate flowers, and I want to complain about it incessantly, as Rhys does. I want my side of the bed, and I want to guard that side rabidly as Nichol does, remaining on *my* side even when I'm alone." Throwing the practical grey blanket to the floor, he crossed the room and knelt beside her. "I want to attend the wedding of my youngest with you by my side, and I want to feel the same combination of terror and excitement Mikhail does every time the word 'marriage' is spoken. I want to exist for more than survival. But I only want these things if you do, too."

She bit her lip, angling her body toward him as she appraised him with the same warm eyes that had welcomed him back out of his Deviant state. "You haven't mentioned wanting a cat."

Leaning in, he brushed his lips over hers. "I want a

cat," he whispered, kissing her chin. "I want a black and white cat." Trailing his lips over her jaw, he tracked the increase of her heart rate and clung to the rhythm. "I want a female black and white cat. And I want to name her Phil."

CHAPTER THIRTY-NINE

Harper rolled onto her side and opened her eyes to find Kaius standing in the middle of the room in his boxers, arms crossed, and blue eyes narrowed as he stared at the opposite wall. "Envisioning a masterpiece?" she teased, wrapping herself tighter in the grey blanket he begrudgingly placed back on the bed a few hours earlier.

"Debating whether we should have a molded archway or a more streamlined design." He glared for a moment longer before turning to her, his serious expression almost worrying until he spoke. "We may need to take out the wall to Rhys's former bunk as well. Phil may want her own space."

Stretching her arms out, she let the blanket slip down enough to snap his attention. "First, the cat doesn't need her own apartment. Second, I never agreed to the name 'Phil'."

His blue irises darkened and ovaled as he stalked back to the bed and tossed the comforter off her naked body, his fangs lengthening farther over his lower lip. "The others have spoken highly of make-up sex," he stated, watching her hands intently as she reached over and pushed his boxers off his hips.

"Is that your way of hinting you want to fight?" She grinned when he kicked the boxers across the room and crawled on top of her, grasping her wrists and gently placing them over her head.

He leaned into the crook of her neck and trailed his tongue along her throat. "Phil is a simple, yet unexpected name."

"Why not something like 'Cleopatra' or 'Tiger'?"

"No."

"Princess?"

"No."

Her breath hitched as he slid one hand along her ribcage and over her hip, her body anticipating what that hand was capable of doing. "How about 'Patches'?"

"How about no?" he murmured into her skin, easing two fingers inside her, and angling them straight to the spot that drove her wild.

She grasped his biceps as he nudged her thighs apart and settled between them, the building pressure in her core already barreling toward its peak while he worked her. "I'm pretty mad right now."

His speed increased, and he pushed himself up on his elbow, his eyes completely blackened with lust. "So am I. Can we make up now?"

Unable to speak, she nodded, her laugh morphing into a whimper when he pulled his fingers from her body and pushed himself deep inside her in one swift movement.

He lowered his forehead to hers and stilled. "Do we want to make up fast or slow?"

"Fast," she panted, lifting her hips in response. "You have a meeting with Nichol in twenty minutes."

"He has a meeting with me," he corrected, pumping into her languidly. "And he can wait."

Gripping his ass, she dug her nails in deep and exposed her throat to him, smirking when he groaned and sped up. "Sure, he can wait. But I can't. Make up faster or we're calling the cat 'Mittens'."

****

Kaius remained anchored to his chair when Rhys shoved the table, sending it skidding across the floor. Continuing, he sat back and crossed his arms. "You will, of course, be kept abreast of her movements and will have access and input to the security details every time Lis is scheduled to make an appearance."

"I already said no to this shit," Rhys snarled, his fangs lengthening in anger. "She has enough going on around here. She doesn't need to be campaigning for some fucking politician who'll use her and throw her under the fucking bus when she's got what she wants." Rhys slammed his hands on the table and glared. "Who the fuck are you to waltz back in here and override my decisions?"

Grabbing the back of Rhys's neck, Nichol yanked him off his feet and pushed him against the wall. "He's our fucking haunt leader, Rhys. Remember that."

"*Remember that*," Rhys mimicked. "We've been getting along fine without him." Craning his neck to look over Nichol's shoulder, he gave Kaius a sneer. "Hear that, hallowed leader?"

Kaius nodded and held position. "Nichol, let him go. Rhys, it's a mistake for you to go against Lis's wishes. I attempted to dissuade her when she approached me, and it took a lot of negotiation to get her to agree to remain within city limits for the time being."

Elbowing Nichol out of the way, Rhys flung the door open. "You had no right to interfere, Kai. This wasn't your goddamn fight."

The door slammed and Nichol spun his chair around

and sat, staring at him long and hard before he spoke. "Go knock his fangs out."

"His anger comes from his fear for his partner's safety," he stated, locking onto Rhys's line in his mind and monitoring his volatile child's rage. "You have been known to become less logical and less open to compromise when Simone exposes herself to risks."

His second wrinkled his nose. "Simone's entire existence is based on risks," he grumbled, pulling his phone from his pocket, and typing out a quick message. "Should we be concerned about Rhys seeking Lis out right now?"

Pausing, he zeroed in on Rhys's line and held it until there was a surge of fear and rage riding an undercurrent of adoration and devotion. "I believe they're discussing it now."

With a grunt, Nichol rolled over to his computer. "He still needs to watch his tongue."

"And he has every reason not to."

****

Harper hesitated in the com room's doorway. The sight of the hauntmates gathered together was an intimidating one indeed.

Molly and Lis sat hunched over Molly's phone, murmuring about floral arrangements and the staining factor of lily stamens. Mikhail's arm was wrapped around Audra's waist as she stood beside Nichol, pointing at the pad of paper in her hand and subtly moving her mate's wandering hand from her backside every thirty seconds.

Bianca and Jagger were deep in discussion with Kaius regarding Boy's whereabouts and the lack of ground footage of the Deviants stumbling through the cities and countryside. Bianca periodically leaned over Dominic's shoulder with whispered warnings as he teased Simone about her recent recruits.

"My training days may be over, but I'd be willing to make an exception for you," a low voice murmured behind her, startling her until she recognized the velvety lilt of Rhys's speech. "Should we petition the boss for a few sessions?"

She smirked as Kai caught her eye and he lifted a single brow, running his thumb over one fang. "Why not? Lis? Rhys has a question."

Lis straightened, lips pursing while Rhys slipped past Harper and pounced on her, nuzzling her throat. "The ice remains thin," she warned him, smiling in satisfaction when Rhys mouthed a quick *sorry* to Harper.

Kaius stood and offered her his seat, the kiss he planted on her forehead bringing every conversation to a frozen halt.

Nichol was first to move, clearing his throat as he rolled his chair to the table. "So this group does know how to shut up. Good to know."

"Well, kind of," Dominic stammered, his eyes still on Kai. "It's one thing to hear about it, something totally different to see it."

Her cheeks pinked and she leaned back in her chair, grateful when Kaius spun his own beside her and straddled it. "Now you've seen it and we can move on."

"No," Nichol interjected. "Your relationship with Harper is the first bullet point on our agenda tonight."

She could see Kai's jaw clench in her peripheral, his eyes hardening. "Then cross it off."

Undiscouraged, Nichol continued. "The unification of the Speaker of the Gods and the Goddess Killer will serve us well in the upcoming election. The FANG supporters are mobilizing in droves to get people out to the polls, and we've noticed an uptick in support among centrists since the anti-vampire camp doubled down on the Deepfryers and strategic assaults on Denver's citizens." Sliding a paper across the table to Kaius, he leaned back in his chair.

"This is a schedule of planned strolls you two will take through the city at various events in the upcoming weeks. We will keep each sighting tightly under wraps until we leak your position to the media. Once the photographers arrive on site, you will continue to do this unexpected, yet marketable cuteness for no more than twenty minutes before you'll vacate the premises."

She blinked and looked between Kaius and the timetable meticulously detailing the when, where, and why of each outing. "You're pimping us out to the paparazzi?"

"Pimping implies we will receive financial benefit," Nichol stated. "This is merely damage control in the face of Khthonios's death and the subsequent Deviant situation we have yet to control."

Kai slid the paper back across the table. "Rhys and Lis are the media darlings. Let them do it."

"Rhys and Lis have saturated the market and their effectiveness in this would be negligible. Besides, they have their own schedule I'm assembling to complement Lis's campaigning itinerary."

Rhys splayed out in his seat. "I get to play the role of the supportive husband who stands in the background of every shot looking dangerous. And hot."

"Except we aren't married," Lis scoffed, swatting his thigh, and rolling her eyes when he leered at her.

Shrugging, Nichol pushed the paper back to Kai. "It needs to be done, Kai. The Kaius haunt leader will be visible to the public, the Goddess Killer will gain redemption from the FANG group while proving her alliance to the species, and we'll have a curated spin to detract from the Deviant shitshow taking over the media right now." He pointed to the top row. "You start tomorrow night at a local animal rescue."

Without thinking, she grinned and squeezed Kai's knee. "We could look for a kitten."

"Yes, Kaius." Nichol smirked with satisfaction. "You can look for a kitten."

CHAPTER FORTY

Harper leaned in close to Bianca to avoid being overheard by the eighteen vampires shouting over each other in the field, their forms silhouetted by the light of the video games being projected on the enormous screens Nichol had set up at nightfall. "This isn't how I envisioned a vampire bachelor party."

"You were expecting more debauchery and less posturing?" Bee smiled, tilting her head to watch Jagger tear across the grass and tackle Dominic.

Swirling her wine in her glass, she laughed, covering her mouth when Kaius paused his sparring match with one of the Minks-Forbes foundlings and waved over at her. "He's patient with the young ones, isn't he?"

"He's had a lot of experience." Bianca angled her glass at the dark-haired vampire creeping up on Nichol, lit firework in hand. "Can you even fathom what it took to raise Rhys through the first decade?"

She braced herself for an explosion and watched an unassuming Nichol remain still until his attacker was primed. In a move too swift to track, Rhys was flipped over his shoulder, the firecracker buried in the dirt in a single motion. Before she could comment, a tiny blur tore past her ankle, and she thrust her glass into Bianca's hand. "Dammit, Phil. Get back here, you little imp. Kai? She escaped again."

The kitten was barely visible in the grass, her black ears blending in with the darkness of the night. Harper tiptoed toward the tiny predator while several of the much larger ones fanned out to block entrance to the forests.

"Don't accidentally step on her," Kaius called out to the Minks-Forbes vamps following his orders. "She's a wily little thing."

"She's a naughty little thing," Harper corrected him, cutting off the kitten's escape to the garage while Kai crouched and held out his hand. "Can you see her?"

He nodded and inched forward, wiggling his fingers patiently until the little ball of energy burst out of the grass and landed on his hand. "She isn't being naughty. She's practicing her tracking skills." Offering the kitten another finger to attack, he grinned. "She wants to be like her daddy."

Getting to his feet with his large hand wrapped around Phil's squirmy body, he murmured something to the young vampires and sent them off to the sparring ring before he crossed the field to her. With Phil cradled against his chest, he wrapped his free arm around her waist and leaned down to kiss her, earning a chorus of groans and catcalls from the gaming station.

"I'll take the beast." She laughed, disentangling Phil from his fingers, and cuddling the kitten tight to her. "You get back out there and enjoy yourself."

After another quick kiss with a little more tongue than she felt was appropriate with an audience, he jogged back across the field, calling out form corrections to the Minks-Forbes vamps.

Bianca nudged the door open and held it with her foot, both glasses of wine still balanced in her hands.

"That little cat is probably the most famous kitten on the planet right now." She cooed at Phil for a moment before she straightened up. "So, shall we report the mayhem and shenanigans of the bachelor party when we return to Molly's celebration? Or do we keep the sordid details to ourselves?"

"We should probably omit the sparring, or we'll lose Simone and Molly to the party out here." She winced as tiny claws pierced her skin. "Remind me again why I wanted a kitten and not an elegant, aloof cat?"

"Because Kaius took to the little hellion the moment he saw her?"

Smiling at the reminder of Kai's reaction to the kitten as she yowled incessantly for his attention from her cage, she nodded. "Right. I was indulging the Speaker of the Gods."

"On camera, with a live audience," Bianca grinned, pausing at the entrance to the former Tender training quarters. "Okay. We'll report the video games, the tree climbing, and the online gambling station, but we're leaving out the fist-and-fang matches."

Nodding as the rest of the women noticed Phil in her arms, she began the grueling task of untangling the tiny claws from her shirt before the kitten was yanked away by her adoring aunts.

****

Kaius stared at the screen and watched as the green dots marking the Deviant hordes continued to converge into a single space in the middle of the Great Basin in Nevada. "What weaponry does he possess? Anything?"

"Fangs," Nichol grunted in reply, pulling up another drone link and cursing. "I can't get any of these fucking things to send a reliable feed once they hit the region north of Mount Callaghan." He sent a pen skidding across the desk, glaring when it clattered on the floor. "A few ATV trails in the area, but aside from a handful of ranchers, the area is nothing but fourteen thousand Deviants. And Boy. What I'm not comprehending is the lack of government mobilization. There's a base within reach, and a threat this big—"

"Is precisely the ammunition the president and his supporters require to remain in power," he snarled. "I guarantee your drones are experiencing inference courtesy of an Executive Order."

The steady grinding of Nichol's teeth resumed, and Kaius opened the least pixelated photos the drones provided. "Any chance we can get some eyes on the region during daylight? Fourteen thousand may be the estimate, but I suspect the sun has taken care of a sizable number of those."

With a terse nod, Nichol hunched over his laptop. "I'll have something in place by dawn."

"I'll be back shortly before sunrise to relieve you for the day." He glanced at the clock. "Harper and I have an appearance at the new lounge on the east side in an hour."

Nichol tossed a note at him without looking up. "Louis needs you to drive all the brats whose names don't start with 'J' into town on your way in. Jonathan will pick up the rest once they wrap up painting the trim in your suite, but the others have appointments at the blood bank that can't be rescheduled, and Aaron has another session with Audra."

Running his hand over his face, he sighed his thanks and turned down the hall toward his suite.

Their suite.

They'd tasked the young from the Minks-Forbes haunt with turning the two bunkers into one, working off the detailed sketch he provided two weeks prior. While Harper was officially in charge of overseeing the progress, Bianca was the strong arm keeping the young vamps on track.

Because unlike his soft-hearted mate, Bianca had no qualms using threats of Jagger's weapons room for those brazen enough to slack off in her sight.

Except for Aaron.

Aaron took to Harper with sullen respect from the start, their wordless interactions rarely more than a polite nod from him or a smile from her. The most volatile of the foundlings, Nichol initially balked at Aaron's participation in the project, citing the young vampire's explosive temper as reason enough to keep him off the work site.

But on Louis's word, Aaron was brought in under tight observation by Kaius until he was satisfied Harper was in no danger.

He lingered in the doorway for a moment and observed the final stage of the construction.

Or, more accurately, he observed Harper.

She sat cross-legged on her side of their bed, studying the medical regulation handbook on her lap in preparation for her new position in the Denver North Vampire Blood Bank. When she stretched one leg out and groaned, Aaron frowned and looked up at her from the floor, holding his paintbrush out of reach of Phil's swatting paws.

"You good?" he inquired quietly, noticeably scanning her for injury.

"Very, thank you," she smiled back before she saw

Kaius in the doorway. "Hey, baby. Ready to go?"

He strode over to her and held out his hand to help her to her feet, acknowledging Aaron's brief nod of respect. "I guess a little alone time is out of the question," he grumbled. "We're driving Aaron, Ryan, Zach, Brandon, and Andy home before we make our appearance." Leaning over to peer through the arched entrance to the other half of their home, he called out to the others. "Hear that? All non-J vamps in my SUV in three minutes. Jeremy, remind Bianca she needs to take Phil with her until we return, so she doesn't get lonely."

Leaving the young ones to sort out their tasks, he escorted Harper toward the garage. "Nichol thinks the new bank will be up and running in two months."

She took a deep breath and nodded. "I'll be ready by then."

"Ready to be the Queen Bee?" he teased, wrapping his arm around her waist. "The Big Cheese?"

Scoffing, she lifted her chin with feigned arrogance. "It won't be easy to go from Goddess Killer to Top Dog, but I shall suffer in silence." Unable to keep a straight face, she grinned. "The better question is, are you ready to wave at me as I head off into the city every night, or am I going to be dealing with the same smothering Lis is going through with Rhys right now?"

He hooked the SUV keys onto his finger and swung them around. "There will be minor smothering due to my inability to remain wholly logical regarding your safety, but I'm already piecing your security detail together and you'll be pleased to know I'm not on the rotation."

Stopping beside the vehicle they were taking into town and tugging him in close to her, she smirked. "Good. You're too distracting."

He ducked his head to kiss her throat, knowing if the young vamps walked in now, they'd be wise enough to double back and wait a moment. "I was thinking Aaron might make a good lead. Under my command, of course." Conscious to avoid smudging her lipstick before their photo stunt, he satisfied himself with running his tongue along the shell of her ear. "His youth is an issue, but he's highly observant, trusts few, and his sparring footage proves he possesses some trainable skills. He's also partial to you and has a healthy fear of me."

Pressing against him, she trailed her thumb along the nape of his neck. "I like that idea. But I don't want that poor boy shaking in his boots if he makes a mistake."

"I'm sure you'll cover for him if he does." He grinned and straightened as a herd of vamps tromped up the steps and flung the door open. "Into the car, gentlemen. Except you, Aaron."

Aaron's back hunched a fraction, his stance instinctively readying for attack, while Kaius opened the garage door and motioned for him to follow. He waited patiently for Aaron to join him, listening in while Harper took control of the mayhem going down in the SUV.

"Your painting skills leave much to be desired," he opened, noting the distance Aaron maintained. "Would you be interested in a position requiring fewer paint fumes?" He could see the internal debate his open-ended question created, pausing long enough for a reply but expecting none. "I've been placed in the delicate position of balancing Harper's need for independence, with my illogical inclination to keep her tethered within the confines of my haunt's security."

Tamping down a smile when he heard Harper

demand the vamps fasten their seat belts followed by a fussing over legroom, he crossed his arms and scanned the perimeter of the property. "Her work site will have a team of its own, but I will be significantly easier to live with if Harper has someone tasked solely with her protection."

Aaron's head tilted a fraction, his nose wrinkling as a gust of wind carried the scent of a decaying animal carcass through the air.

"Your duties would include escorting her to and from work, remaining within protection reach at all times, monitoring the site for potential concerns, escorting her on errands when I am unable to attend, reporting to me, and scooping Phil's litter box."

With the naming of the final duty, Aaron side-eyed him. "Would I answer to you or Miss Harper?"

"Both."

Glancing at the SUV, the young vamp's lips drew tight. "But in cases where the orders are contradictory, who would trump who?"

"Provided the mandate does not place Harper at an increased risk of harm, her directives will take precedence. If you accept the position, she will be your boss."

Aaron shoved his hands into his pockets, his shoulders squaring. "Yeah, I'll accept." He was halfway to the SUV before he looked over, the hint of a smirk on his sullen face. "Boss said last week that the litter box is your responsibility and to go to her immediately if you tried to pawn it off on one of us."

****

Harper buried her head into Kaius's shoulder, conscious of the familiar faces discretely angling their cameras their way while the heavy bass of the lounge's music pounded in her ears. "Have we smiled and nodded long enough?" she murmured into his shirt as his arms wrapped tight around her.

"Damn," he whispered into her hair. "You were smiling this whole time? I was channeling the whole 'lethal indifference' aura." When she laughed, he released her, keeping one hand on her hip. "Let's go. I've been craving a little one-on-one time with you since sunset."

It was an experience she had yet to become accustomed to, the parting of the crowds as they walked toward the exit. In a city dedicated to the continued existence of vampires, there was still significant awe when one of the Kaius haunt made an appearance.

And sightings of the haunt leader himself continued to draw interesting reactions.

While most people remained subtle in their observations, others approached them without hesitation, requesting autographs, offering services, and courting favors. The detractors they encountered rarely attempted contact, their spiteful words and flyers limited to the sidewalks outside the establishments she and Kai entered. FANG supporters, while more brazen in their attempts to be noticed by the Speaker of the Gods, were quick to bow, the most ardent dropping to a knee when they passed by.

Or, more accurately, when Kaius passed by.

She, on the other hand, met with tight-lipped appraisal and reluctant regard frequently followed by a hopeful look at the vampire at her side.

Dozens of cameras lifted in their direction as he opened the door of the SUV for her. The quick smirk he gave her when her skirt slid up her thighs was captured by photographic trigger fingers before he returned to the stoic expression he donned for anyone not in his haunt.

"Watch for the people close to the curb," she warned as he eased onto the gas.

With a chuckle, he nodded. "Yes, dear. Now where to?"

"Aren't we heading home? Nichol texted me an hour ago to remind you to stay on schedule because you have a busy night ahead of you when we get back," she said, opening the text and holding it where he could read it.

Pulling off the main road onto a narrow side street, he shrugged. "Do you want to head home?"

"Well, not really," she replied. "But Nichol said."

Parking in the middle of a quiet industrial zone, he scanned their surroundings and unbuckled his seat belt before looking pointedly at the back seat. "You may call the shots with those young vamps, Little Miss The-Litter-Box-Is-Kaius's-Job, but I still trump Nichol. So if you want to test out the springs in those leather seats, there's nothing Nichol can say to stop me."

Catching on to what he was gunning for when he threw his door open and got into the back, his fangs already lengthening, she bit her lip. "A little alone time?"

"I tried to find a private island within driving distance of here but came up empty." He grinned as she crawled into the back seat and straddled his lap. "So a quickie in the backseat of an SUV will have to do. For now."

"I suppose I'll have to endure it until I buy my own island." She giggled when he fumbled with the clasp of her bra.

Nuzzling her throat, he skimmed his fangs across her skin, sending a shiver through her. "We'll pick one up for our honeymoon. Phil will love it."

A word about the author...

Katja Desjarlais is an unapologetic music addict with an obsession for bad Bach puns despite her irrational aversion to Baroque. Her favorite words include 'plethora' and 'dapper', and she is physically repulsed by the word 'moist'. Katja's interest in the paranormal can be traced to her early childhood film choices and to the revolving book collection on her phone.

Desjarlais lives in the Okanagan Valley with her husband, three children, and two black cats. Her ideal summer vacation is spent traipsing through the United States with her family and attending heavy metal concerts.

katjadesjarlais.wordpress.com